W•CLARK
PUBLISHING

The Pussy Trap 2: The Kiss of Death

By

Ne Ne Capri

Wahida Clark Presents Publishing, LLC
60 Evergreen Place
Suite 904
East Orange, New Jersey 07018
973-678-9982
www.wclarkpublishing.com

ISBN 13-digit 978-19366493-0-3
ISBN 10-digit 1936649306

Library of Congress Catalog Number 2012913339
  1. Urban, New Jersey, New York, Bronx, Brooklyn,
      Atlanta, GA, African-American, Street Lit – Fiction

Cover design and layout by Oddball Design
Book interior design by Nuance Art.*.
Contributing Editors: Linda Wilson and Rosalind Hamilton

Printed in United States
Green & Company Printing, LLC
www.greenandcompany.biz

Dedication

To my Princess Khairah. Everything I do is for you. Mommy loves you.

Acknowledgements

All praises is forever due to most high that strengthens me to do all things. To my Beloved, you are the air in my lungs, thank you for all your support I could not do anything without you by my side. To my mother Birdie, I love you, I am grateful that I have you in my life thank you for all that you do for me and Princess Khairah. To my Dad, I am still daddies "Pretty Lady" I love you. To my baby sister Angel I love you, you are growing into a beautiful woman stay focused. Wahida Clark you continue to motivate me to be a better me, thank you for being you.

To my Nana I am almost who you wanted me to be (smile) I miss you RIP. Nobel we did it again, thanks for sacrificing long nights to read my work. To my aunt Jackie thanks for being one of my biggest supporters. Uncle Neville stay out of trouble at least until I get there. Welcome to the world Yuri I love you, you have the best parents Iman and Boobie I love you. Princess you already know, thank you for everything. Uncle Nigee just knowing you love me makes my heart smile.

Tiko Tionne I got your back always know that. Tiombe I am so proud of you stay strong. Chucky hurry up home we got work to do love you. To My cousin Kisha, thank you for looking after Khairah while I do my work, I can rest easy knowing she is safe when I'm away. Hey Baby Jay (Jacinqua) aunty is so blessed you are in my life remember "Don't look back, we are not going that way." My baby brother "IRoka" I love you from a special place in my heart we will always have the wooden wall (smile). Hey Jess love you. WCP Divas thanks for holding us down. Erica MsKayne, SlowMo, Char, Micole, Jacole Coco, I'Kia, and Tiffany. If I missed anyone charge it to the head not the heart. My girls at Bo Robinson, you can do it take one day at a time. My Baby Draya, and Alisha I'm holding you to that college thing. To my KeKe I miss our tea dates you are my idol. To my girl Kimberly Williams who use to always say "it ain't for sale, but it damn sure ain't for free" you are the realest person I have ever met RIP. Special shout out to Cyrus enjoy!

Also check out my short story "Shattered" in Love is Blind an anthology published by Boo Jackson to fight against Domestic Violence 100% of the proceeds will go to a battered woman's shelter in New Jersey. Speak out. Silence kills. Thank you for allowing me to be a part of something great.

Special shot out to my Label mates: Intelligent Allah and Cash, Y'all helped me set my pen on fire! Thanks for all the edits and advice. Anthony Fields and Mike Jefferies thank you for the support and shout outs, I'm holding you down. Shahid Pushbuttinz, New Jersey's finest stay up. Nuance Art.*. you a beast on these graphics ma, they better Holla at you. Davida from oddball designs this cover is official. DC Book Diva I see your work tell Eyone Williams I'm coming to the top hold me a seat. #TeamAnimal. #TeamTreasureBlue. #TeamCartel. #TeamAshleyandJaquavis. Thanks to all the book stores and real readers, who support our work, thank you. To the whole WCP team the sky is the limit. Street team... Stand up!!! Can't wait for the summer #Trappin...

"Plan Your Work, Stay Wise, and Work Your Plan."
Hit me on: Twitter@nenecapri and Facebook NeNe Capri

1
Black Night

"That's the wrong fucking answer!" Night yelled, smacking his helpless victim in the face with a police baton.

His victim sat with both legs and hands tied to a chair alone and helpless. "I told you I don't know shit!" he yelled. Blood trickled from his nose and mouth and his partially opened right eye now threatened to shut.

Night pulled the man's head back and stood over him breathing heavily. His soul-piercing eyes gave the man death's invitation. "Heaven ain't got no place for nigga's like us. So bust hell wide open, nigga! I'll see you there."

Night pulled out an icepick and stabbed him in the chest repeatedly. When there was no more movement, Night stepped back with blood dripping from his shiny instrument of pain. "Y'all came for the wrong muhfucka!" He spat in the dead man's face, dropped the icepick in a bag, and exited the house with Savage and Pete right behind him.

Later that night. . .

KoKo and Night sat on the couch in his apartment going over a few last minute details and smoking a blunt. KoKo sat up, placed the rest of the blunt in the ashtray and asked, "Did you take care of that problem?"

"I never met a problem I couldn't solve."

KoKo nodded in agreement. "A'ight, hold shit down. I have to leave town for a couple days. I'll hit you when I get back."

"Stay outta trouble," Night playfully ordered.

"Trouble is a bad bitch, but she don't want none of me." KoKo smiled as she walked out the room.

Night laughed, but inside he was worried as hell. KoKo was making too many moves too fast, a dangerous invitation for a nigga on the come up to slide in and weaken the fold. All he could do was keep his promise to Kayson and do everything in his power to keep her safe.

— 2 —
Haunted

"You got the time?" the man with the sinister look asked Kayson as a gun emerged from the car window. Time seemed to slow down as he and KoKo stood by the car looking at the gun that now threatened their life.

Boom! Boom!

KoKo and Kayson fell to the ground as the car pulled over and the doors opened, releasing the assassins to finish the job. When she got up and looked, at Kayson, he was bleeding from his chest and coughing up blood. "Nooooo . . . Kayson, oh God. Please not now. Don't leave me! Don't leave me!" she yelled as she cradled his head in her lap. Her heart beat a million thumps per second as she watched Kayson struggling to hold on to life.

KoKo tossed and turned and mumbled over and over in her sleep, "Kayson. Kayson."

"KoKo. KoKo. Wake up, baby," the man in her bed commanded as he tried to wake her.

She sat straight up. Sweat dripped from her forehead and tears fell down her face as she frantically scrambled to locate her gun under the pillows.

The man lying next to her grabbed her arms and said, "Baby, wake up. It's me. Calm down."

She adjusted her vision. Seeing it was not Kayson, but a

close replica, only made her heart ache and yearn for a few seconds before that fatal blast that stole Kayson away from her. Quickly, she jumped out of bed and headed for the bathroom. Unnerved, she locked the door and turned on the light and began dousing her face with water. Gazing up into the mirror, she hated who she saw, a merciless killer who went through life mourning the death of a man long gone. Tormented by the fear of love and loss, KoKo was unable to love the man who was torn out of his sleep night after night. Her heart would not allow it. If it was not the fucked up nightmares about Kayson, it was the constant flashbacks of plunging the knife in and out of her sister. Her anguish was well-deserved payback for all the shit she and Kayson had done. But damn, would God ever let her settle with the house? All she could do was pray that little Quran would grow up to be better than they both were.

Knock. Knock. Knock.

"Baby, are you a'ight?" the voice came through the door.

She hesitated before answering, "Yes. I'm good. I'll be out in a minute."

KoKo grabbed a pair of jeans and a tank top from the bathroom closet and quickly put them on. She opened the door, only to stand face-to-face with the sexy, concerned man on the other side.

"You gotta stop running, baby," he said.

KoKo didn't say anything as she headed to her side of the bed and put on her shoes. "I'll call you later," she said, grabbing her gun, keys, and money off the nightstand.

"Look, I understand that you're still dealing with some shit, but at some point you're going to have to put that nigga to rest."

KoKo glared at him. Deep inside she knew he was right, but this damn sure wasn't the time to bring that point to light. "Like I said I'll call you later."

She stepped forward to move past him, but he grabbed her by the arm and made her stand there. "Look at me. I'm not trying to hurt you. I got mad love for you, girl, but I can't compete with no fucking dead man. I'm the one holding you at night when you're going through these fucked up nightmares and shit. I'm here, baby. Living, breathing . . . " He put her hand on his chest.

KoKo snickered. Here this nigga was standing in the middle of the floor, butt ass naked trying to plead his case. Not even knowing that he himself was bait. Just another piece she was strategically moving across the chessboard. "Is that all?" she asked just as smoothly as she slid her hand down his chest. She headed for the door, not waiting for a response.

"KoKo. KoKo!" was all she heard as she slammed the door.

A few seconds later, she jumped in her car and threw on Kayson and her wedding song "Ready for Love" by India Arie. Then she grabbed a blunt out the ashtray, lit it up, and pulled off. As she drove away, she flashed back to what Kayson's mother, Monique had told her a year ago and the mission she was on to find everyone involved.

One year earlier . . .

6

KoKo stood at the foot of Monique's bed, gun in one hand and her father's chain in the other. Monique trembled as her heart pounded with fear, yet relief flooded her conscience at the same time. She had been holding painful secrets for almost twenty years, and she was ready to release them.

"Sit down, baby. And put the gun down. It's not necessary. I have been waiting for you to ask me some questions that will help release both of our demons," Monique said just as softly and soothingly as her usual conversations were with KoKo.

KoKo pulled a stool over to the bed.

"I don't know where to start," Monique stated as she stared off at the wall.

"The beginning would be a good place," KoKo spat, still heated at what she had already found out.

"Okay. Okay. The beginning it is." Monique took another deep breath. "I had just graduated college and landed a job at a top accounting firm on Wall Street. Because I have always been a label whore . . ." She paused to laugh. "I needed money coming out of my ass. So I got a second job at night bartending on the Upper East Side to support my thirst for the best. One night as I was about to get off, in walks what I can only describe as the sexiest nigga on the planet. Standing at 6'1", about 200 pounds, light brown skin, hazel eyes and he was wearing a neatly trimmed goatee. He looked like walking moneybags dressed in a two-piece charcoal gray suit that I could tell was very expensive. He had a few men with him that looked to be of the same caliber. Then he walked over to the bar and changed my world.

"Excuse me, beautiful. Can a thirsty man have a drink?"

he asked, looking at Monique like he wanted to lick her from head to toe.

"The bar is about to close, but I guess I can send a few rounds over there," Monique said, feeling like a little girl in his big world.

The man took out a thousand dollars, slid it across the counter and said, "Keep it open until we're done, and I'll make it worth your while." He smiled and Monique almost melted.

"I'll see what I can do." She smiled back, grabbing the neatly stacked hundred dollar bills. Then she turned to pour them a couple shot glasses of the best Bourbon the house had. She put them on a tray and turned and placed the tray on the bar.

"How did you know that I would want Bourbon?" he asked, very impressed.

"The best usually drinks the best."

"Is that right?" He gave her a sexy smirk. "Can I have you this weekend? I have a taste for something good and from what I can see it's in those jeans."

Monique's light colored face turned beet red. She didn't know what to say or do. "The only thing for sale up in here is liquor. Not pussy." As she put both hands on the bar, he placed his on top of hers.

"Lean up here so I can tell you something." Monique reluctantly complied. The closer she got to him, her stomach filled with butterflies. The strong scent of Fahrenheit colonge stimulated her nostrils, while the intensity of his gaze made her knees weak. He placed his soft lips to her ear and then whispered, "I don't pay for pussy. I walk with a magic wand that can make a woman cum on command. You have a look in your eyes that tells me that you haven't been fucked good in years. I want to relieve you of that. I promise on Monday you'll have no regrets." He placed a light kiss on her earlobe. Pulling back, he made eye contact with her. "I'm going to finish up this meeting. I'll let you know when I'm ready to go." He slid his hands off hers and smiled.

Monique stood there speechless. Then she mumured, "Damn this muthafucka is smooth as hell." She waved the waitress over and sent the drinks to his table. She finished cleaning and then took a seat, watching him dominate the gentleman at the table, wheeling and dealing until he got everything he wanted. He was powerful and commanding. Monique definitely wouldn't pass up the opportunity to be with him.

When the meeting was over, the men stood and shook hands and left. The sexy gentleman grabbed his suit jacket off the chair, put it over his arm, and headed to where she was sitting. He said, "So do we have a date or what?"

"On one condition." She paused and rose from her seat. "You have to promise not to stalk me after I put this hypnotic on you."

"Oh shit, it's like that?" he said with a hint of excitement in his voice.

"All I can say is on Monday you will have no regrets."

"Is that right? Well, let's go before you get attacked right here."

Monique and the stranger headed to the door. As they

approached the exit, she heard her best friend Lisa yell out, "Mo. Are you okay?"

Monique turned and started to answer, but the smooth gentleman beat her to it. "She's all right now, but later she's not going to be."

Lisa laughed. "Sheeit . . . I hear that. Call me if you can, girl," she said.

Monique smiled and then they disappeared. While they waited for his chauffeur to pull up, Monique crossed her arms and shook a little as the late night New York air chilled her skin. The kind gentleman put his coat around her shoulders and pulled her to him.

"I don't even know your name, Mr. Stranger." She looked up into his eyes.

"My name is Mr. Wells, but my friends call me Tyquan. Don't worry about remembering it now because you'll be calling it out so much over the next couple days that you will know it well."

"You sure are very confident in your abilities."

"No, not confident. Convinced." He took her hand and slid it down the length of his dick. He could see her breasts elevate as she slightly inhaled. "See. And he ain't even woke yet."

A lump formed in her throat as a small amount of fear built up in her gut.

Tyquan smiled. "Don't get scared now. I'll be gentle." He winked.

The car pulled up and they got inside and drove off. Once they reached the Waldorf Astoria, they were escorted to the penthouse. He tipped the bellhop and then led Monique inside.

Tyquan looked her up and down, and all he could think was, Damn, she is well put together. How someone so small could have all that ass is beyond me.

"Do you make it a habit of bringing women to your room for weekend sexcapades?" Monique asked as she walked to the window to see the view.

"Actually, I never bring women to my room. I'm a very busy man. But you, I want." He unloosened his tie and took off his diamond cuff links.

"Is that right?" She tried to imitate him as she walked around the room smelling the different floral arrangments and looking at the beautiful paintings and big soft couches.

Tyquan unbuttoned his shirt and took it off along with his pants. When Monique turned to face him, he was in his boxers, six-pack bumping, smooth skin shining and looking 'fione' as hell. "So Mo, can you come shower with me?" he asked, standing there looking like a god.

"Sure can." She started to pull her shirt over her head.

"Nah, baby. I want to unwrap my own gift." He walked over to her and slowly pulled her shirt over her head, exposing her perfect 36B breasts and small waist. Carefully, he unbuttoned her jeans and eased down her zipper. Monique watched his every move and tried to control her breathing. He went to his knees and gently slid her pants down her thighs and just stared at her pussy print through the red laced thong. He placed soft kisses on her thighs and continued to slide her pants down until she was able to step out of them. Tyquan was so turned on by her soft skin and manicured feet. He stood back up, pulling her to him. Her soft breasts touched his chest

and his dick became rock.

"I think he likes you," he said, placing his lips to hers and kissing her so deeply and passionately that he took her breath away. She pulled back, almost panting.

"What's the matter?" He began kissing her collarbone.

"I never do things like this. I guess . . . I'm a little scared." She melted in his arms.

"Don't worry, baby. I told you I would be real gentle." He picked her up and carried her to the bathroom.

Once they entered the shower, he let her body slide down his. Staring in her eyes, he requested, "Can I let your hair down?"

Monique nodded yes.

He took off the clip and her hair fell down to her lower back, long, black and wavy. Tyquan loved long hair. He grinned his approval because Monique was passing all of his tests. He released her breasts from her bra and placed his mouth over one and gently sucked until he moved to the other one. Monique closed her eyes and bit her bottom lip as her breathing increased. He popped the strap to her thong, and she gasped as it dropped to the shower floor. He continued to suck her nipple as he circled his hand on her clit. The water showered over them and Monique felt like she had stepped outside her body.

"Turn around. I need something sweet on my tongue," he said as he turned her. She placed her hands on the wall and bent over slightly. He took off his boxers and went to one knee, grabbed her butt cheeks and went to work eating her pussy like there was a trophy to be passed out afterward.

"Oh . . . My . . . God . . ." Monique yelled out over and over as she tried to hold on without falling over. "I'm about to cum . . . " she said. "Ahhhh," she shouted for the third time.

Tyquan was in his glory. He had made her cum three times and hadn't even given her the dick yet. Standing up and rinsing her juices from his face, he watched Monique keep her balance by placing her hands on the wall. With her head down and stomach heaving in and out, he eased behind her and slid his dick inside her wet pussy. Her intense moans matched her tightness, which confirmed that no one had been up in her in a long time.

Monique tried her best not to cry as the feeling of pain and pleasure overtook her body. Tyquan stroked long and deep from the back as he placed soft kisses up and down her back.

"Tyquan . . . oh my God . . . right there."

"Right here?" He picked up a little speed.

"Yesss . . . Yessss . . . There . . . " she said as she began to cum again.

He went in deep, grinding in the spot until she came, screaming and crying at the same time. He pulled out and turned her around and held her in his arms. "You know you belong to me now, right?"

"Maybe," she said, playfully.

"Well, let me seal the deal." He picked her up and placed her legs around his waist. Then he entered her and went to work. Tyquan had her up against every wall in the bathroom. Finally, he carried her to the bed and made her wish there was a trap door or some kind of escape from his merciless stroke. When he was done, she couldn't see or move. He rose up and looked down at her body, limp and satisfied.

"Now you have to make me cum." He began kissing and sucking her lips.

All Monique could think was, Oh my God! This nigga is charged the fuck up. She said, "I don't know if I can take anymore."

"Well, you got forty-eight more hours to please me. You better pray and ask God for mercy because I don't have none. I'm about to go into overdrive." He slid back in and fucked her into a coma.

*****

When the weekend ended, Tyquan drove Monique to work on Monday morning in his limo. She stepped out in her $2,000 dollar suit he had sent to the room for her. He came around and hugged her tight. "Any regrets?" he asked, placing a single kiss on her lips.

"None, baby. Not one," she said as she reminisced about the weekend.

He reached in his pocket and handed her his card with all his information and ten thousand dollars.

"What's this for?" Monique looked down at the money as she began to immediately feel used.

"It's not like that. I want you to buy yourself some nice things so you can be ready for me when I send for you."

"Send for me?"

"Yes. I have to leave town. But I will be stationary in about three weeks, and I'm going to send for you. So you can bring your beautiful ass to me so I can see those pretty legs on my shoulders."

"What makes you think I'll cum whenever you call?" she asked with a sexy smile.

"You came all weekend. My reputation speaks for itself." Tyquan kissed her again. "If you need anything, call me." He turned her loose. "Go to work before you make me late for my flight." He smiled as he watched her walk away.

From that day forward it was just as he said. He would send for her whenever he was stationary. This went on for a year. Then the unplanned happened. She became pregnant with Kayson, and Tyquan was perfectly happy about it. He got her a bigger place, furnished it, and bought her a car so she would be able to get around. When Kayson was born, Tyquan was right there and named him. He stayed until he was two weeks old. Tyquan continued to come back and forth until Kayson turned three. Then the visits became too far and too few in between, but he would always send her money by a trusted friend.

When Kayson turned four, Tyquan came by and they had one last weekend together. With teary eyes he explained to Monique that he had to go away for both of their safety. Monique burst out crying as the pain of his words pierced her soul.

"Why did you make me love you only to rip out my heart like a cancer?"

"Baby, it's not like that. I love you. I don't want anything to happen to you. I'm not who you think I am. Trust me, it's for the best."

He looked over at Kayson, who was fast asleep in his mother's bed. He kissed his cheek and turned toward Monique and said, "Take care of my son. He is going to be somebody."

They hugged a few times and then he was gone. Every Thursday someone would either show up at her house or job with thousands of dollars, and she would bank it for Kayson and herself. At first, different people would do the drop offs, but then a regular started to come every week. That regular was Malik, KoKo's father. Malik would not only come and give her money, they would talk and laugh, and she would even cook him dinner sometimes.

KoKo sat staring at Monique with glassy eyes. Monique paused took a deep breath and then continued. "Malik began to tell me about his situation with Keisha and his wife Sabrina and how he had two daughters, one with each of them and how he loved them both," Monique said to KoKo. "His revelations made my situation with Tyquan not seem so bad, until one night while sitting and talking he leaned in and kissed me so passionately. I gave in and those Thursday drop offs became more than just stop and go. He would spend the night and give me what I needed—some good dick and companionship."

KoKo looked on in silence.

"When Kayson turned five, we started spending time with you and your father." Monique looked at KoKo. "Then one night when he was supposed to bring me money he didn't come. Instead, his buddy Nine came and gave me Malik's chain and a large amount of money. Then he delivered the most devastating news to me that I had ever received. Your father was dead. I felt like shit. Nine stayed with me for a little while and then he stood to leave. He let me know that if I

16

needed anything to call him. Nine was what I call the holder of secrets. He knew everything, and his lips were like Fort Knox. If you can ever find him he will tell you everything you need to know. He used to say, "I'll let the children grow up and claim their own revenge."

KoKo sat there trying to remain calm while listening to this woman baring her soul like she was talking to one of her friends, when in actuality she was another one of her father's dirty secrets. "Wait a minute. You mean to tell me you were one of my dad's mistresses?"

"I guess in a way I was." She paused and chuckled. "I loved Malik. It was impossible for anyone to not love him. He was that type of character."

"So what you're saying is if I find this nigga, Nine, I can get to the root of who put that hit on my father and mother?"

"I know you will. He has been waiting for you to get to this point."

"Why didn't Kayson tell me?"

"He was onto something, and I think that's what got him killed. He didn't want to tell you until he had the nigga in a body bag. Malik had become a father figure to him, and he felt he owed you and him some justice. Don't be angry with your husband. Kayson loved you more than life and just wanted you to be safe. He gave his life for you, KoKo. You find these muthafuckas and make them pay."

KoKo sat straight up and took a few more deep breaths in an attempt to stop the tears from falling down her face. "On the life of my son. They will pay," she avowed.

THE PUSSY TRAP 2: THE KISS OF DEATH

One year later . . .

KoKo had been heavy into her business with the Russians and the Colombians now pushing black heroin in New York along with crystal meth. She still upheld the deal Kayson had with the Japanese, flipping counterfeit money. Her real estate ventures were racking up nicely, along with the businesses in different states, not to mention all the property Kayson left her in Dubai. However, she was trying to get into a different bed. KoKo had made a trip to Atlanta to check on opening a club. She figured this was going to be a perfect trap spot. Not only was she going to have the most jumping spot in the 'A', but she was going to recruit one of the baddest bitches in Atlanta to run it.

That Saturday night, KoKo was cruising Downtown Atlanta headed for the strip club, Magic City. The air was warm and the streets were jumping like a typical summer night. As she pulled her Rolls Royce Phantom onto Forsyth Street, all she saw was a block filled with niggas on the prowl, and high post bitches trying to get chosen. Then there were chicken heads waiting to be plucked. However, KoKo's focus was dollar signs. Each muthafucka out there had a price on their head, and she was adding it up. She pulled up in front, parked, and jumped out wearing jeans and a fitted T-shirt and blazer, accompanied by high-heeled ankle boots. Being as though she had created all these legitimate businesses, she had gotten into the habit of dressing up, and the bitch would throw it on like lotion.

KoKo handed the parking attendant three yards and headed

to the front door where this big Afro-Cuban bouncer named Chico The Crusher stood at 6'3", and weighed 300 pounds. He had the reputation for mashing a nigga out if he thought they were going to act up.

"What's up, KoKo?" he asked with a smile and then kissed her on the cheek.

"Sheeit . . . I can't call it."

Chico opened the velvet rope so she could enter. Bitches were sucking their teeth, rolling their eyes and whispering, apparently swoll because they had been standing in line for hours and here came little KoKo walking right past them.

KoKo turned and looked at them like dirt. She smirked and then asked Chico, "Is she here tonight?"

"Yeah, just go inside and Janice the hostess will take you to her."

"A'ight, make sure they take care of my baby," she said as she looked over at her car.

"I'ma treat it like it's mine," he said in his thick Spanish accent.

KoKo smiled and moved through the doors. Once inside, she was amazed by the crowd. It seemed like business was jumping. She knew that her spot would be a sure "'nuff moneymaker.

Janice, the club's assistant manager, walked up to KoKo and said, "Good to see you. Follow me." Janice knew KoKo was about business. She wasn't about all that small talk, so she made sure to get her to where she needed to be as quick as possible.

KoKo followed her to a room with a double mirror where

she could witness Goldie dealing with the girls before they went out to perform. It was Goldie's tradition to give them a pep talk, or as she called it "putting the pimp hand down." She figured she would warn a bitch first, so she wouldn't have to put her foot in anybody's ass later. KoKo looked at the women rushing around half-dressed in g-strings, pasties, and an array of other costumes. Some females had on masks or were covered in body glitter. She murmured, "Ain't this some shit." Then she watched Goldie do her thang.

"Look, y'all need to handle y'all business. Don't be out there trying to date these tricks. They here to spend money and y'all here to make it. We don't walk up to an ATM and suck its dick, so don't do that to the customers. You have to stroke that muthafucka's mental, and if he ain't trying to go in his pockets to pay for the fantasy then you politely move on. Don't let me hear about no fucking crack head moves at the end of the night."

Every one nodded in agreement. Goldie looked around. "A'ight hoes, let's get that money."

Everyone hurried to finish getting ready when this chick named Loren came over to Goldie.

"Goldie, I was wondering if I could get a couple hundred advance on my check until next week?"

Goldie frowned and said, "Why do you need an advance? I pay you well. You don't have no fucking kids or major shit to pay for, plus you leave here with a different nigga every night. What's the deal?"

"I'm broke, Goldie, and I have some shit I need to take care of," she said as she folded her arms and shifted her weight to one side.

"Bitch, how the fuck are you broke?" Goldie asked, pointing at Loren's pussy. "You sittin' on a fucking gold mine. I can't see how the fuck you talking about you broke."

Loren stared at Goldie like she was crazy. Then she thought, *No the fuck she didn't.* She started to say something, but was cut short.

"Why the fuck you looking at me like that? I just don't get it. I can't see how you could be broke. You fucking, ain't you?" Goldie waited for a response. "Ain't you?" she reiterated.

"Yeah," Loren said matter-of-factly.

"Well, bitch, if you fucking and ain't getting paid, you ain't just a broke bitch, you stupid." Goldie looked around at the girls and raised her voice even more. "I don't understand how you bitches be having niggas jumping all up and down in yo' ass and then you got bills due and shit."

One of Goldie's top workers said, "Oh shit, they done got Goldie started."

"It puzzles me . . . Y'all bitches be out here fucking for trinkets. Sheeit! I make a muthafucka pay for every stroke. How you gonna be fuckin' and be broke?" Goldie looked Loren in the eyes waiting for a response, but cricket sounds occupied the room. "Hell no, I can't give you no advance. Shit, I don't suck dick to pay your fuckin' bills. You betta go ask the nigga whose dick you keep in your mouth and shooting loads into the back of your throat to advance you something." Goldie turned to walk away. As she got to the door, she yelled out, "Silly bitches, get to work. Time is money."

KoKo was more than impressed. She needed this ruthless, no-nonsense type bitch on her team. KoKo looked at Janice and then said, "Take me to her office."

When KoKo walked into Goldie's office, she was sitting at her desk smoking a Black and Mile and drinking a glass of Bacardi bomber.

"So I hear you need someone to run your new club?" Goldie asked, looking at KoKo and feeling full of herself.

"Bitch, I don't need shit," KoKo said, looking Goldie dead in her eyes. "Who the fuck do you think I am? One of them bitches you was scolding like a fuckin' child? You acting like you caught me sucking dicks for five in the back." KoKo took her nine from the small of her back and slammed it on the table. "This is the only dick I can make bust off and get me all the money, power, and respect I need. And I don't have to give up no pussy to get it."

Goldie kept eye contact and tried to be cool on the outside, but on the inside she trembled.

"Now, either you can handle being on my team or you can't. However, don't ever get what I want confused with what I need." KoKo looked her up and down and then chuckled. "Do I need you? Sheeit. Unless you gonna grow a ten-inch dick then you'll never have anything I need." She put her gun back and headed to the door. "I'll be in touch."

Goldie watched KoKo exit. She took a deep breath and held her chest. "Shit. That bitch is crazy." She quickly downed her drink, reached in her drawer and grabbed a blunt and lit it up. Taking a deep pull, she sat for a minute and thought about her encounter with KoKo. Then she asked, "Can I work for a bitch like that?" She tossed the idea around momentarily. "Hell yeah," she finally answered.

A few minutes later, Chico walked into Goldie's office and asked, "So what do you think?"

"Man, she pulled a fuckin' gun on me."

Chico laughed. "Yeah, that's KoKo. She don't play. Damn, she pulled out on you? What you do to make her do that?"

"All I said was 'I heard that you need me to help run your club.' Then she went off. I thought I was going to make the ten o' clock news," she stated and then laughed.

"It is always best to ask her, 'how can I assist you'. She don't need nobody. That bitch is a boss. And she ain't afraid to take a nigga out to maintain her throne," Chico said with a certain amount of strength and fear. He knew he was strong in his spot, but he also knew that KoKo had a strong reputation and an organization to match. Them muthafuckas would kill the president in the middle of a speech on prime time, and then walk up to the prison, knock on the door, and do their time with no regrets.

"Well, I think I can handle my shit. If she decides she wants me, I'll be ready." Goldie put the Black to her mouth and took another deep pull. She turned in her chair to watch the monitors.

Chico nodded. "Just don't cross her," he said before turning to walk out of her office.

Goldie ran everything through her head and decided she wanted to be on Team KoKo.

~ 3 ~
Nine

KoKo spent the rest of the week in Atlanta, scouting out a spot for her club. When she got back to New York she headed to Jersey to follow up on some leads. As KoKo rode down Central Avenue heading to "The Valley" in Orange, New Jersey, she toiled with thoughts of what digging up her past would reveal, and with everything she had going on, was she ready to face it? Knowing she had come this close to unmasking the truth, she quickly concluded there was no turning back now. She turned left on Scotland Road and headed to Beach Street. When she made the right and went under the bridge, the house was just a half block down. She parked, surveyed the area, and got out the car. KoKo walked up on the porch and rang the bell.

After about two minutes, she saw someone peek through the window in the door. The locks clicked and the door started to open.

"Hello, is Nasir home?" KoKo asked, a little unsure if this was where she was supposed to be. Nothing about the man's expression seemed inviting.

Finally, the man chuckled. "Nasir, huh? Come in, young lady." He stared at her for a few seconds without blinking. *Damn she looks just like her father,* he thought.

KoKo entered the house and had to admit it was hooked the

fuck up. From the outside it looked average, but when she stepped inside it was immaculate, modern, and laid out with tall ceilings and expensive fixtures. The interior of the home looked as if it were cut right out of a magazine. The man walked into the living room and sat in a green, butter smooth leather chair.

"Have a seat," he instructed KoKo and pointed to the couch in front of him. KoKo sat down as she looked around at the pictures on the wall. It was apparent that he was a family man. The house felt warm and full of life.

"So how may I help you, young lady?" Nine asked as he sat back waiting for her to reveal her hand. KoKo looked over his unblemished mocha skin and neatly shaven face. He was dressed in a pair of freshly pressed brown slacks and dress shirt, and age definitely agreed with his 5'10" medium build.

"I don't know yet, but from what I was told, you have something you have been waiting to tell me. If my sources were right then I will be relieving you of twenty years of secrets," she asserted.

"Well, Princess, I have been waiting for you. And yes, there are some things I have to give you and tell you."

"Well, let's go. Because from the looks of it you ain't getting no younger. And I don't want you to check out before you spill your guts." She gave him a sinister stare. KoKo didn't trust anyone, and until she found out his exact role with her father that's how she would remain.

Nine enjoyed her confidence, knowing it was another trait she had inherited from her father. "Princess, if you are going to be the boss I hear you are, patience is going to be needed,"

Nine advised.

"Is that right?" KoKo smiled.

Like a guru, he sat calm and unfazed by her little threats and anxious attitude. They sat for a minute engaged in a stare down. Nine reached into a mahogany cigar box and pulled out a Cuban. He then lit the cigar, inhaled, and watched the smoke ascend from its end. "So, Miss KoKo, you have grown into a beautiful and powerful woman."

"I'm all right."

"Look, I'm not going to bullshit you. Your dad and mom were killed by a very powerful man. Let me start by saying your mom was very undeserving of her fate. And your dad—that shit was just a greasy ass execution."

"Wait, hold up. I thought my mom was tortured."

"No. It was very quick and painless." Nine recounted the memory.

"I was told that she was kidnapped and tortured."

Nine had a confused look on his face. "Who told you that?"

"Never mind names. Give me the accurate."

"Your mother was Sabrina. Keisha was tortured. That was your dad's mistress and your sister's mother. Your dad was married to your mother. One morning she got in your dad's car, and it blew up before she pulled out the driveway. A death that was intended for your father."

KoKo digested the information. "Well, why is Keisha's name on my birth certificate?"

"Situating paperwork is always a bitch. I guess you have a lot of work to do. I will tell you this—things were done to keep you and your sister safe from whoever was looking for

26

your family. She was adopted by a Seattle family. You were sent to a New Jersey family."

"Hold the fuck up!" KoKo moved to the edge of her chair, obviously agitated. "The lady that raised me wasn't my real grandmother?"

"No."

KoKo's head was spinning. Her whole life flashed before her eyes, and everything she knew and held dear was lies. As she sat trying to digest the information she had just received, she heard the door open. A woman entered with two little children full of life running up the stairs with bags in their hands.

"Hi, baby," the woman yelled. "Oh, we have company." The woman moved fast, headed in their direction.

"Where you been? Out making me a poor man?" Nine looked at the bags dangling from her hands and arms.

"Cut it out. You know what today is. You said I could have whatever I wanted," his wife said as she kissed his lips. She turned her attention to KoKo and said, "Hi, sweetie. Has he been hospitable to you?" She reached out to shake KoKo's hand.

KoKo mustered up a half smile. "If that's what you want to call it."

The woman laughed. "Well, the lady of the house is here now. Would you like something to drink?" she asked as she turned to walk off with the bags.

"No ma'am. I'm about to leave."

"Okay, if y'all need anything just holler." She went toward the steps and turned to address KoKo. "Oh, I'm Tina. I didn't

27

get your name."

"That's cool. I'm anonymous," KoKo said and then stood up.

Tina paused with a puzzled look on her face. Nine was impressed at how KoKo handled herself.

"Baby, wait for me upstairs. I'll be done in a minute."

Tina knew what that meant and headed upstairs.

Nine kept his eyes fixed on the steps until he heard the bedroom door close. He turned his attention back to KoKo. "Come into the basement with me. I have something to give you. It will answer all your questions."

They headed to the basement and she took note of the decor. Pool table, projector screen TV, plush carpet in the sitting area which looked like a small theater. Also, the walls were decorated with sports memorabilia. A fully loaded bar and a music system made it the ultimate man cave. Nine went behind the bar and grabbed a bottle and two glasses. KoKo hopped up on one of the stools and held her glass while he poured. Nine picked up the universal remote and turned on the stereo.

"I made a promise to myself that when you came I would give you everything you needed." He paused and took a swig of his drink as KoKo sat quietly listening. "Your father was one of the most loyal niggas I have ever met. If he gave you his word, you could put your life on it. However, he trusted to a fault." KoKo nodded. "He loved Sabrina, but he shared something with Keisha that is a once in a lifetime love. She had his back and rode for him hard. When all those events happened, it killed him. He was a dead man before he died."

"What events? Who killed him?"

Nine took a deep breath and sorted the facts in his mind. "I will provide you with everything you need to get started. I'm confident that you will follow the path I set into play. Your enemy will be helpless. Just promise me that when you find the man responsible, you make his grandchildren feel it."

"You already know." KoKo tossed the rest of her drink back and then stood up.

Nine threw his drink back also. He reached up over his head where the glasses hung and grabbed an envelope and a folded piece of paper. He wrote an address on it, closed it, and slid it across the bar. "This will help you. Read it when you leave. My business is done with you. I wish you all the happiness in the world."

KoKo picked up the envelope and the folded piece of paper. "I'ma follow this little plan you set into motion, but I promise you this. If I get to the end of the rainbow and the pot of gold got your name on it I will kill you and your wife and your children."

"I wouldn't have it no other way."

KoKo shook his hand and then turned to walk up the stairs.

A smile formed on Nine's lips. It seemed like just yesterday she would put her arms out for him to pick her up, and now she was making a threat on his life. "I will tell you this. You are your father's daughter. Happy hunting, Princess."

KoKo didn't respond, but inside she was tickled that she had just gotten closer to the justice her parents deserved. Within seconds, she dashed up the stairs and walked through the living room toward the exit. Before she reached the front door, she began planning her enemy's demise.

~ 4 ~
Game Time

"Y'all niggas ain't shit!" KoKo spat as she slammed her ace on the table. It was game night and the money was definitely on the table.

"You poppin' all that shit. You better pay me my money," Mugsy yelled, slamming a three of spade on top of it. "Get that shit outta here."

"You ain't talking about nothing, nigga," Night yelled, slapping a four of spade on top of it.

"I see that bullshit. Yo' ass better not renege either, nigga," Mugsy yelled back.

"Don't worry about what I got in my hand, nigga. Just play your cards." Night came back at him.

Savage stared at his cards.

"I don't care how long you stare at 'em, they ain't gonna change. Put something on the board, nigga."

KoKo laughed. When they played cards it was like war. Night always talked shit, and Savage always got mad. She sat at the head of the table and smiled, confident in her and Night's partnership. They would come in there and take niggas money every time they graced the table. KoKo watched the room, making sure shit was cool while Night dealt the next hand. Several tables had card games going on, and ever so often, a sore loser ass nigga would make a scene and try to get out of paying, and tonight would be no different.

"Nigga, fuck you. I ain't paying you shit," this Queens nigga named Dolo shouted.

"Muhfucka, you gonna pay me my money," Butchie said, coming right back at him.

"You crazy as hell. I saw you looking at the cards, nigga."

" . . .Fuck outta here with that bullshit. This nigga dealing me cards like he dealing them to you. How the fuck I'ma see what's in this man's hand?"

"Like I said, I ain't paying you shit," Dolo said, trying to get out of the five thousand dollar hole Butchie had just put him in.

"Muhfucka, either it's gonna come out your pocket or your ass, but you gonna pay me my money," Butchie stated, trying to remain calm.

Scales looked back and forth at them both. He started to say something, but didn't get a chance. KoKo strolled in their direction, already on her way over there.

"Is there a problem?" she asked.

"Yeah, this nigga got shifty eyes, and I ain't paying him shit," Dolo responded.

"Fuck is you talking about?" KoKo asked.

Dolo looked at the seriousness in her eyes as she approached the table. Her stare remained unwavering, and on her heels were Night and Savage.

"Say some shit, muhfucka," she spat as she now stood beside him.

"Look, KoKo, this ain't got nothing to do with me and you.

Let me settle it with this man."

"Fuck you mean? You up in my place creating a fucking disturbance, and then got the balls to part your fucking lips and tell me this ain't got nothing to do with me. What the fuck is this nigga drinking?" She looked at the bartender who just shrugged in response. "How much this nigga owe you?" She turned her question to Butchie.

"He owe me five."

"Pay the man," she instructed.

Dolo stood and glared at Butchie through slanted eyes, who had smoke coming up off those neatly twisted dreads. Dolo took in some air, reached in his pocket, and pulled out a stack.

"Make it double for the fucking inconvenience," KoKo instructed.

Dolo looked at her sideways. "Double? I'ma pay what I owe."

KoKo squinted and cocked her head to the side. "I would ask you to repeat yourself, but I heard your punk ass loud and clear."

"I ain't got no beef with you, KoKo."

"You right. You got debt with me. His money is now my money. You don't owe him shit. You now owe me." KoKo pulled out Midnight and rested it at her side.

"You ain't gotta do all that, KoKo." Dolo put his hands up in surrender.

"Run this nigga's pockets," she ordered.

Savage shook him down and pulled two fat knots from his front pockets.

"Come on, KoKo, that's all I got."

33

"Shut the fuck up!" Savage yelled and handed the money to her. She looked at it and threw it at Night.

"Now get the fuck outta here! You banned from the game from now on, and don't let me see you on the block."

"You crazy as hell. Fuck that! I gotta make back my losses," Dolo stated.

KoKo leaped on him and whacked him on the head with the pistol. The first couple hits to the head forced him to the ground. Then she busted both eyes, mouth and nose before Savage joined in, stomping him in the stomach and chest.

Dolo passed out. When KoKo saw no more movement, she stood up huffing and puffing.

"Damn, ma," Night said, watching KoKo walk to the bar and grab a towel to wipe off her gun.

"Get this piece of shit outta here." She tossed the towel on his face.

"You all outta breath. Maybe you need to do some pushups or something," Savage teased.

"Sheeiit . . . that's light work. Let that be a lesson to the rest of y'all niggas. If you owe, pay!" KoKo yelled, looking around the game hall.

Savage gave the signal to the cleanup crew. They wrapped Dolo up in a large piece of plastic and hauled him out.

"Hurry the fuck up, Savage. You still getting that ass spanked on this table," Night yelled.

"Fuck you, nigga," Savage yelled back.

KoKo walked over to Butchie and handed him his five grand. "That was an expensive ass card game and he paid with his life. Now you owe me yours." She then moved on. Butchie

34

was now in KoKo's debt, and from what he witnessed, he damn sure wasn't going to cross her.

— 5 —
Secrets

After the card game, KoKo went home to review the contents of the envelope she got from Nine. She had been putting it off, but tonight would be the night. After exiting the shower, KoKo snatched her towel and began drying her skin. She grabbed the remote and turned up Nina Simone. Messing with Kayson, she had acquired a love for old but classic music. She placed her towel on the sink and began to apply lotion to her skin. Then she strolled naked to her walk-in closet and grabbed one of Kayson's Big A T-shirts and crawled onto her huge bed. She sat back, grabbed a blunt off the nightstand, and lit it up.

After taking a few deep tokes, she stared at the envelope, looking at it as if it would open itself. Conflicted, she was caught between the thought of just saying fuck it, move on, and the revenge in her veins that hungered to bring death to the niggas who had made her an orphan.

After smoking half of the blunt, she poured herself a glass of Ciroc. She drank it down and then placed the glass on the nightstand. Leaning forward, she grabbed the envelope and tore it open, pouring its contents on the bed. Pictures, article clippings, court documents, insurance policies, and a list of names and some information on each person lay in the pile.

She placed the policies aside, and began organizing the articles by date. The first clippings were highlights of Sabrina's assassination and Keisha's death. The last articles were about Malik, and most of them ended with the comments, "There are no leads," or "Motive appears to be a drug deal gone wrong."

Quickly, she read through them. A hot surge ran from the tip of her toes to the top of her head as the names and events surrounding the articles cut her to her soul. She reviewed court documents that didn't hold much information because almost everyone involved was dead. Then she began to go through the pictures—pictures of her mom and dad, and also of her dad with his crew at a few parties. A few photos showed Monique and Malik at a restaurant, which appeared as if they had been taken by an investigator. That brought questions to her mind.

The last batch of photos showed KoKo and Star at separate times in different places. Another picture featured a woman holding a baby boy, and then another lady holding a baby girl. On the back it read, "Daddy's baby 8-15." Questions flooded her mind about who the other children were and if they belonged to her father or his enemy. KoKo placed the pictures and articles back in the envelope. Then she grabbed the insurance policy, seeing her and her sister's name listed as beneficiaries. The amount of the policy read $1.5 million that they were to share equally, but not until they turned twenty-five. She glanced down at her dad's signature. Chills prickled her arms. He signed his name the same way she did, even down to the dot over the 'i'. KoKo smiled and a tear welled up in her eye. Quickly, she brought her hand to her face and caught it before it rolled down her cheek.

Taking a deep breath, she turned the page and saw a name in the witness section that gave her pause. "Monique Wells," she said. "This bitch is full of secrets." KoKo looked over the list of names and internalized them. For the first time she was brought to the realization of her enemies. She vowed to find and kill each one and anyone who crossed her path in search of them. KoKo had seen enough for the night.

As she organized the last of the information to place it back into the envelope, one picture slid from between the pages and fell onto the bed. Her brows wrinkled with curiosity. She placed the envelope down and reached for the picture. A man with a light brown complexion, short dreads, and a scar that went from the side of his eye down to the middle of his cheek stood shaking hands with another gentleman. Nine was in the background looking on. She turned the photo over to see if there were any words on the back, but there were none. Hastily, she poured everything back onto the bed and shook everything out to make sure she wasn't missing anything, but nothing else surfaced. She knew she would have to make another trip to see Nine, and this time a gun in his mouth was going to make him spill his guts one way or another.

— 6 —
A Deal is a Deal

KoKo spent the next couple of weeks in New York making sure her ship was tight. Then she was off to Atlanta to close on a few pieces of property. And right away she ran into a snag.

"Muthafucka. Don't play with me. I told you what I needed and you said you could make it happen," KoKo yelled at the twenty-one-year-old timid real estate agent.

"Miss, I told you we can't sell the Buckhead property, but you are welcomed to look at any of the other six houses we have available."

"Nah, fuck that. When I spoke to you on the phone, you said the shit was a go and that everything would be ready for me to sign when I got here. Now you talking some shit I can't comprehend," KoKo said, full of anger, ready to bust his punk ass in the mouth.

"Yes ma'am, you're right, but when I spoke to the boss he let me know we were not going to be able to do it," he said, trying to shift the blame off himself.

"Look, rookie. When I asked your punk ass was it a go, you should have checked with your boss and then got back to me. Instead of sucking my dick so hard for that commission with all your fucking yes, yes, yes, shit." KoKo was pissed. She was on a time schedule and he was fucking with it. She wanted to pull out and put something hot in his ass.

Rock, the owner of the real estate company, watched the transaction from his office window. His interest was piqued. But urgency kicked in when KoKo went for her cell phone to answer a call, and he saw a gun sticking out from her waist. He stepped out the door and tried to calm the situation.

"Excuse me, Miss. May I help you?" he asked as he approached her with caution.

KoKo looked in his direction, a little taken aback by this 6'2" chocolate man with the chinky eyes, big smile, pretty, white teeth and fit body in an Armani suit.

Aside from the real estate company, Rock also owned a construction company and an office park occupied by fifteen businesses, not to mention the numerous properties he owned around Atlanta, Marietta, and Buckhead. KoKo was getting ready to rape the real estate company and use to her advantage.

She examined this fine specimen, who strongly resembled the actor Idris Elba. She asked, "Why everybody I run into in Atlanta wanna help me with something?"

Rock stood confident and said, "I can't speak for them, but when I see a beautiful woman in distress I come to her aid."

"Is that right? Well, I'm not in distress. I'm pissed the fuck off, and unless you can get me that property, then give me my quarter mil' and I'll be on my way."

Rock smiled, enjoying this little lady asserting her position. "Come into my office and I will do what I can to get you what you want."

KoKo said, "I hope so, because I would hate to have to fuck your boy up."

"Nah, baby. That won't be necessary. I got you. Come this way."

KoKo gave the young boy a dirty look and then followed Rock to his office. He got on the phone and made a few calls, wheeled and dealed, getting her exactly what she wanted. As she stood to leave, he said, "Since I got you what you wanted can you give me something I want?"

"And what would that be?" she asked, looking at him with a serious expression.

"Dinner."

"All you got me was what I paid for. Why is that deserving of more of my time?"

"I want to sit and look into those eyes while they are not spitting fire." He gave her a sexy grin.

KoKo tossed that around for a few seconds. "I'll get back to you on that." She turned to walk away.

Rock watched her switch that fat ass out of his office. KoKo stopped at the door and said, "Have my shit ready by Friday and I will give it more consideration."

"I'll have it ready by Wednesday, and I'll be ready to take you out Saturday night."

"If you can do that then I'll take you out," she said and walked off.

Rock sat at his desk fantasizing about her as he watched her hop in her car and ride off. He then picked up the phone and put his foot in anybody's ass he had to in order to make his promise become a reality. He was not going to miss a date with the woman whom he could only describe as mesmerizing. And he wanted to get up close and personal.

41

THE PUSSY TRAP 2: THE KISS OF DEATH

Little did he know getting close to her could be deadly.

7

Chico

Chico turned off Flatshoals Road and onto Boring Road, cruising the neighborhood with Reggaetone blarring, windows vibrating, and seat back. He threw up his deuces at a few of the young boys who looked on and admired his gleaming hunter green Cadillac MLK with the shiny rims as it approached the corner. When he hit Pheasant Drive, he made a left heading toward his house. Pulling into his driveway, he noticed an unfamiliar vehicle with tinted windows. As he approached with caution, he immediately reached into his console and grabbed his .45. Relaxation set in when he noticed KoKo sitting behind the wheel. Placing the gun on the seat next to him, he deaded the engine and jumped out with a big smile on his face. KoKo opened her door and stepped out her car smoking a fat spliff.

"What's up, mami?" Chico said, greeting KoKo with a hug. "What brings you to the A so soon? I thought we were supposed to meet next weekend."

"You know me, always about business," she stated, breaking their embrace.

"Out here bringing down my property value." He referred to the heavy weed smoke permeating the area.

"Sheeeiiit. I was passing out samples before you got here."

Chico burst out laughing. "Come inside," he said as he

headed up the steps and opened the door.

When they entered, a big ass pit bull rushed toward them barking furiously. KoKo didn't even blink. She pulled out her nine. Chico grabbed the dog in mid-air by his collar in an attempt to calm him down. Dragging the dog off, Chico cursed in Spanish and called for his wife. He dragged the dog to the basement door and pushed him down the stairs and slammed the door.

"My bad, KoKo. I told that bitch to keep his ass locked up in the daytime." He looked at KoKo, who was only slightly fazed. "Damn! You was going to kill my dog?"

"Hell yeah! I don't fuck with dogs like that. I was getting ready to send his ass to the big dog house in the sky," she said, placing her gun back in the holster.

Chico chuckled as he led her to the den.

Seconds later, his wife came downstairs with an evil look on her face like she had been sucking on lemons. They swapped a few heated words, and then he slammed the door in her face. "So what's up, Miss KoKo?"

"I need you to run security for the club."

"Hell yeah. I was waiting to see what you had for me."

"And I need you to put me down with them esés down in the SWATS."

"What you need?"

"Just a little space to move some shit while I'm down here."

Chico listened attentively.

"I know you got a family, so I don't want you directly involved. Just set up a meeting and I will handle the rest."

"Sheeitt . . . I ain't no fucking porch gangsta. If I'm in then I'm in one hundred percent." He looked at KoKo with sincerity.

KoKo took a minute to process his offer. "A'ight. But I need to warn you. My shit is dirty. And if you care about anybody you better secure them a safe spot because I'm about to turn shit up in the 'A'."

"I fucks with you, KoKo. Let's get this money." He put his hand out to seal the deal.

"That's what's up. Oh yeah, put some protection on Goldie, and expect a black Nightmare to visit you in a couple days."

"Who?" he asked.

"Don't worry. You will know him when you see him." She stood up and headed to the door.

Chico followed as he turned over in his mind the money and danger headed his way, and the blood in his veins started to stir. He felt alive. It had been awhile since he had tested his guns, and he was ready to get shit started.

"Oh yeah, and don't sick your bitch on me again."

"My bad, KoKo. I'll make sure she's locked up next time."

"That's not the bitch I'm talking about. When I rang the bell, your wife gave me a dirty look and talked a little shit. She don't know me like that. Tell that bitch to gather some respect. I don't want you to have to spend your first check on dental work."

Chico got an instant attitude. He had been telling his wife to man up and have his back because some shit was changing. "Don't worry, I'ma put shit in check."

"I'll see you in a week." KoKo jumped in her car, backed

out the driveway, and sped off.

— 8 —
It's On

Goldie drove into the car dealership wearing a pair of black leggings and a hot pink tank top. Prada thong slide ons enhanced her French pedicure. The bitch was well put together, twenty-four-inch waist, forty-inch hips with an ass big and firm. Her shapely legs had just the right thickness, no cellulite, all muscle from thigh to calve. A red bone with light brown eyes and a head full of neatly styled blonde dreads to hint at the name Goldie.

She jumped out of her souped up Yukon and proceeded to switch that big ass up and down the parking lot, looking at the cars and trucks.

Curupt and Geek were sitting in the office looking out the window when she caught their attention.

"Who the fuck is that?" Curupt asked.

"Shit, I don't know but I wanna find out," Geek said as he got up to get a better look.

Curupt stood up. "Nah, I got this playa."

"Cock blocking muthafucka," Geek yelled and started to laugh.

"Nigga, you know your dick too small to handle all that ass," Curupt shot back.

"Sheeit . . . that ain't what your mama said."

"Why you think she stopped fucking with you?" Curupt joked.

"Fuck you, nigga."

Curupt walked out the office and right up to Goldie. "How you doing today, Miss? I'm Craig but my friends call me Curupt.

"Hi, I'm Renee."

"Can I help you find a vehicle today?" he asked, holding out his hand.

She shook his hand once and released it. "I don't know. Can you?" she flirted.

"Shit, I hope so? What do you need?" Curupt said.

"What are you offering?"

"Everything you see."

"Well, I need something to ride," she said and licked her lips.

Curupt's mouth watered. "What are you looking for? Something big or something small?" He used his hands to demonstrate size.

Goldie turned her back to him so he could get a good ass shot. She pointed at her Yukon. "You see all that? Can't you tell I like them big?"

Curupt's eyes were glued to her ass and the hot pink thong he could see through her tight ass leggings. Goldie turned just as he was starting to look back up. She gave him a big smile as she thought, *This nigga is going to be easy.*

Curupt stopped his fantasy long enough to say, "I specialize in big things, but can you handle it is the question."

"The bigger, the better."

Curupt grabbed his throbbing dick as he enjoyed their word play. "Let me grab some keys and I'll take you for a test drive."

"I hope you have time, because I like to ride long."

Curupt grinned a big ass Kool Aid smile on his face as he thought, *Are we still talking about cars?* "I'll be right back, Renee. Pull your truck over there." He pointed to an empty space and walked back inside the dealership.

Goldie jumped in her truck and parked. She grabbed her shades, hit the remote lock, and posted herself up so they could continue to get a good look at her.

Geek watched Curupt enter with his chest stuck out and his head held high. "Damn, man. She trying to give a nigga some pussy," Curupt said.

"Get the fuck outta here!" Geek stated.

"Hell yeah. We just had a conversation that almost made a nigga bust his zipper."

"See, I told you to let me go out there. You can't even handle a bitch giving you words. How you gonna handle her giving you pussy?"

"That's a'ight, because when I'm laying deep in it and she's calling my name 'cause a nigga hitting that spot, I damn sure won't be thinking about your non-pussy getting ass." Curupt grabbed three sets of truck keys and headed outside. They walked up to a shiny, candy apple red Mercedes Benz truck and opened the door.

"Can you help me up?" she asked, turning her back to him and placing her hand on the door and one foot on the footrest. Curupt got up on her butt and placed his hands at her waist.

She smelled so good and felt so soft. Goldie brushed her butt against his semi-hard dick to see what he was working with. Nothing about his size disappointed her. He pressed lightly against her, and then lifted her up into the seat. She was impressed with his strength. His big muscular arms handled her just right. She thought, *I'm going to have fun setting this nigga up. Perfect body, good on the eyes, and a big dick. Damn! Thank you, KoKo for hooking a sistah up.*

Curupt went to the other side and got in. "Don't tear my shit up."

"I'll be gentle." Seductively, she looked in his eyes.

Curupt wanted to jump in the backseat and fuck the shit out of her right there. She was turning him on with her every word and movement.

Goldie pulled off and headed to Interstate 285. Twenty-five minutes later they returned, and she pulled up next to her truck and said, "Thanks for the ride."

"You like it?"

"I like everything I see." She gazed into his eyes and Curupt had nothing to say. "Cat got your tongue?" she asked playfully.

"No, but it can have my tongue."

Goldie smiled. "Draw up the paperwork." She grabbed the door handle and jumped out. She sashayed over to her truck, opened the glove compartment, and pulled out $70,000 and then handed it to him. "Make it happen." She turned and walked away.

"Yo, how do I get in contact with you?"

"You don't. I'll contact you." She hopped in her truck and

peeled out.

Kim, Curupt's secretary stood watching the transaction between him and this mysterious woman from the reception area window. Her breathing began heavy as suspicion rose in her gut.

— 9 —
Following Leads

After KoKo reviewed all the information she received from Nine, she began hunting down her prey one by one. KoKo sped down the highway and exited I-280 on the Clinton Avenue exit. She drove alongside Freeway Drive until she came to Oakwood Avenue. She turned left and proceeded through the light, passing Oakwood Avenue School. A hint of nostalgia brought a smile to her face. An image of her and her childhood friends playing double dutch on the playground and at the after school program at the Friendship House flashed in her mind.

Spotting the brown house near the corner as directed, she began looking for a parking spot but there were none. She then decided to pull into the BP gas station across the street. After parking, she checked her guns and her surroundings before popping the locks and exiting the vehicle. KoKo crossed the street and walked up the stairs onto the porch. She rang the bell twice and then waited to see what this visit would reveal.

After a few minutes, a figure appeared in the curtain accompanied by the sound of locks clicking. Once the door opened, there stood a tall, slim woman with a short boy cut colored dark red. Four-inch nails garnished the tips of her long, skinny fingers. She held an old-fashioned filter with a personally rolled cigarette between two fingers. Gold chains adorned her neck, and bracelets decorated her wrist. She reminded KoKo of Jada Pinkett's mother, just darker.

"Hello, how may I help you?"

"I'm a friend of a friend. I just need a few minutes of your time."

Pat looked her up and down with apparent disdain. Sucking her teeth, she said. "And a minute you will get." She opened the door a little wider, allowing KoKo to pass through. She locked the door and then walked past KoKo.

"You can come in the kitchen."

KoKo followed, carefully taking note of the interior of the house. It was clean and up to date. She then took a quick inventory for any pictures. Several were on a mantel that she wanted to make sure she got a closer look at. Once in the kitchen, Pat took a seat and crossed her legs as she continued to pull on her cigarette. She gestured for KoKo to have a seat. KoKo pulled the chair out and sat across from her. The silence was thick as each woman tried to feel the other one out.

KoKo broke the silence. "I'm Malik's daughter."

"I know who you are," Pat stated and took another long pull on her cigarette. Without looking up, she reached forward and dutted the ashes. She took a deep breath and exhaled hard. Her eyes met KoKo's eyes. "So what is it that you need from me?"

"Answers. Nothing more. Nothing less."

"Uhm. Well, I don't know shit. Didn't know shit twenty years ago, and I don't know shit today." She twisted her lips back and forth with major attitude.

KoKo folded her hands together tight in an attempt to not go off, but it was getting harder by the minute. "Look. I'm not trying to make you relive no trauma. I just need you to answer a few questions."

"Like I said, I didn't know shit then and I don't know shit now. Plus, how are you going to walk up in my house and demand shit from me when it was your sorry ass father who's the reason my niece is dead?"

"What? You mad because he ain't fuck you? Or did he?" KoKo developed an evil grin on her face.

"You need to leave my house," Pat said calmly as she tried not to curse KoKo out.

"Struck a nerve, huh?" KoKo taunted.

"I don't know what you're talking about and apparently neither do you."

"Oh, you don't? Let me jog your memory. You sat in your niece's face day-in and day-out, skinning and grinning, listening to her talk about how much she loved that man and all behind her back you was sneaking and fucking my father."

Pat's breathing quickened. KoKo had successfully drawn blood. Now she just sat back, waiting to see what would come out of Pat's mouth next. "I loved my niece and would have never done anything to hurt her. Your time is up and I need you to leave my house."

"You's a scandalous ass bitch. And you're going to die a lonely death." KoKo rose from her seat. "Out of respect for my dad and my sister I was going to look out for you, but I can't have a lying, conniving bitch like you on my team. So rot in hell, bitch." KoKo pushed in her chair. "I would kill your dumb ass, but a bitch like you ain't worth my bullets."

Pat stood up fast, knocking her chair to the floor. "You can't judge me. You don't know me. I did what I had to!"

KoKo slammed the door shut on her way out. She realized there were things hiding behind Pat's tough persona, and she was getting ready to find out what they were.

Minutes later . . .

"I need to talk to you," the voice came blaring through the receiver.

"Hold up. What the fuck is you hollering for?"

"That bitch came to see me today."

"What bitch?"

"Little KoKo," she said with venom in her voice.

"Oh yeah. And?"

"Why does she know shit that only you know?"

"Why you ain't ask her?"

"Nine, I buried all secrets with my niece. I settled with the house. I am not in a position to deal with this bullshit."

"Well, you better get in position. Because it's just the beginning. I have my orders and I'm going to carry them out. I suggest you do the same." He hung up, not waiting for a response.

"Shit!" Pat yelled and threw the phone across the room. She quickly lit another cigarette and inhaled hard. "Think, bitch, think," she repeated as she sat trying to compose herself. Then it came to her. "Yeah, these muthafucka's are not going to throw me under the bus. I'm about to trump they asses." With that, she got up and grabbed her keys and left out.

— 10 —
Get Down or Lay Down.

Almost a week had passed, and KoKo had managed to get a good footing on her enemies and get a lot of new shit jumping in the 'A'. It was time to sit back and watch shit unfold.

Goldie walked into the lobby of the Marriott hotel in Downtown Atlanta wearing a strapless sundress, high heel sandals, big shades and a floppy hat, which she removed as she entered the building. The cool air hitting her skin was a welcomed relief. It was one of those suffocating hot days in the A. She walked past the front desk and headed straight to the elevators. Pushing the up button, she flipped through her phone checking the messages. When the doors opened, she pressed seven and was on her way. Once she reached 715, she gave the special knock. Moments later, the door opened.

"What's up, boss?" Goldie asked as she shut the door and followed KoKo into the room.

"Ain't nothing. Just trying to make shit happen. What you got for me?" KoKo sat in the chair.

Goldie sat on the end of the bed and started her spiel. "I was able to recruit ten of my best from the club, and I have to interview seven more girls tomorrow. But I plan on club hopping tonight to see what's biting. I went by the club this afternoon, and everything is on schedule. It looks really nice."

She paused briefly. "I checked out old boy and got his schedule down pat. I will be paying him a visit in a few days. Other than that, a bitch is just lining them up and knocking them down."

"Any of them bitches prospects for what I want handled?"

"Hell yeah."

"It sounds good. Make it look good." KoKo moved to the refrigerator and grabbed a bottled water. She opened it and took a long gulp before placing it on the desk. "I have a lot of shit riding on you. Don't fuck up." She picked up the water and drank it until it was empty.

"I won't." Goldie nodded in agreement as KoKo tossed the water bottle in the trashcan.

"Keep your mouth shut. No pillow talk. No 'I need to get some shit off my chest' confessions, and under no circumstance do you talk about any of this shit over the phone. Pay attention. Watch your back at all times, and when shit seems like it ain't lining up, back up, think and regroup. Lastly, if you need me, hit a bitch up. Don't try to do the impossible and fuck up then call me. Because if I have to stop doing what I'm doing to clean up, somebody usually gets fucked up." KoKo looked her in the eyes with intensity.

"I got you," Goldie responded.

"I hope so." KoKo grabbed a stack of money from the table next to Goldie. "Here. Make sure your shit is up to par. Also, for those three girls that will work close to you, make sure those bitches are official. And I want to meet with y'all in a couple weeks. But until then, I'm invisible. This is your shit."

"You used the name Renee Givens, right?"

"Yes."

"All right. I'ma have someone bring you the paperwork tomorrow at noon. Don't fuck up."

Goldie stood and reached for the money. "I got you, KoKo."

"Don't have me. Just do what the fuck I tell you." KoKo moved toward the door. "That's it. I'll see you in a week." KoKo unlocked the door and opened it.

Goldie smiled as she headed for the exit. "Enjoy your day, Miss KoKo."

"You do the same. And remember my words." KoKo watched Goldie exit. She shut the door and locked it. Lying across the bed, she grabbed the remote and turned on the TV.

"Today on I-285 North there was a car discovered on fire. After firefighters were called in, the blaze was brought under control. Two bodies were found in the trunk totally unrecognizable. According to Atlanta's chief of police, there is a full investigation underway. We will bring you more details as they come in. Back to you John."

KoKo picked up her phone. "Hello?" Chico's voice came through the phone.

"I see the weather is going to be hot tomorrow," KoKo said, acknowledging that she saw the news.

"Yeah, I'ma try to stay cool."

"A'ight. See you when I get back." KoKo disconnected the call.

KoKo clicked the television off and said out loud, "Let the games begin." These muthafauckas were either going to get down or lay down.

— 11 —
I Owe You One

KoKo had been back from Atlanta for a week and decided to stop by Nine's house to see if she could ask him a few questions. She stood on the side of Nine's house looking through the windows, which revealed that he had picked up and moved out. She walked around to the back to get a better look. When she got to the back porch and peeped in the kitchen, she saw the same thing, an empty room. "Shit," she said as she began heading back to the front of the house. *What the fuck is going on?* Although she wanted to do a little investigating, it would have to wait because she had some very important business pending.

*****

Rock sat in the backseat of the Mercedes S600 looking through the panoramic sunroof, watching the stars and sipping on a glass of Cognac. He was anxious to see what type of date KoKo had set up after she sent for him with specific instructions on what to wear. The car pulled into Atlanta's private airport and drove up to a jet that had Boss Lady written in black Old English lettering. The car came to a stop and the chauffeur got out and opened his door. He stepped out onto the red carpet and looked up and saw the sexiest pair of chocolate legs leading up to a short, white, off the shoulders dress.

"Damn!" he mumbled.

KoKo smiled with her hands behind her back.

Rock adjusted his tie and headed toward the steps. When he got to the top, he leaned in and kissed her on the cheek. "Hey beautiful," he said, looking in her eyes.

"Did you enjoy your ride?" KoKo asked in a sensual tone.

"Yes. But I wanted to see your face."

"Well, you're seeing it now," she said, giving him an innocent, sexy smile. "Come in and have a seat." She guided him into the plane to a butter soft leather chair, which sat in front of a circular table covered with a white tablecloth. Candles and a white plate set with gold trim, gold cutlery, and crystal champagne glasses also dressed the table. Rock opened his jacket and sat down.

"We will be taking off in ten minutes, Miss KoKo. Would the gentleman like a drink?" Sarah, the flight attendant asked as she stood by the table with her hands clutched together.

"Yes, I will take a short glass of something dark," he stated without taking his eyes off KoKo.

"Yes sir, I have the perfect thing. Would you like anything, Miss KoKo?"

"No thank you."

Sarah walked to the back to retrieve his drink as the other attendant closed the door. The captain announced the takeoff and for them to fasten their seatbelts. After they were clear, Sarah brought Rock his drink. KoKo and Rock were heavy in conversation for the next hour, discussing how they could intertwine their business. When the first round of drinks were finished, their meal was brought out, grilled chicken over mushroom risotto and steamed spinach with walnuts.They ate and talked as the plane flew over several states. Sarah collected the dishes and refilled their glasses. They stopped in Miami, refueled, and then headed back to Georgia. When they reboarded the plane, KoKo went to the bathroom. When she returned, Rock had removed his tie and jacket and moved to the large leather recliner across from them.

"Come sit right here," he said, patting his lap.

KoKo strolled over to him and placed her soft ass right on the rock. "I think your little friend is waking up," she said as she shifted from side to side on his now hard dick.

"He likes to rise for the occasion."

"That's a good thing. Real women need a dick on Everlast."

"You talk a lot of shit," Rock said smoothly as he ran his hand up her thigh.

KoKo grabbed his wrist and said, "The first one was free. The rest will cost you."

"Oh, it's like that? What's it going to cost for me to be able to put my tongue somewhere very private?"

KoKo observed Rock carefully. *Look at him setting his own self up.* "Look, I need you to handle some very important business for me. I need a few houses, and I need them fast and I don't have time to go through a lot of red tape. So I need you to take care of all that quickly. There will be a large bonus in it for you."

"I don't do it quick. I like to take my time so I can get it right, and therefore, everyone involved is satisfied."

"Good. Then we have a deal?"

"Give me the figures, and I will see what I can do." Rock got quiet as he stared into KoKo's pretty eyes.

"What are you thinking about?" KoKo asked.

"How good your nipples are going to taste in my mouth when I'm deep inside you listening to you moan."

"What makes you think you will get the opportunity to experience all that?"

"Oh, trust and believe, I'm going to get the experience and so will you," he said, allowing himself to rise to full potential.

KoKo's back arched slightly as she felt his thickness between her butt cheeks.

"Excuse me, Miss KoKo. We are about to land. We need you to return to your seat and buckle up," Sarah announced as she came into the cabin.

KoKo removed Rock's hand and got up. His eyes were glued to her ass as she walked to the seat next to him. Sarah's eyes roamed back and forth at Rock's dick as she collected the empty glasses and bottles from the table. Rock caught her looking and smiled. Sarah looked away as her white face turned cherry red. KoKo chuckled. "You better be careful, Sarah. You know he's a single man."

"Not for long," Rock replied, looking over at KoKo.

Sarah made a girlish giggle and walked off to her area.

"You over there scaring that little girl."

"You gonna be scared of me, too," Rock stated with full confidence.

"Now you talking shit."

"When I get the chance, I'm going to do things to you that are going to make you thank God you're a woman."

KoKo laughed. "We will see," she said. *If this nigga only knew.*

The plane landed, and their time together ended. They both released their seatbelts. Rock stood up and grabbed his jacket and put it on. KoKo stood and assisted him by fixing his collar. Rock turned and took her by the waist.

"Thank you for the date."

"This is the first of many," she shot back.

"Next time it's on me," he said, pulling her into his arms and hugging her tight. She felt so good in his arms he didn't want to let her go. KoKo allowed him a few minutes to enjoy her. Rock whispered in her ear, "I plan on making you mine." He placed light kisses on her ear and neck while rubbing his hands up and down her back. Rock closed his eyes and began caressing her butt.

"What if I was planning on giving it to somebody else?"

"You might as well give it to a real man that knows what to do with it." He ran his hands through her hair. Grabbing a handful, he pulled her head back and placed several kisses from her throat to her chin. He locked eyes with her, but suddenly heard, "The limo is ready, Miss KoKo." The other attendant stood at attention, ready to escort Rock out of the plane.

"When can I see you again?" he asked as he released her from his embrace.

"I'll be in touch." KoKo turned, grabbed his hand, and walked him to the door.

Rock smiled and kissed her hand. He then proceeded down the steps to the awaiting vehicle.

THE PUSSY TRAP 2: THE KISS OF DEATH

KoKo watched her mark exit the tarmac with a plan formalizing in her mind.

Golden Paradise . . .

Over the next week, KoKo feverishly got ready for the grand opening of her club. She had recruited all the baddest bitches in the 'A' to work as servers and private entertainment for the VIPs. KoKo walked around the club checking out the final details. She was very pleased. Soft, white leather circular and L-shaped couches, crystal chandeliers, glass tables accented with gold, and custom mirrors hung everywhere, gave it that finishing touch. KoKo went to each VIP room and gave it a once over. Two of the rooms provided hot tubs for the show the strippers would give the honored guest. The other four rooms were equipped with limo tinted windows and poles, along with an array of toys to quench every desire.

"So what do you think, KoKo?" Chico said as he approached her.

"It's all good. We just have to make sure to fill this muthafucka up come Thursday night."

"Don't worry. The publicist is off the chain. She put together a hell of a guest list, and if everyone shows up this shit will be off the chain." He grinned big.

"Well, handle your handle and make sure everyone is on point."

"Let me ask you this. Is Goldie on point?" Chico asked.

"She straight. I got her on something, but she will be ready on Thursday."

When KoKo looked up, Goldie walked in the door with three bad bitches on her side. KoKo gave them all the once over as they approached. "Boss. This is Zori," Goldie said, introducing the first girl who stood about average height, weighed 145 pounds, red bone with shoulder length hair and all curves. "And this is Shameezah." She introduced the chocolate brown Jamaican girl with a tiny waist and ass for days. She was no taller than a minute. "And this is Porsha," Goldie said, pointing at the 6'1" light brown hued sister. She wore her hair long on one side and shaved on the other. Thin as a rail, her 40DD breasts caught everyone's eye.

KoKo looked at them for a few seconds and then rendered her verdict. "I want you to brief each one on what I want them to do. Take them to that house in Buckhead. Get into your roles. The work starts in a week. I'll be in touch."

The three women nodded in agreement. They had been well advised on how to deal with KoKo and from what she was paying, they were more than ready.

"Y'all ready?" Goldie asked. Again, they nodded as they turned to follow her to the exit.

"Keep an eye on those bitches. If they get outta pocket, you know what to do," KoKo said to Chico and then made her exit.

— 12 —
Recognition

Back in New York, KoKo was sitting in her office at her desk when Night came walking in.

"What's up, ma?" he asked as he took a seat.

"Sheeit . . . I can't call it," she said, looking up from some paperwork. "What's good with the count?"

"Everything is on point. Niggas responding like we need them to." He paused and looked around the room as he went into his vest and pulled out an envelope. He set in on her desk.

KoKo picked it up and looked inside. "What the fuck is this?" she asked, face all frowned up.

"I picked that up from Wise. Shit light as hell ain't it?"

KoKo took a deep breath.

"Yeah, my thoughts exactly. Everytime I go down there, I only see Wise and not Aldeen." Night waited for a few minutes to see what she would say. "Just say the word KoK."

"Nah, I got it. What else is up?"

Night nodded and then went to his next order of business. "I've been meaning to bring your attention to that nigga, Boa."

"Yeah, he's been on my radar."

"I want to bring him a little closer to the top."

"Is that right?" KoKo paused to think about the plan she was putting together, and if he was anything like she had been hearing, she could use him. "Well, set something up. I need to get in this nigga's face. Then we can see if he is qualified."

Night smiled.

"What's funny?" KoKo asked.

"Nothin' really. They tell me that he is a lot like Kayson used to say you were when he first snatched you up."

"What's that supposed to mean?" She chuckled and grabbed the drink she had poured for herself.

"You know your ass used to run around killing everybody on GP."

"Nah, playa. I only kill when necessary."

"Yeah, right. You just like the way it feel to cease a nigga from breathing." He paused and then grabbed the blunt from behind his ear and lit it up. "Nah, on the real, he is a real solider. If we can get him to calm the fuck down, he can be of some service. That nigga just took a chunk outta Brooklyn's ass last night." Night passed her the blunt.

"I sent them niggas a warning. They took my kindness for a weakness," KoKo said as she took a few deep pulls and passed it back.

"Yeah, Boa was sitting in on one of their little 'why all y'all work for a bitch' meetings. Then he aired out the room."

KoKo gave a half smile. "Yeah? Well, keep him close to you."

"I got him. He's a lil crazy. But I can handle him,"

KoKo thought about the report she had gotten a few days ago about those niggas talking shit. The fact that Boa took initiative and handled a potential problem only put a merit on his checklist. "Set up the meeting and let me worry about calming him down."

Night laughed again. "You gonna fuck around and hurt that boy."

KoKo just grinned. "Anything else? I have some work to do."

"Nah. I'm heading Uptown. I'll catch you later." Night put out his blunt, placed it back behind his ear, and then headed toward the door. He turned and said, "Be careful, KoKo. You know they building these niggas different these days."

"I'm not worried. Kayson taught me well. Remember, trappin' is not between the legs, it's between the ears."

— 13 —
Boa

A lot of changes took place when Kayson left the scene, and one of the biggest was bringing in new recruits. Boa was one of them. He had risen to the top of the ranks and his name was weaved all through the fibers of the organization. It was time for KoKo to get to the ground level and get a face to face. She wanted to catch him in action and see if his reputation was official. She figured if he was what they said he was, he would be very instrumental in what she was getting ready to pull-off.

KoKo pulled up a few blocks away from Sticks, a private pool hall she had set up in Manhattan. Here, they all hung out when they needed a little down time. She carefully observed all the activity going on. To her right, Savage engaged in conversation with this tall, light-skinned brother that held a strong resemblance to Kayson. It appeared that everyone was coming to him with information like he was in charge. "Boa, huh?" she mumbled. *Nigga want to be me.* She chuckled.

KoKo checked her guns and then jumped out and hit her alarm. As she got closer, everything seemed to get more organized. Savage elbowed Boa to let him know she was approaching. He circled his finger in the air and niggas started to scatter to their position. As she got closer, she and Boa locked eyes and almost immediately there was a connection.

"What's the verdict?" she spat to Savage, who was Night's head guy and responsible for making sure all the workers stayed in line and the money was right.

"It's all good, ma."

"Is that right?" She gave him a look that said she knew something that he wasn't telling her.

Savage picked up on it and then said, "Let me talk to you."

"I thought so."

They stepped aside. "That nigga Diesel has been getting way out of line. He should be here in a minute. He wants to talk to you about getting his own crew and area and moving from under your control."

"Is that it?" She raised her eyebrows.

Savage hesitated before speaking. "Nah, he asked why all these strong muhfuckas was taking orders from a bitch." Savage didn't want to say anything because he knew that KoKo would start a war. Plus, he had his orders from Night to bring him all the heavy shit.

"Riddle me this, my nigga. Why the fuck did I just have to ask you three times for one piece of information?" She gave him a dirty look. Savage immediately knew he fucked up. "When I ask you it's because I already know. I ain't got time to be jogging your fucking memory. When I ask you. Tell me."

Boa stood there ear hustling and smiling on the inside. He was working for a bad bitch, and he wanted to be more than just a worker. He figured if they could team up they could fuck the shit out the business with no vaseline.

KoKo turned her attention to Boa. "You got some shit you

want to reveal, or do I have to be a fucking psychic to find out?" KoKo asked him. Then she looked at Savage again real dirty.

"Nah, Boss. I'm an open book. You can have whatever I got." Boa put his hands up in surrender as he looked her up and down, licking his lips as if she was on the menu.

KoKo caught the transaction. "Well, put your lips away. I like my ass kissed in private." She walked inside the pool hall.

"Oh shit!" Savage said and then grabbed Boa's arm. "Nigga, that's some dangerous pussy. Don't do it."

"Nigga, please. Every woman got a spot that if you hit it right, she'll calm the fuck down and submit."

"That might be true. But that's KoKo. Niggas hit that spot then wake up dead than a muhfucka." Savage chuckled and walked inside, leaving Boa a minute to consider what he just said.

Boa took it in and thought, *Sheeit . . . if a nigga got to go, why not do it deep in some good pussy.* Then he went inside.

The pool hall was filled with about twenty of KoKo's team members and a bartender. While KoKo was working the room getting information, Boa and Savage took a seat at the bar, ordered a drink, and started talking.

"Boa, rack 'em," KoKo said. She began screwing her pool stick together and set it on the pool table. She took off her jacket and threw if over a bar stool, exposing the two nines she kept in a shoulder holster. She grabbed her pool stick and then positioned herself at the pool table.

Boa racked the balls, grabbed a stick, and stood across from her.

KoKo chalked her stick, set the cue ball and cracked the balls, sinking three in one shot. "I got stripes." She lined up her next shot and started her teaching session. She wanted to see where Boa's head was at. "How do you stop your enemy?" she asked, meeting his gaze dead on.

Boa thought for a minute. "You join him. The closer you get, the more you find out. It's better to have an enemy in your pocket than a bullet in your back."

KoKo nodded. "If the enemy doesn't conform, then what?" She sank another ball.

Boa leaned over and sunk one himself. "Kill 'em. It's better to have a dead enemy than a live stalker."

KoKo nodded again. "You left out one thing." She paused, sank another ball and said, "Dead men can't make money." Everyone got quiet. "Always get a nigga's throne before you burn down his castle." She sunk another ball. Everyone nodded in agreement, and Boa stood there savoring his lesson when Diesel came walking in with his little entourage.

"Oh, so I'm right on time. Just the person I wanted to see," he said, walking toward KoKo as she continued her game.

"Is that right?" She paused and looked over the pool table to see what to hit next.

"Yeah, that's right. I have a proposition for you. Can I speak to you in private?" he said, rubbing his hands together.

"Sheeit. You been running your mouth publicly, and now you want to talk in private. This *is* private." She stood erect to make eye contact. "Speak."

Everybody tensed up, ready to air his ass out. The people he walked in with could feel the tension.

Diesel took a minute but then thought, *Fuck it.* "I want my own shit. Our previous arrangement worked for then, but this is now, and I figured that I should have earned enough respect to go for self. I figured I would ask first, and then take if not accommodated."

"Well, you know what?" She leaned in to sink another ball. KoKo stood back up. "I just might have been open to a discussion, but you already made up your mind, so why the fuck are you in my face?"

Diesel began rubbing his hands together and shifting his weight from one foot to the other. A bead of sweat ran down the side of his face with all eyes on him. He thought about changing his mind, but he had already made his choice, so he had to go with it. "Look, I'm coming to you like a man. I didn't have to tell you shit."

Savage got up and at the same time the bouncer locked the door.

Diesel looked at the sudden movement and realized it was no turning back now. "Look, KoKo. I ain't trying to disrespect you. I just want my own shit."

"Well, if you want it you're going to have to take it."

"Bitch, I don't owe you shit ... . I—"

Boa hit him in the mouth with the fat end of the stick and it knocked him down. A stream of teeth and blood flew out his mouth. Boa beat him over his back and head as Diesel tried to crawl away. Everybody pulled out their pieces and had Diesel's boys dead in their scopes. His boys just put their hands in the air to surrender. They had so many guns in their face that they just stood down.

KoKo came over to Boa and said, "That's enough."

"Nah, fuck this pussy ass nigga." He hit him again. Diesel blacked out, lying in a puddle of his own blood and piss.

"Well, you should have just killed him then."

"A dead muthafucka can't feel pain. I want this nigga to feel me!" he growled as he stood over him breathing hard and holding the broken pool stick.

KoKo nodded and pulled out her gun and put two in Diesel's head. Then she said, "Yeah, that's true. But remember you said an enemy is better in your pocket than stalking your life? Well, you were his next target. He was after your crown."

Boa gave her a look that said 'damn and thanks' at the same time. Then he said, "What about his throne?"

"I already own it. And now I'm giving it to you." She turned to Darnell and Najim and said, "Y'all now work for Boa."

They gave a slight nod of agreement and walked over to Boa and shook his hand. KoKo had already found out about Diesel weeks earlier. His own boys had flipped on him. They were actually responsible for getting him to her.

As KoKo placed her gun back in the holster, she grabbed her pool stick. "Eight ball left side." She sunk it effortlessly. "That's game," she yelled as she grabbed her jacket. "I'll find a way for you to thank me later."

Boa tried to hide his excitement, but he could not help but give a small smile.

Night walked in from upstairs and looked at KoKo. "Is it done?"

"Yes it is. Bring Boa to me later. We got shit to do. Savage, get somebody to clean this shit up."

KoKo walked over to the bar, drank a shot of Brandy, and then walked out with Night on her heels. He stopped in front of Boa and said, "Be ready at 10:30." Then he kept on going.

Boa stood there amazed. He was starting to see why they called her The Boss.

Later that night . . .

Darnell and Najim found themselves in a dirty warehouse in Brooklyn. They had been snatched up as soon as they left the pool hall. Boa's goons had them tied at the feet, hands behind their backs, mouth gagged and standing straight up with truck tires around their bodies.

Boa came walking in the room and stood there looking at them while gritting his teeth. Mugsy, Boa's right hand, came over and snatched the tape off their mouths. They took the opportunity to plead their case.

"Boa, come on, my nigga. KoKo is straight with our loyalty," Darnell yelled out.

"Nigga, please. Y'all served up your boy on a silver platter. What assurance do I have that you won't turn on me if given a chance?" Boa said, his voice dripping with sarcasm.

"You got my word. That's all I got. I never crossed the organization," Darnell pleaded.

Boa stared him down and nodded at his boy who came over and poured gasoline all over them.

Darnell and Najim spat and gurgled up fuel while choking

and begging for their lives. Boa walked over to where they were as their pleas went ignored. Boa took out a cigar and a book of matches. He lit up, looked them both in the eyes and said, "Appeal denied."

"Boa, please don't!" Najim yelled.

"It's already done." He threw the match on the puddle of gas and walked away. The sound of their screams of pain only fueled the beast within him. Boa turned to get a visual to feed his thirst for torture. Black smoke arose from their heads. They made their final squawks as he took a deep pull on his cigar. The tobacco scent mingled with the stench of burning flesh. A wicked grin appeared on Boa's face. "I ain't got shit for traders but death. Fuck them niggas," he said and walked out the room.

Interrupted . . .

At two in the morning, KoKo was sitting in the back of the pool hall when she looked up and saw Boa coming her way wearing a serious face like he was on a mission. He walked up to one of the barmaids, whispered in her ear, and then continued walking toward KoKo. He slid in the booth next to her and put his arm on the back of the bench.

"What can I do for you?" KoKo asked in an aggravated tone.

"Nothing, I'm just a little hungry," he said, staring in her eyes.

"Is that right?"

"Yeah, that's right," he said, looking her up and down.

KoKo didn't change her facial expression. "First of all, take your fucking arm down. Second, this is called KoKo's time. Hence the fact that a bitch is sitting here by herself. Lastly, you missed that 10:30 meeting, so you're dismissed."

"You too sexy to be so fucking mean." Boa kept his eyes on her and moved his arm a little closer.

"And you too young to die."

"Damn. Why a nigga gotta die because he see something he need in his life?"

"I gotta hand it to you. You're a bold muthafucka. And I gotta applaud your courage. But let me ask you this—Are you willing to mess up your happy home? Because KoKo don't share no dick."

"Why we talking about my home? I'm trying to get over to your house."

KoKo chuckled. "That's what I thought. Like I said, you're dismissed. Come see me when your bitch gives your balls back." She looked over at Mugsy and nodded. As he approached the table, she grabbed her wine glass by the stem and brought it to her mouth. Taking a sip, she savored the flavor and then looked at Boa.

"You still here?" Although the question left her mouth, on the inside she was thinking, *Damn, this nigga fine as hell.*

Boa gave her that sexy smile. "I bet your pussy be wet all day." He looked her up and down once more. "I'ma have fun licking up every drop."

Boa's forwardness turned KoKo on, but she refused to show it. For the first time she was thrown off guard and had nothing to say. But being the bad bitch she was, she quickly recovered.

As he slid out the booth, KoKo shot back, "Yeah, and I bet ya ass will be outside in the daylight with a flashlight and a mattress strapped to your back with candles on your shoulders looking for a bitch."

"Oh shit. I'ma call this nigga Kraftmatic," Mugsy said and burst out laughing.

"Sheeeit . . . I'ma make that pussy send me a thank you card," Boa shot back as he slapped hands with Mugsy and then moved out.

"Oh yeah, you owe me a hundred stacks for that unauthorized assassination."

Boa shot her a smile. "Oh, I'ma pay you all right," he said and then turned to make his exit.

KoKo smiled and took another sip as she watched him walk out. *He's almost ready.*

— 14 —
Unpredictable

Boa had showered and changed. He was now sitting in the back of the game room watching the action, drinking and enjoying Maureen running her hand up and down his dick. She whispered all kinds of offers in his ear.

Boa smiled as he reveled in her trying every trick imaginable to get him to take her home with him. He had come to the conclusion that he was going to have her get on her knees right there and taste the rock. However, that all came to a screeching halt when he looked up and saw Night and Savage walking toward his table. Their patience was wearing thin as he was supposed to have met them two hours earlier to go meet KoKo.

"Damn, nigga you hard to keep up with," Savage yelled over the music as they approached the table.

"Nah. All you got to do is follow the pussy trail, and there I am sitting and enjoying." He smiled and looked over at Maureen, who gave him a girlish grin. She was sure she had won her an evening. But Night shot that dream to hell with his next statement.

"Let's go, nigga. KoKo been waiting on you for two hours." His stare was cold and disappointing. He had vouched for him, so his rep was on the line, and he would rather kill this nigga before he let him fuck up his reputation.

Boa looked at Night's expression and dropped his smile. He moved Maureen's hand out of his lap, quickly sending a signal to little Boa to chill. He took one last sip of his drink and then stood up. He looked down at Maureen.

"I'll catch up with you next time, shorty."

Maureen grimaced, apparently upset. She stood and whispered in his ear, "Too bad for you. I was going to suck your dick so good, you were going to forget where you lived."

Boa smiled and said, "Put me down for Wednesday."

"Maybe," she shot back. She squeezed between Night and Savage and was gone.

As she disappeared, Savage turned to get a look at her ass, "Sheeit . . . That's a hell of a piece of ass to just dismiss."

"Nah, I got a date with the Boss. Ain't no pussy sweeter than power pussy." He stood up and walked past them. "What we riding in?" he yelled as he headed to the door.

"KoKo is going to fuck that nigga head up," Savage stated.

"He better pray that's her plan. KoKo is the black widow. He'll mess around and wake up with his dick in his mouth," Night said. He then headed for the door.

"Oh shit!" Savage grabbed his dick. "That's some shit I can do without." He followed behind Night.

***

The car ride blared Busta Rhymes and The Game's song "Doctor's Advocate" from the speakers along with weed smoke scenting the vehicle's interior. Boa sat back looking out the window and wondering what KoKo wanted with him.

KoKo's mansion parallelled Kayson's mansion out in

Yonkers. When they pulled up to the gate, Night rolled down the window and hit the buzzer. The camera scanned the vehicle and the gate opened. Boa was impressed. They drove up to the garage and it lifted, giving them entrance. All he saw was wall-to-wall cars sitting on the sexiest rims he had ever seen. Night got out and headed to the elevator, put his hand on the security recognition pad, and the doors opened.

"Damn. Where the fuck we at? The Pentagon?" Boa laughed.

Night and Savage didn't respond because they were in business mode. Boa picked up on it quickly, and he too got serious. When they got to the second floor the doors opened. Night stood between them and pointed to the left.

Boa got off the elevator. "Why y'all not getting out?" he asked with a bit of suspicion.

"Don't get all worried, nigga. It's just KoKo," Savage said with a smile.

"Go ahead. You already late," Night reminded him as he maintained a serious mood. He stepped back on the elevator.

Savage laughed. Just as the doors closed he said, "Watch your back."

Boa looked down the dimly lit hall. He started to walk in the direction he was sent in, but he was taken aback by the interior design. When he got half way down the hall, the wall ended and glass began. He looked through the rose tint and saw an all black marble indoor pool with red lights coming from the bottom and mirrors all around. "God*damn*!" he murmured. As he reached the end of the hall, two huge, dark red lambskin couches decorated the sitting area. He took a seat and continued to look around at the paintings on the wall. The one that caught his attention was right across from the couch—a big canvas photo of KoKo sitting on a beach in an all-white bikini with her head back, hair hanging long and silky. It appeared the sun was just about to leave the sky. Beautiful. She had a full arch in her back and those chocolate legs were sexy as hell.

KoKo stood in the shadow watching his every move. Boa sat forward and took a few deep breaths as he kept looking at his watch. Just as he was getting ready to let impatience drive him back toward the elevator, KoKo spoke from the shadow, "Are you lusting at me, Mr. Barnes?" She stepped into the light.

Boa looked in her direction. "Nah, I just know a beautiful woman when I see one," he said and stood up. She walked toward him wearing a black, knee-length form-fitting body dress. Her scent caressed his nostrils before she reached him. The whole mood said 'sex me.'

"So I guess you know I got you out here for a reason?" KoKo said as she walked toward her office and pushed the doors open.

Boa walked behind her as he watched her perfect heart-shaped ass sway from side to side. *Is she wearing panties?* he thought as he enjoyed the view. "So what? You need me to put in some work?" Boa said, not taking his eyes off her body.

KoKo looked back over her shoulder. "I don't need shit. I want to bring you closer to the top." KoKo rested up against her desk.

"You ready to share your throne?" Boa looked her over.

"It's only room for one ass on my throne, and that's mine. But I will let you sit in it from time to time."

"No problem. If you're going to sit that ass on my lap . . ." He looked in her eyes, reveling in the sexual tension between them.

"Look. Mr. Barnes, this is just business." KoKo's tone said otherwise.

"If it's just business, then why me?" Boa moved closer.

KoKo allowed herself to relax enough so she could appear a little shy. She was setting up the bait, and from what she could see, he was getting ready to jump head first into her trap. "I need somebody by my side. I have to have somebody I can trust." KoKo paused as Boa got right up on her. "You need to calm down though. Your temper can blow this whole mission."

Boa kept his eyes locked on hers. "Can I taste you?"

"Mr. Barnes, you're treading in dangerous waters."

"Well, why don't you try drowning me?" He leaned up against her, allowing her to feel the lethal weapon he carried in his pants. He placed his hands on her waist and continued his seduction.

"Why do they call you Boa?" KoKo asked as she placed her hands on top of his.

"It's Boa like the snake. When I see a threat I ambush my prey before they can strike. Poison is not my weapon of choice. However, I'm deadlier than a muthafucka. Plus, once I have something I want, I hold on real tight. So they started calling me Boa." He was all up on her. "There are a few other reasons . . . that, you'll find out in time."

"Will I?"

"Let me show you." He took her hand and ran it down the length of his dick.

KoKo stared him right in the eyes, showing no emotion. But secretly she thought, *Damn, this shit is almost to his knee!* This was accompanied by the thought that she hadn't had sex in a little over a year, and she wanted Boa to be the recipient of all that release. She silently allowed him to have his pleasure, and then she broke the silence. "Am I supposed to be impressed?" She removed her hand.

"No. Not impressed. Frightened," Boa spat back.

"Is that right?" she said in her Kayson voice. "Aren't boas supposed to be deadly? Why would you want to hurt all this, sexy?"

"Nah, he's not for pain. He's for pleasure." His eyes roamed all over her body and then locked with her eyes.

KoKo couldn't shake the fact that his demeanor reminded her of Kayson. His confidence and downright cocky attitude were a definite turn on, but it was the resemblance that was so scary.

"Did they check you before you came up here?"

"Nah, but feel free to feel a brother up," he said.

"Turn around," KoKo seductively ordered. Boa stepped back and took the position, placing his hands behind his head. KoKo moved smoothly behind him and began patting him down. Boa stood there enjoying the precision of her touch. KoKo leaned forward, resting her breasts on his back as she ran her hand down his stomach and then along his dick, nice and slow. In two moves, she unzipped his jeans, slid her hand inside, and started to stroke him to full potential.

"He feels more like a threat. Are you sure he's for pleasure?" KoKo barely whispered. She continued massaging his now massive hard-on, applying the right amount of pressure.

"Yeah, but even his pain feels good. Come here for a minute," he said, moving her hand from his pants and guiding her in front of him. Placing his hands on her waist, he sat her on the desk. He caressed the small of her back as he slid her to the edge, pressing that steel against her now throbbing clit as his hands began to roam over her body. KoKo and Boa were in a stare down as the sexual tension between them became suffocating.

"I want you to take over dealing with the Russians. I want to wage a war between them and the Italians. I need to step a little further back into the shadows." She began tutoring him on the job at hand. Then KoKo nibbled and sucked that spot under his chin. "It's going to be dangerous. You have to stay focused." Boa closed his eyes as he reached between her legs and ran his fingers up and down the lips of her pussy, playing in her wetness. KoKo continued to talk while caressing him as she enjoyed his touch. She was on fire.

"You want me to show you another reason why they call me Boa?"

"Yes," she whispered.

Boa gently pushed her back and pulled the chair up from behind him. He pulled her dress up her thighs, placed her feet on his shoulders, gripped the back of her thighs, leaned in and went to work. His tongue slid easily over her clit as she circled her hips to his rhythm.

KoKo looked down, watching as his soft lips covered hers. His tongue was soft, long and flexible as it moved effortlessly, pleasing every inch of her sweetness. Her pussy felt like it was smiling.

Once her breathing changed, he placed his mouth over her clit and rotated between soft and hard sucks. He paused and ran his tongue from the bottom of her pussy back to the top and then began sucking her clit again.

"Ssss . . . mmmm," KoKo moaned. The response sent chills up his spine. KoKo began riding his face, stimulating her spot. Within moments she felt the contractions coming on. Seconds later, her legs shook as she started cumming and skeeting all over his mouth.

"Damn!" Boa responded as he watched KoKo recover from that mind-blowing orgasm. He released her legs and reached for his zipper and let the snake lose.

KoKo was all over him, kissing and sucking his neck and pulling at his shirt and pants. She wrapped her legs around him, clamped her thighs to his waist and bit hard into his neck as he fumbled around in his pocket in search of his plastic.

Just as he ripped the side of the pack open with his teeth and prepared to strap up, Night's voice came blaring through the intercom, "KoKo, we on our way up."

KoKo released Boa from her grip and pushed him back.

"Hold up, ma," Boa protested in an attempt to keep her there.

"It's always business first, Boa," KoKo said and slid off the desk, pulling her dress down. KoKo walked over to the phone and hit the response button. "Come on," she said and then headed to the bathroom. She closed the door, leaving Boa with a hard dick and a wet hand.

"What the fuck?" Boa said out loud, quickly putting his rod back. He threw the condom in the garbage, fixed his clothes and stood next to the bathroom door.

KoKo emerged about five minutes later, fully dressed in jeans, a shirt, and boots. She looked up at Boa, who was obviously disappointed.

"You got that off!" Boa spat.

"I'm KoKo, baby. I always get off." She reached up and rubbed his face. "Go ahead and clean up. They'll be up here in a minute. I don't do late," she stated. She headed to her desk and sat down.

Boa walked into the bathroom and shut the door. He stood at the sink looking in the mirror while washing his hands. *How the fuck I let her get away from me?* Then he saw a big ass hickey on his neck. *What the fuck!* He turned his head to the side. "Latreece." His thoughts went to his girl for a few seconds. Briefly he panicked, but finally said, "Fuck it." He ran water over his face and then grabbed a paper towel and dried off. Just as he was about to emerge from the bathroom, he heard Night and Savage talking. He hesitated but then opened the door and walked out.

Savage looked at Boa and smiled. He pointed to the hickey on his neck. "What the fuck happened to you?" he asked with a slick smile on his face.

"I fell," Boa said, walking to the couch.

"I bet you did. Was it on something or in something?"

"Fuck you, nigga. Where's KoKo?" he asked, still feeling a little slighted.

"She had to go. She said don't get dirty. She can't afford to lose time over bullshit. Come on. We have to go take care of something. Then she wants you to give orders to your crew to fall in under Savage until you get back," Night instructed.

"Get back from where?" Boa asked.

"We'll explain that to you in the car. Let's roll," Night said, walking off toward the elevator.

Boa was confused as hell. Within a matter of hours KoKo had managed to fuck his head up, take control of his crew, and leave him with a hard dick and no explanation. He had to admit that for the first time a bitch had him by the balls.

— 15 —
Opening Night

On Thursday night, the curtains were opening and KoKo was ready to perform.

"KoKo, it is packed up in this muhfucka," Chico yelled in the phone as he watched the crowd pouring into Golden Paradise.

"I'll be there in about ten minutes." KoKo hung up and prepared her mind for her arrival at Golden Paradise. She took a few more sips of champagne and two more pulls off her blunt and then put it out. Looking in the mirror, she applied a fresh coat of flavored lip-gloss. She combed her hair, sprayed on some David Yurman, and then popped a Listerine strip in her mouth. The gold Bentley pulled in front of the club and cameras flashed from everywhere. There were two long lines, one from each side of the door. KoKo stepped out onto the red carpet and began walking the long runway between the two velvet ropes.

Chico watched KoKo switch down the red carpet in a two-piece white pants suit with the low cut jacket showing off her perky breasts. Niggas were hollering and bitches were hating. He heard the girl standing close to him say to her friend, "Damn, she must be a celebrity or something."

When KoKo reached Chico, he smiled from ear to ear and

said, "Goddamn!"

"Is my section ready?" she asked.

"Si, Senorita," he responded.

He took her hand and led her inside. When she stepped in the club, all she could do was smile. The music was pumping and people were dancing and drinking. The VIP sections were full, and the champagne was flowing. She shook her head up and down in satisfaction.

The signal was given to the DJ, and he quickly threw on KoKo's favorite song, "I'ma Boss" by one of Atlanta's hottest underground emcee's, Boss Chic. He shouted out, "We got the Boss Lady in the house. Show some love for Misssssss KoKooooo." He shined a spotlight on her, and the crowd started clapping and whistling.

KoKo waved, walking toward her private section, escorted by two of Night's boys. As she walked the club, she noticed all of the celebrities in attendance. She passed the first glass enclosed area and had to drop in. "Are you gentlemen enjoying yourselves?" she asked.

"We would be enjoying ourselves a little bit more if you would join us," Floyd Mayweather said and threw her that big smile. He reached up and grabbed her hand.

"This night is about y'all. I will send someone over in my place to make sure you have a very good night." She winked and prepared to walk off.

"All we need is a little bit," Fifty yelled out and flashed his sexy smile.

"Then I'm the wrong bitch to fuck with. Because I need way more than a little bit."

The men started laughing.

"Enjoy the evening. Let me know if you need anything." She waved four sexy, half-dressed females over who came right away with several bottles of champagne. KoKo nodded and walked away. She spotted Big Boy and Andre 3000 and waved without even breaking her stride. In another section, she saw Ludacris and his entourage. She gave them the same treatment and kept it moving. As she got closer to her section, Lil' Wayne and some of the Young Money and Cash Money crew were in the building. She leaned over to Big Mike. "Put them in that last VIP room with the tinted windows, and send a crew in there with some bud and some bitches and keep the drinks coming."

As Mike delivered the news to Lil Wayne, he looked up and she mouthed, "YMCMB." He nodded and stood up to be escorted to VIP.

KoKo winked and left the area. Before she went inside her section, she looked over to a far corner at a small group of men. "Can't be," she said to herself with a slight smile as she headed in their direction. When she approached the men, her assumption was confirmed. Her dog, DMX was chillin' in her establishment.

"Y'all good?" she said over the music.

"Yeah, we good, baby," DMX responded.

"I can put y'all in a private area."

"Nah, we good right here. I like to be with the people. You know I'm feeling the love."

"A'ight, if you need anything let me know."

"Will do." He stood up and hugged KoKo. She returned the

embrace.

"You my nigga," KoKo said, throwing him a smile that he returned. She left the table, stopping to send a few drinks their way.

After making her rounds, she stood in front of the VIP section and took one last look at the crowd to make sure she didn't miss anybody. KoKo turned to walk inside the glass enclosed area and take a seat.

Watching the action, she could only think about how proud Kayson would have been to see her making moves to legitimize their money. In a short period of time she had opened one club and awaited the opening of her Miami location. All the real estate she was accumulating would only solidify her goal. And with the many businesses she helped different members of the organization start, things were really lining up. It was only a matter of time before she would be able to walk away from all ties to the drug game and just focus on her son. "This is all for you, Kayson," she said, holding her glass in the air and then taking a sip of the wine the waitress had poured her.

Night walked through the doors smiling from ear to ear. "These niggas up in here spending a grip."

"Hell yeah. And my crew is working the room, blueprinting mickies."

"Mickies?"

"Yeah, niggas that you can get to do whatever you want."

Night started laughing. "Business as usual."

"Hell yeah, it's always business. These muhfuckas came out for fun. I ain't rich enough yet. I'll party when all my money is working for me. Right now a bitch got to work hard."

Night shook his head in agreement. "Well, tonight at least enjoy yourself a little," he said, pulling on a blunt."

KoKo put her hand out to take the blunt and said, "You enjoy it for me." She sat back and crossed her legs, watching the action. Night whispered something to her bodyguards and left the room.

For the rest of the night, KoKo sat in the VIP section as different members of her crew came by to congratulate her and give her reports. Around 2 a.m., Goldie came by to give her the count. They grossed over $100,000 between the door, food and bar, and they still had three hours to go. KoKo dismissed her and had Chico to escort her to her car. She sat back as the curtains closed. She lit up a blunt, thinking, *The 'A' is definitely getting ready to bless a bitch, and they ain't even going to see it coming.*

Fear . . .

"You didn't have to come all the way out here."

"I had to talk to you face to face," Pat revealed as she walked over to the couch and took a seat.

"Look, we have gone over this enough times. You know what you're supposed to say. Handle your business."

Pat stared at the wall for a few seconds. "She knows shit that only me, you, and Nine know."

"So the fuck what! If you don't confirm, then all she has is suspicions. Stick to the plan."

"It's easy for you to say. You're all the way the fuck up here." Pat stood up and walked over to the window where she lit a cigarette and took a few pulls. "I just want all this shit to go away. I'm tired of the lies."

"Look, don't fall apart on me now. You knew this day was coming. Just stick to the script. It's almost over."

Pat continued to stare out the window. Her mind was full and her spirit was heavy. The secrets she had been holding for the last twenty years had grown in her belly like a tumor, and she was dying to rid herself of the pain of deceit.

~ 16 ~
Living Foul

At three in the morning Boa gently turned his key in the door so as not to wake Latreece. He had been gone for three days, and he knew he was going to hear her mouth. Slowly he opened it and peeked inside. When he saw no light or movement, he cracked the door more and slid inside, closing it very lightly behind him. He adjusted his eyes to the darkness, slipped his feet out of his boots, and then proceeded to tip across the living room. When he got to the middle of the room, the light came on and he paused, squinting his eyes from the blinding light.

"Why the fuck is you creeping through the house like a damn cat burglar?" Latreece said, standing in her two-piece pajama set.

"I didn't want to wake you."

"You are such a liar," she said, apparently fed up with his recent activity.

Within the last few months, Boa had begun getting sloppy. Latreece had found a pack of condoms in his overnight bag he used to go out of town, and she received several phone calls from random bitches, not to mention the other signs of his infidelity that had become magnified. Now he was creeping in the house at three in the morning looking guilty as hell. Boa kept on walking and went to the walk-in closet, took off his clothes, and headed for the shower.

Latreece came and stood by the shower. "Got to wash the evidence away, huh?"

"Go 'head with all that."

Latreece snatched the shower door open. "Do you enjoy making a fool out of me?" she shouted, full of rage. Just as she started her rant, her eyes settled in on the mark on his neck. She felt like the wind had been knocked out of her. She wanted to continue, but couldn't. Up until now everything was speculation, but tonight she had gotten an in your face confirmation and immediately felt sick to her stomach.

"I fucking hate you!" she screamed and stormed out the bathroom. Latreece went straight to her dresser and began snatching her clothes from the drawer in an attempt to get dressed and leave. Tears fell from her eyes at a rapid pace, and her heart felt like it wanted to leap from her chest.

Boa came storming out the bathroom. "I'm sorry. Hold up. Let me explain."

"Explain what? How you just crawled out the next bitch's pussy and then came home to me with that bitch's pleasure mark on your neck?" She glared at him with pain in her eyes. "Why Boa? Why do you enjoy hurting me?" she said, shaking her head.

"Baby, it was a mistake. This stripper bitch was all up on me, and then she just bit me," he said, rubbing at his neck.

Latreece chuckled. "What type of fool do you take me for?" She turned and walked to the closet to retrieve her shoes.

Boa was torn. The last thing he wanted was to hurt

Latreece. She had endured so much and didn't deserve what he was taking her through. The part that hurt him most was seeing the disappointment in her eyes. "Shit!" Boa said, coming up behind her and hugging her tight.

"Get off me, Boa!" She tried to resist his advances.

"I need you to forgive me," he whispered in her ear.

"Boa, stop. I need to get out of here. I can't stand to look at you right now," she protested while struggling to break from his grip. He pressed up against her, dick out and ready.

"Let me make it up to you," he said, planting kisses on her neck.

"Boa, don't. Let me go," she asserted with tears streaming down her face.

Boa reached up under her shirt and began caressing her breasts. She grabbed his hand and tried to move it. "Let me make it all better," he seductively whispered.

Latreece felt defeated. He felt so good up against her, his strong hands on her breasts and warm lips on her neck and ear. His rock hard dick threatened to bust through her shorts. Boa had managed to get a hold of her nipple and slowly kneaded it between his fingers. While she was distracted with trying to free her breasts, he rushed his other hand down the front of her shorts and began circling her clit. "Let me go, Boa," she said with both pleasure and anger in her voice. She tried one last time to be free. Boa was fed up with the small struggle. He turned her around, pushed her up against the wall and started kissing her rough and deep. She surrendered her tongue to him and was rewarded with his passion.

Boa broke the kiss, looked her in the eyes and said, "This is your dick." He took her hand and wrapped it around his hardness and squeezed. Then he started to stroke himself with her hand.

After a few strokes she said, "I can't tell it belongs to me."

With that, he picked her up, carried her to the bed and threw her on it. Grabbing her by the ankles, he yanked her into position then forcefully pulled off her shorts and climbed on top of her like a wild man. He inserted himself deep inside her and went to work.

Latreece screamed and moaned and came for hours as Boa fucked her in every position possible. By the time he was done, the sun was up and she was sexed out.

He lay on her back, slowly stroking her as her limp body had no more energy. "You forgive me?" he whispered.

Barely able to respond, she mumbled, "Mmmm. Yes. Yes. I forgive you."

"It's all about you, Treece," he said in her ear and picked up his pace in an attempt to cum one more time.

"Mmmm . . ." she moaned as he went deeper.

"I love you!" he growled as he came long and hard.

The deep stroke brought one last orgasm on for her as well, and she yelled out, "I love you, Boa! Oh my God!"

Boa pushed as deep as he could and stayed there. Kissing the side of her face, he told her, "This is your dick."

"I know," she whispered as a few tears escaped her eyes.

Boa rolled off her back and onto his own. Latreece snuggled next to him and dozed off. He lay there thinking that here he had a woman lying beside him whom he loved, who had had his back for the last three years. He wasn't willing to fuck that up by chasing KoKo. He decided at that moment he needed to keep it professional. Little did he know KoKo wasn't going to allow it. Boa was already in too deep.

— 17 —
Uninvited Guest

"Stop, Boa!" Latreece yelled out, laughing and squirming in Boa's arms as he continued to bite and tickle her.

"Say you love me."

"I do. I do. I love you," she yelled while grabbing his hands to stop the torture. Boa stopped, briefly allowing her to regain her composure. Then he started all over again.

Boa had spent the last two days in the house trying to get back in Latreece's good graces. They were lying on the couch watching TV and laughing when the doorbell rang.

"Whyyyy?" Latreece yelled out as she attempted to sit up.

Boa pulled her back into his arms. "Stop Boa, I have to get the door." Boa started kissing her and running his hand up and down her back.

"Buzzz . . . Buzzz . . ." the bell rang again.

Latreece broke from his grip and headed to the door. "Don't your little friends know it's daddy time?"

"Don't hate 'cause I'm loved. Plus you had me for two days. They probably want to see if I'm still alive."

She turned and smiled and proceeded to open the door. "Just a minute," she yelled and then looked through the peephole and her whole attitude changed. She took a deep breath, unlocked the door, and cracked it. There stood KoKo in a pair of fitted jeans accenting her shapely bowlegs. A strapless fitted tank showed off her cocoa smooth, slightly muscular shoulders and arms. A pair of three-inch designer heels displayed her manicured feet. Latreece looked at her iced out chain that read, KoKo. She had heard about KoKo, but from the rumors she thought that maybe she may have looked real butch. But she had to admit KoKo was well put together.

KoKo locked eyes with Latreece and said, "Is Mr. Barnes home?"

"It depends on who's looking," Latreece shot back with a fake smile.

"It's his boss," she said, maintaining her serious face.

The women stood in a stare down until Boa yelled out, "Who is it?"

"It's your boss," Latreece said, eyebrows raised. She opened the door, exposing Boa lying on the couch.

"What's good, KoKo?" He sat up. "Let her in, ma." Latreece put her hand out as a gesture for KoKo to proceed in. KoKo walked inside. Latreece looked her up and down as she went past and a strong feeling of jealousy rose up in her gut.

"So what's up?" he asked, uncertain of what KoKo was trying to pull. He knew she had balls, but no one ever knew when she was going to use them.

Latreece came and sat beside him, wondering the same thing. *This bitch is bold as hell.*

"That watch looks good on you," KoKo said to Latreece.

"Yeah, Boa gave it to me," Treece said, beaming and looking at Boa.

"I know. I bought it," KoKo stated with a serious look.

The color drained from Latreece's face and so did the smile.

"Yeah, it's for the wives. Don't fuck up," KoKo warned and then turned her attention to Boa.

"It's time to punch the clock, nigga," she said and then laughed. "You all 'love-nest' up in this muthafuacka." She sat back, crossed those sexy bowlegs, and pulled a blunt from her clutch and lit it up.

Latreece was on fire. Her leg shook as she bit on her bottom lip displaying a small attitude.

Boa looked back and forth between the two and could feel the tension getting thick. He said, "Let me go get dressed." Then he stood up.

As he passed, KoKo smacked his ass with the back of her hand. "Hurry up, soldier. We got shit to do." She took another long pull on her blunt.

All he could do was smile. KoKo was that bitch. "You ain't paying me that much," he mumbled then headed to the bathroom.

Latreece was ready to check her, and the fact that Boa didn't say anything and kept on going made Latreece even madder.

"We usually don't smoke in here," Latreece stated as her eyes lowered and her mouth twisted from side to side.

"Is that right?" KoKo said, taking another long pull while staring her down. "Well, where do *we* smoke at?" she asked, sarcasm dripping from her voice as she blew smoke in Latreece's direction.

"Well, Boa smokes in the bathroom."

KoKo grinned and kept on smoking.

Just as Latreece got ready to say something else, the house phone rang. "Excuse me," she said, and then got up and headed to the kitchen. She was ready to get out of KoKo's face.

"What's up, girl?" she said into the phone and paused briefly. " . . .Giiirrl. That nigga had me up in here doing all kinds of shit to me." Latreece began loading the dishwasher and cleaning the kitchen while engaged in her phone call.

Just then, KoKo heard the shower come on. She got up and sashayed her sexy ass down the hallway and into the bathroom. She locked the door, and then little by little she opened the shower door and stood there smoking her blunt and watching Boa lather up that sexy body. The water and soap ran down his muscular back and his ass.

"I'll be back later on. What are you going to feed daddy?" Boa yelled out as he ran the water over his face and then turned around. "Why you ain't saying nothin'?" he asked as he opened his eyes to find KoKo standing there.

"What the fuck?"

"Don't mind me. I'm just enjoying the view," KoKo said smoothly.

"For real, KoKo?" he asked, turning the water off and reaching for his towel.

"Where is Latreece?" He looked past her at the door.

"She said 'we smoke in the bathroom,' so here I am. Don't fuck up my moment with bullshit questions." Boa wrapped up in his towel in an attempt to cover up. He pulled the door all the way back then tucked the towel in on the side.

"Don't put it away on my account," she said in a sexy tone.

"You know your ass is dead wrong," he said while staring into her eyes.

The excitement of having his woman in one room and the woman whose pussy he had been fantasizing about lying in for months standing in front of his face only made his dick hard. Boa began to think about how good she felt to him and the moans she made because of him just using his tongue. The more he thought about it, the harder he became.

"Let me get some of that." He reached out for the blunt. KoKo pulled her hand back and dutted the ashes in the ashtray. She placed the blunt in her mouth and moved in closer to Boa. She blew him a shotgun allowing her lips to lightly touch his. The smoke hit his lungs hard as he inhaled, releasing the smoke from his nose as he stared into her eyes.

KoKo removed the blunt from her mouth, placed it on the ashtray and then broke the trance by saying, "Is that the snake you wanted me to meet?" She reached in his towel and began to stroke his dick, applying just the right amount of pressure. "I think I might want this for myself," she whispered as she seductively stroked his handle. Boa put his hands behind his back as he enjoyed the action.

"What if it already belongs to someone?" he said in a deep and sexy mumble.

"I always get what I want, Mr. Barnes. And I have no problem with taking it." KoKo quickened her pace as she heard a slight hiss from his lips.

"I want you to take it," Boa said, allowing himself to reach his limit.

"You gonna let me take it, Boa?" she moaned, turning her wrist and picking up speed, causing Boa's breathing to become heavy. She continued to stroke him until he was cumming. KoKo slowly slid her hand up and down the length of his dick, allowing the wetness to guide her stroke. Holding their intense gaze, she said, "You hooked a sistah up the other night. I just wanted to return the favor."

"You know when you finally give me that pussy, I'ma fuck you so good you ain't gonna know your name."

"It sounds good. Make it look good." She threw the challenge on the table to see if he had the balls to get some with his girl in the next room.

Boa smiled. "You a bad bitch."

KoKo released him from her hand, grabbed him around the neck, and placed a kiss on his lips. "There ain't another bitch on the planet like me. And don't you forget it."

She seductively turned to the sink and washed her hands. Turning back, she looked at his dick and said, "Um. Um. Um. It should be illegal for a nigga to walk around with all that dick. Oh yeah, that's going to be KoKo's." She nodded. "Hurry up. I don't want to have to fuck your bitch up." With that, she walked out the bathroom.

Latreece suddenly became suspicious with the silence. "I'll call you back," she said into the phone and then hung up. She came into the living room and went on high alert when she didn't see KoKo. She immediately walked to the hallway toward her room and saw KoKo switching those hips coming down the hall. She was giving Latreece fever.

"Umm . . . excuse you," Latreece stated.

"Thanks for the hospitality. Tell Boa I'm in the car," she said in a serious tone and kept walking.

Latreece watched as she grabbed her clutch and left the apartment. Livid, she stormed toward the bathroom, and when she opened the door Boa was sitting on the toilet in his jeans, smoking the blunt KoKo left behind. "Why the fuck was that bitch in here while you were in the shower?" She had one hand on the doorknob and one on her hip in full argument mode.

"Smoking. You told her we smoke in the bathroom," Boa stated matter-of-factly. Then he stood up, put on his tank top and a T-shirt on top of it. He slid his feet in his boots and laced them up. Then he walked over and kissed her on the forehead and moved past her. "I got to go." He went in the room, grabbed his money and his gat, preparing to leave the house.

"When will you be back?" she asked, her voice cracking as if ready to cry. It was something about KoKo that she didn't like, and she certainly didn't like how Boa's whole attitude changed whenever her name came up.

"Later on." Boa gave her a big hug and kissed her on the lips. "Don't be jelly, ma. KoKo is just one of the guys." He released her and headed for the door.

Latreece watched him bop his cool ass out the door while thinking, *Yeah fucking right*. She felt Boa slipping, and it was just a matter of time before he slipped and fell in some pussy he would not be able to get out of. And from what she could detect, KoKo was the one with that power.

— 18 —
Real Estate

For the next two weeks KoKo kept Boa close. She was carefully grooming him to meet the Russians. Even though she had been working with them for years, they were still very hard to deal with. KoKo had to make sure Boa's attitude calmed down before the introduction. In the meantime, she had to get back to the 'A' to make sure things stayed in line.

Back in Atlanta, KoKo was sitting in Rock's office finalizing the property she had purchased from him. She looked over the paperwork pinpointing the many lines she had to sign. He stood looking at her like she was his favorite dish.

"Sign here, here, and here," Rock said to KoKo as he pointed to the signature portion of the documents. This would be the fifth piece of property that Rock got for KoKo. She was having them rehabbed to flip.

"Nice doing business with you," KoKo said as she stood up and put her hand out for Rock to shake.

"Nah, Miss KoKo. I deserve more than a handshake." He looked her up and down.

KoKo gave him an innocent smile. "Yeah, you've been a good boy. Let momma give you a small reward. She opened her arms and he stepped into them and wrapped her tightly in his embrace. KoKo felt so good in his arms. Even she had to admit the strength of his warm embrace made her kitty tingle.

"You need to let me take you out tonight," he whispered in her ear. She closed her eyes as his steamy breath caressed her neck.

"Not tonight, baby. But I promise I will reward you for a job well done." She pulled back, bringing this little tryst to an end.

"You scared?"

"What exactly am I supposed to be scared of?"

"A real man."

KoKo smiled. "Let me see your hand," she stated as the smile slowly left her face. Rock put his hand in hers. She placed it between her breasts. "You feel that?"

"I don't feel nothing," he said, enjoying the warmth of her smooth skin.

"Exactly. The only thing worse than a real bitch is a fearless one." She pulled his hand down. "When the time is right, you're gonna wish I was afraid of you." She turned to leave his office.

Rock leaned up against his desk and folded his arms. "Enjoy your property."

"Oh, don't worry. I will." She looked down at his bulging package and looked back up at his sexy smile. "Just be patient. I got you," she said, exiting his office.

Rock stood for a minute, fantasizing about her and when he would get to cash in on her promise.

— 19 —
Thank You

Curupt pulled into the driveway of the address that Goldie had given him. He looked at the house and then put the truck in park. Opening the door, he stepped out and headed up the steps and hit the bell.

After about forty seconds, he hit it again. He waited but no one came to the door. He stepped back and looked through the window next to the door. Music echoed in his ears but Curupt didn't see any movement inside. As he was about to ring the bell a third time, Goldie came walking toward the door wearing a two-piece red bikini and a pair of red high-heeled sandals. Her white sheer robe fluttered in the breeze as she moved.

Curupt developed a huge smile on his face as Goldie opened the door. "Hey Mister," she said, holding the door open, and exposing her thick, smooth legs. Curupt looked her over from toe to head, stopping at her fat coochie print and then her tiny waist. Her C cup breasts and pretty face easily won her a dime rating. Her dreads were twisted neatly and pulled back into a bun.

"I thought I was going to have to drive that shit back to the dealership."

"Oh, my fault. I was sitting by the pool. Come in," she said, turning to expose that fat ass.

Curupt watched it jiggle. *Damn I wish I was that g-string.*

"Lock the door," she yelled and walked to the kitchen to grab the rest of the money. Curupt came in behind her. He pulled an envelope from his pocket that included paperwork for her to sign and the temporary tags and registration. After the exchange, he handed her the keys.

"I filled it up and had it detailed. My man also put a system in. When you ready to change those rims let me know."

Goldie handed him an envelope. "Thanks, I appreciate it."

"Nah, the rest is on me," he said, pushing her hand back.

She smiled and slid it back. "You trying to get on my good side?"

"Yup."

"Well, it's working." She smiled wider, looking at him intensely with her pretty brown eyes.

"You wanna get wet?" she asked.

"Hell yeah!"

Goldie took him by the hand and led him to the backyard. She walked over to the poolside bar and poured him a drink. Curupt took it and began sucking it down. Goldie took off her robe, placed it on the chair, and then stepped out of her shoes. Picking up the remote, she changed the satellite station to R & B and sashayed over to Curupt. She placed his empty glass on the bar, and then slid her hands up his shirt and pulled it over his head. Slowly sliding her hand down his stomach, she rested it at his waist and then unbuttoned and unzipped his jeans.

"Can you swim?" she asked while looking into his eyes.

"Yup. But I got to be in deep to enjoy the stroke."

"The deeper, the better," she shot back.

Curupt grinned as their interaction began to heat up. Goldie pulled at his jeans and they dropped to his ankles. He stepped out his sneakers and then his jeans. Goldie began caressing his dick.

"We don't allow pets in the pool."

"He won't bite."

"I hope he does," she said, turning and heading toward the water. She dived in the pool. He pulled his shirt off and dove in after her.

They swam around, playing and splashing until they ended up in a far corner of the pool. Curupt had Goldie up against the pool wall with her legs wrapped around his waist. They were laughing and talking when she locked lips with him and began grinding on his dick. Curupt breathed heavily, ready to put in some work. Goldie began kissing him deeply while caressing his neck. Curupt pulled at the side of her bathing suit in search of her sweet walls. He pushed his fingers deep inside. She gasped in pleasure and kissed him harder, sucking on his tongue and lips. He continued to push them in and out faster and faster until she moaned louder and louder. Once she came, he quickly pulled out his joint and slid up in her and did damage. Goldie was pressed up against the wall unable to move. As the water rose and rippled around them, all she could do was hold on and enjoy. Curupt continued to stroke deeply until she was cumming and shaking. Then he had a release of his own.

"I want to thank you for the truck," Goldie whispered in his ear.

"What was that?" he shot back.

"That was an appetizer. Let me give you the main course."

Curupt pulled out and let her down.

Goldie adjusted herself, took him by the hand and led him out the pool and into the house.

Once in her bedroom, she stood in front of him and released her top and then her bottoms. He stared at her perfect landing strip and immediately wanted to bury his face between those thick thighs.

"Drop your boxers," she commanded.

Curupt wasted no time obliging her. Goldie walked over to him and ran her hand across his chest and down his stomach. She manuevered until she was standing behind him. Goldie reached around his waist, grabbed his dick, and began stroking him back to full potential. Curupt watched her hand massage him back to attention. Then Goldie lowered herself behind him and began planting kisses on each one of his butt cheeks.

"You ready to get your world rocked?"

"Hell yeah," he said in a deep, raspy whisper.

Goldie grabbed his waist and then ran her soft wet tongue between the crack of his ass. She heard a hiss leave his mouth, so she repeated the process, and then nibbled and planted a few more soft kisses. Reaching between his legs, she began gently caressing his balls as she again ran her tongue from the bottom to the top of his crack. Goldie grabbed his dick and pulled it downward. "Open your legs," she commanded and he complied.

Once she had his dick in full view, she positioned herself in a low squat and began licking and sucking the head. She sucked harder, applying pressure with her jaws and taking more of him in her mouth. Her hot wet mouth sent chills up and down his spine. She slid him out of her mouth and then sucked gently on each one of his balls. When she felt his knees wobble, she began to suck and tease the tip of his dick with her tongue.

"Sssss . . . Oh shit!" he moaned as she continued to work her show. Goldie picked up speed as his breathing increased.

She sucked, slurped, and bobbed until Curupt was on the brink. She released him and slid between his legs, placing him back in her mouth and then to the back of her throat. With speed and accuracy, she sucked until she heard him say, "I'm about to come." With that, she took him as far as he would fit and gripped his ass with one hand and gently rubbed the line between his balls with the other. When she felt him grab her hair, she looked up and saw his eyes closed and face contorted.

"It's coming. It's coming." He grabbed harder and at that moment Goldie stuck her middle finger in his ass and pushed it in and out as he released hot and sticky to the back of her throat. "Ahhhh . . . Oh shit!" he shouted as he tried to recover.

Goldie eased him out of her mouth, released his ass, and slowly removed her finger. Rising from her squat, she looked at him and smiled.

Curupt didn't know what to say. He stood there conflicted. He didn't know whether he should fuck her up for putting her finger in his ass or marry her since that shit blew his mind.

Goldie knew she was taking a chance, because that shit

could always backfire. But she knew she had to put something on that ass that would give him that come back.

"Do you feel thanked?" she asked.

"Yeah, I'm good," he responded, still out of breath.

Goldie headed to the bathroom and hopped in the shower.

Curupt stood there for a few more minutes before joining her. He stepped in the shower and slid the glass door closed. Curupt came up behind her, wrapped his arms around her waist and began kissing her neck and rubbing her breasts. "Bend over," he commanded.

Goldie secured her hands on the wall and braced herself. Curupt slid up in her wetness and pulled her back and forth into him. In search of her spot, he pumped faster and faster.

"Yes. Yes. Fuck me," she yelled and his dick answered with long, deep strokes with skill and speed.

Curupt panted and Goldie moaned. They were in a zone. He was thrusting and she was throwing that ass.

"I'm about to cum. Keep it right there," she ordered.

At the same time, he felt another gut wrenching orgasm coming on. Just as they were both about to cum, Curupt pulled out and went up in that ass, Goldie barely flinched. She took that dick and came so hard her body shuddered. Curupt busted right after her and then pulled out. He fell forward onto her back and began planting kisses up and down her spine.

"Do you feel thanked?" he asked out of breath.

"Yeah, I'm good," Goldie answered, trying to catch her breath. She turned and wrapped her arms around his neck and kissed him sloppily. "This dick belongs to me now."

"And this ass belongs to Curupt," he said, palming her ass

with both hands. They stood there kissing and caressing and then carefully lathered each other up. All Goldie could do was count the dollar signs. Curupt was getting ready to make her a rich bitch.

~ 20 ~
Little Italy

"Buongiorno," Andres said as KoKo approached. He sat at a table in his coffee shop sipping on a cup of espresso.

"Ciao," KoKo responded as she leaned in and he kissed both of her cheeks.

"How are you signorina, KoKo?" he asked in his thick Italian accent. Night stood firm behind her. He couldn't stand dealing with the Italians. And his attitude always displayed it.

"I'm good. Just trying to make this money."

"In that way we are definitely alike. Please be seated." He pulled out a chair for her. KoKo sat down and Andres sat across from her and crossed his legs. He took a sip of his espresso and then proceeded with the business at hand. "So are we almost ready?"

"Just about. I need about a week to collect that info, and then we will be in business. Everything looks good and I foresee no real problems. I need your people to be on point. I'm putting my best on it, and I'm not risking my family." She looked him in the eyes.

"Again, we share the same interest. I am also putting my best on this, and you have my word that as long as your men don't buckle mine won't fold. The time and place is set, let's make it happen."

"We have a deal." She leaned in and shook his hand, knowing that trusting him one hundred percent was out of the question. And Italian's pretty much felt the same way. A nigga could work for you, but at the end of the day they were not family. So risking her men was not his concern. But it was hers, and she was certainly going to make sure her people were safe. She was going to have men on her men and men on his men and then some men on them.

KoKo stood up, preparing to leave.

"Let me take you to lunch when this is all over," Andres asked.

"I don't mix business with pleasure," she said very firmly.

"When this is over we won't have any business between us," he continued his forwardness, causing the hair to stand up on Night's neck.

"And there will be no pleasure between us either."

"Posso farti sentire veramente ben," he said, which loosely translated that he could make her feel real good.

"I don't know what the fuck you said. But I earned my bones on my feet not on my back. The only long thing I'm interested in that you have is money."

Andres smiled, impressed by this sexy, powerful woman. He wanted her even more. But KoKo wasn't having it. With her point well stated, she headed to the door with her plan secure in her mind. Her first stop was to Goldie's place. She had to make sure she had Curupt's ass lying down.

— 21 —
The Lions' Den

That Friday night, Boa, Savage, and Chucky were on the prowl. The three of them out together always spelled trouble.

"Nigga, get the fuck outta here!" Savage said to Boa as they stood up against the wall talking shit. KoKo had turned a five-level parking garage into a motorcycle club called the "Lion's Den."

Boa's henchmen, Chucky, ran his hand over his clean, glistening baldhead as he took a crack at Boa. "Nigga, you know good and well Treece had that ass up in the house washing floors and walls. Punishment-ass-nigga. We ain't heard from you in like three days," he yelled.

"Fuck y'all. I had to take care of home," Boa shot back.

"Yeah, until you got a surprise guest," Chucky replied, pushing his hand deep into the pocket of his black jeans. The thin leather jacket he wore over his white 'A' T-shirt concealed his gun holster. If he ever pulled his gun, the conversation was over.

"KoKo crazy as hell," Boa said, looking over the crowd and shaking his head.

"Hold up, nigga. KoKo came to your house?" Savage asked, laughing. His dreads were twisted down in the front and hanging neatly just past his shoulders, bringing out his shiny chocolate skin.

"Hell yeah. I almost shit a brick. I ain't know what she was gonna do," Boa said and chuckled.

"KoKo don't give a fuck. You lucky she ain't take that dick and make Treece watch," Savage said. He and Chucky slapped hands three times.

"Sheeit . . . I been trying to talk Treece into a threesome for two years. A nigga would have been in heaven," Boa said, grabbing his dick.

Just as they were reveling in Boa's sticky situation, they saw that familiar black and pink Ducati with the word 'Boss Lady' written in the back under the seat. KoKo was pulling through the bike display area headed in their direction. She parked her bike in front of them and pushed down the kickstand. Turning off the engine, she removed her helmet, swung her hair from side to side, and then placed the helmet on the seat. Boa stared at her, reminiscing about their last encounter.

KoKo stepped off the bike and immediately got the attention of everyone within eye range. People whispered and elbowed each other and pointed. In her black, three-inch heeled Pajar ankle boots, she walked over to where Boa, Savage, and Chucky were standing. The showstopper that had people talking was the black leather cat suit jumper she wore that showed off her sexy bowlegs. The front was zipped down two-inches past her cleavage, accenting her perky breasts.

"What's good?" KoKo said as she approached her boys.

"Sheeit . . . I can't call it," Savage answered, reaching in to give her a hug.

"Why you all quiet, Boa?" she asked, locking eyes with him. She took in his dark blue jeans, white T-shirt, black bulletproof vest and black boots. His face was clean-shaven and he rocked a fresh cut. Visible was that one dimple that always lit up Boa's face when he smiled.

"You know Boa just got off punishment. Pussy-whipped ass nigga," Savage spat and then laughed. Chucky burst out laughing with him.

"Oh, is that what it is, Boa?" KoKo asked.

"Nah. I ain't pussy-whipped yet. But I wanna be," he said, giving her that serious look and then a sneaky smirk.

Savage and Chucky stood there waiting to see where this shit was going, because it was getting intense.

KoKo said, "When a real bitch bless you, you don't get whipped you get tranquilized."

"I want that too," he said, not losing eye contact.

"Can you hang out tonight?" KoKo asked.

"The question is. Will you. Be able. To hang?"

KoKo just smiled. "We will see. Y'all come up to the office so we can blow some smoke."

As they headed to the elevator, KoKo admired the stunts and bike tricks. The ground and first level were for stunting. Dudes were shouting them out and hollering out "Boss Lady" as they passed. They all nodded, heading toward the elevator. When they got close, the doors opened and they stepped on. The security guard remained straight-faced the entire time. His demeanor was serious as hell. He didn't talk to anyone, not even KoKo. He made sure he was always on point. The doors closed. He pressed number five, put his hand on the security pad, and put in his code. They all watched the goings on as they rode up in the glass elevator. The second floor was set up Vegas style with casino tables, slot machines, pool tables, and several card tables along with two full bars. The third and fourth floors were dance halls. The third floor played hip-hop music and the fourth floor played reggae. KoKo's office occupied the infamous fifth floor.

Stepping off the elevator, the security guy said, "I put the delivery on your desk." He held his arm against the doors to keep them open.

"Thanks," she said as they exited the elevator and the doors closed behind them.

When KoKo reached her office, she entered her code and the doors slid open. As they entered the office, they were smacked in the face by the fragrance of vanilla and lavender. The huge space was all white and glass. Pretty vases with flowers and green and black rocks at the bottom dressed the wall shelves. An all glass and mirror bar sat in the corner. A huge white desk sat in the middle of the room with a large white chair behind it, and three leather chairs sat in front of it. KoKo headed to her desk as everyone else moved around the room.

"Who's pouring?" KoKo asked, sitting in her large comfortable chair while reaching for the package on her desk. She opened it and pulled out the plastic bag containing a quarter pound of Acapulco gold and another bag with Black Russian. She started to smile and then said, "Who's rollin'?" She tossed the bags to Savage.

He caught them and a huge smile came across his face. "I got this," he said, walking over to the bar and pulling out a box of Philly flavored wraps. He began filling them with that green.

"Any reports?" KoKo asked.

Savage said, "Yeah, everything is in place for Boa to meet the Russian."

KoKo nodded her head in agreement.

"The Russian's son been running his mouth about trying to work with someone new, so this should be cake," Chucky said, going to the bar and pouring them all glasses of dark liquor. He brought them to the desk and set them on the glass top.

Boa wondered how all this was going to affect his life. As he saw it, there was no turning around from there. He was ready to do whatever he had to do to move up in the organization, but his real quest was KoKo. Boa had his eyes and his mind on her for over six months, and he was ready to cash in.

They each grabbed a glass. Savage walked over and laid ten mixed blunts on the table. KoKo grabbed one and lit it up. She took a deep pull and then coughed. "That's what the fuck I'm talking about," she choked out as they all started laughing.

"Gentlemen, raise your glasses." They all put their glasses together to make a toast. "I'm about to make y'all some rich muthafuckas," she said as they clinked their glasses together and then took the shot to the head. After the first couple rounds, everything became a blur. They started reminiscing and joking. Within two hours they drank two bottles of Patron and smoked an ounce of each of the bags. They were officially fucked up.

"Oh shit! I can't feel my legs!" Savage said and then started cracking up. They all lay back in the leather chairs in front of her desk. KoKo reclined in her chair with her feet on the desk.

"I haven't been this fucked up in years," Chucky slurred.

"Y'all niggas can't hang," KoKo said in a calm voice. That shit they just did was child's play compared to how she had been drinking since Kayson's death.

"You trying to have a nigga on dialysis out this muthafucka," Savage said. They all started laughing. "I'm going downstairs to find me something soft to lay next to tonight." Savage rose from his seat.

Chucky followed suit. "I hear that. Let's see if we can find two." He rose up and stretched. "Thanks for the private party, Boss."

"Anytime. I hope y'all niggas throw some Listerine in your mouth before y'all go down there singeing a bitch's eyebrows," she said. They smiled and shook their heads.

"Yes, mother," Savage said sarcastically as he headed to the bathroom. Chucky went in after he came out. "Y'all coming?" Savage asked as he and Chucky headed for the door.

"We'll be down in a minute. I gotta holla at Boa," she responded. Once they were gone, KoKo and Boa gave each other a stare down.

"Why don't you come downstairs and dance with me," Boa said.

"You ain't scared your little girlfriend is going to find out?"

"Let me worry about that."

"So you admit to being worried?"

"The only thing I'm worried about is you not being able to walk a straight line in the morning." He walked over to her side of the table.

"I'm counting on it. Ain't nothing worse than a nigga walking around passing out bad dick. If a bitch can get up and clean the house and go on with business as usual, then the muthafucka need to kill himself."

Boa just chuckled.

She walked around the desk brushing up against him, and then headed to the bathroom. KoKo quickly washed her face and hands and combed her hair. Then she brushed her teeth and applied some lip-gloss and perfume. Boa went in after her and hooked himself up. Then they cleaned up, locked up, and headed downstairs to the reggae floor. When they stepped off the elevator, the music was bumping and the weed smoke was thick. Couples were grinding and winding on the dance floor. The neon lights had KoKo in a zone. She took Boa by the hand and led him into the middle of the dance floor. He grabbed her waist and placed her ass on his dick, and she began winding her hips to Beres Hammond's song "Step Aside." The words were perfect.

Step aside now, another man wants to take over.

Because you don't know what you got so now it's time to lose her.

KoKo was giving him some serious action, and he was rocking right with her. Then her favorite song came on. She turned around, put one arm on each of his shoulders, closed her eyes and began winding that waist. Boa put his hands on her hips and enjoyed that slow grind as his dick began to swell. They were damn near fucking on the dance floor. KoKo sang along with Nadine Sutherland's lyrics to "Babyface."

This is for my babyface. You got a cute baby face.

We have so many things in common. Yet we are two different people.

Boa's dick was now at brick breaking capacity, and KoKo was sliding up and down on it just right. They danced to a few more songs and then Boa whispered in her ear, "We need to get up outta here."

KoKo put her hands on his back and pulled him to her, pressing his dick right on her clit and grinding hard and slow. She wrapped her arms around his neck. "You ready to see if I can hang?" she asked as she pulled his neck to her mouth and nibbled and kissed right under his chin.

Boa closed his eyes and grabbed her ass, forcing her to grind harder on his now pulsating steel. "Come on," Boa said, turning her around to shield himself. He began walking her to the elevator.

Night watched as they moved to the elevator and began moving toward them. "KoKo, you good?" he asked as they stood waiting for the doors to open.

KoKo winked and said, "No. But I'm about to be." She allowed Boa to walk her on the elevator.

Night nodded and watched the doors close. He took her cue that she was in control of the situation, so he got on the walkie to put security on point.

Once the doors closed, Boa moved her into a corner and

began whispering in her ear, "You gonna let me feel your legs shake tonight?"

"You gonna fuck around and your legs gonna be shaking, so you better bring it," she said, breathing heavy in his ear.

Boa licked his lips as he gazed into her eyes. The doors opened and they headed to where their bikes were parked. Savage, Mugsy, and Chucky stood in the bike lot. Each one of them had a female up under them and was engaged in heavy conversation.

"We about to bounce," Boa said as they approached.

Savage looked up and said, "A'ight, I guess we'll catch y'all later." He gave Boa a pound. "Don't hurt 'em, KoK."

"You always starting shit, Savage," KoKo said as she headed to her bike.

"I start it. You finish it."

"You already know."

KoKo put on her helmet while Boa peaced out the rest of the crew. When he got to KoKo, he said, "You ain't driving me with your drunk ass."

"Let me ride you now, and you can ride me later."

Boa smiled. He put two fingers up to his mouth and whistled, catching the attention of one of the staff members. The guy came over and Boa gave him his keys and instructed him to take his bike upstairs and lock it up. Then he got on the back of KoKo's bike. She adjusted her gloves and checked her gun, making sure it was secure in her ankle holster. KoKo slid her leg over the bike and positioned her ass right on his dick.

Right before Boa threw on his helmet, he said, "When you let me ride you, I want it just like this, and you will need those handle bars 'cause it's going to be a rough one."

KoKo smiled. She couldn't wait to put that power on him. Then she pulled the bike up, kicked up the kickstand, and hit the ignition. The roar was loud and sexy as she slowly began exiting the garage. Boa held on tight, leery of her driving as fucked up as they were. But he just said fuck it and said a little prayer. KoKo picked up speed and flew out of the exit, whipping through the streets like a pro. Riding like a daredevil. Boa just went with the flow. When they stopped at a red light, he ran his hands up and down her thighs. All he could think was that every block was getting him closer to where he wanted to be. Deep in something hot.

An hour later . . .

KoKo opened the door to the apartment and she and Boa came stumbling in.

"Oh shit!" KoKo said as she tripped over the end table while reaching for the light.

"Damn, you a'ight?" Boa said while trying not to laugh.

"Yeah, I'm good. You know a bitch be trippin' sometimes," KoKo said and they both burst out laughing.

"Shit, it's hot in this muthafucka. Hold up." KoKo went to the air conditioner and turned it to a comfortable temperature. Then she reached for the remote and hit the music system, putting her satellite radio to the R&B station. Usher's "Can You Handle It" blared from the speakers.

Boa looked around at the immaculate condition of her apartment. Everything matched. There was a nice color scheme of dark pink and brown. The couch was huge, dark chocolate brown with large brown, pink and black pillows dressing it. The soft carpet threatened to swallow his feet with every step. Boa admired the fish tank that covered the whole wall. Tinted lights illuminated the underwater world, which housed three baby sharks. When Boa's eyes made it back to KoKo, she was unzipping her jumper and taking her arms out. Boa walked in her direction.

"So what's up? You got something for me?" KoKo asked while grabbing at Boa's clothes. He could see she was fucked up. The last thing he wanted was to take advantage of her due to his respect for her position. So he subtly tried to defuse the situation.

"You drunk as hell. Let me help you out your clothes and get you to bed," he said, grabbing her wrist from his waistband.

"Shit, sounds good to me." Boa picked KoKo up and carried her to the bathroom. He assisted her in undressing as she continued to touch all over him. He was trying his best to fight temptation, but she was making it impossible. Once the water was right, he helped her into the shower. Soaping up the washcloth, he then began washing her from head to toe. Water splashed all over the place. Before he knew it, water soaked his shirt and pants and his dick was hard as hell.

Damn, her body is bangin'. Be cool, Boa. Be cool, his mind raced.

"Come here," KoKo said seductively. Water and soap covered her body. Her perfect breasts sat up looking both suckable and inviting. Boa's eyes wandered all over her body, resting at her neatly shaven pussy. Her lips were screaming 'taste me.' Each second in her presence weakened his resolve, breaking him down.

"Nah, ma. Let me finish so you can get some sleep," he responded, turning her around to get the last of the soap off her skin.

With her back to him, she looked over her shoulder and slowly licked her lips. "A bitch bad from the back, ain't she?" KoKo asked.

Boa's dick jumped, giving his zipper a fit, but he didn't respond. He turned off the water, grabbed a towel, and put it around her.

"Stop acting all scary and come here," she demanded, grabbing at his zipper. KoKo nibbled on his chin while releasing the beast from its enclosure.

Boa closed his eyes and enjoyed her finger play. With the last bit of fight in him, he pulled back and said, "Maybe another time."

"What? You afraid of little ol' me?"

"Nah, I just don't do drunk pussy. I like fair playing grounds." Honestly, he was battling with the feelings he had for KoKo while trying not to violate the promise he made to Treece. KoKo had his head fucked up. He struggled to keep it business, knowing that once he crossed that line it was no turning back.

KoKo got serious quickly. She locked eyes with him and said, "There are three things that I handle well. My money. My liquor. And a big dick. So are you going to come up off it, or am I going to have to take it?" she asked, giving him that 'nigga what' look.

"You talk a lot of shit. And I want to fuck you so bad I can taste it. But you ain't ready for this."

KoKo chuckled. "Just as I thought. All that dick and you a bitch," she said as she tightened her towel and moved past him heading to her bedroom.

Boa paused to process her words as he watched her sashay away. He took a deep breath. *That was the invitation I needed.* He pulled his shirt over his head. Stepping out of his pants and boxers, he reached in his pocket and pulled out a Magnum and slid it on inch-by-inch and then headed in her direction. Eddie and Gerald Levert's "Baby Hold On To Me" played in the background.

KoKo bent over, lotioning her legs when Boa came up behind her. She stood, face-to-face with a sexy, butt naked man on a mission. He picked her up and threw her on the bed. She took in a chest full of air as her adrenaline started flowing.

Boa climbed on top of her with force and pinned her arms to the bed. He used his knee to spread her legs. "I'm ready to make this pussy mine. You ready to let me have it?" he whispered as he kissed and sucked her breast.

"I'm ready to get this nut off my back. Let's go." KoKo continued to talk shit.

Boa began to glide inside her wet walls. She held him tight as he began to break down the tension between them. Once he hit bottom, it was over, and her moans confirmed that she was enjoying every stroke.

"Which inch of this feel like you fucking a bitch?" Boa taunted while listening to the sweet sounds of pleasure drip from her lips. Each power stroke caused her to back up a little, which only made him thrust harder. "Ssss . . . Nah ma, don't run from this dick," he taunted as he looked down, watching his dick as it went in slowly and came out sticky.

"Mmmmm . . . Make me cum, Boa," KoKo moaned.

Boa placed his mouth over one of her nipples and sucked gently, pushing deeper with every stroke.

She wrapped her legs around him and flipped over, placing herself on top, taking Boa totally off guard. He gripped the small of her back and guided her body enjoying her power. Removing his hands from her back, she pinned him to the bed. "My turn," she panted as she rode his dick slowly and from side to side with a little bounce.

Boa locked his fingers in hers and pumped every time she came down. He flicked the tip of his tongue back and forth over her nipple and then engulfed it in his mouth. Rotating from one to the other, he had KoKo on fire, and the rhythm of her ride confirmed it.

"Oh shit! Right there!" she moaned.

"Cum on this dick for me," Boa said in between moans of his own. Then he pulled his hands from hers and firmly gripped her ass. He stroked up hard, pulling her down on him with intense power.

"Yes, Boa," she moaned as he hit that spot. Within seconds, she was cumming hard. KoKo's body twitched and shook. She rose to the top of his dick then skeeted up his stomach.

"That's what the fuck I'm talking about. Let Boa have all of it."

"Mmmm . . . " KoKo continued to ride in an effort to bring

on another one and without much effort she was cumming again. Her tight muscles around his dick caused him to squeeze her tighter with every thrust. Boa pulled her close to him and nibbled on her neck and shoulder.

"You trying to fuck a nigga up," he said as he savored her very essence.

KoKo whispered into his ear, "You ever been to death row?"

"What?" Boa responded, nearly out of breath and ready to bust.

"Well, come over here and let me give you something lethal," she said seductively as she rose up allowing his dick to slip from her grip.

"Hold up," he stated with slight panic in his voice as he grabbed at her waist in an attempt to get back inside her.

KoKo pulled away from him and got off the bed. "C'mere," she requested with a sexy smirk. Boa rose to his feet with his throbbing hard-on leading the way.

"Sit down." She pointed to the short ottoman with the thick cushion over by the wall. He walked over and took a seat. KoKo glanced at Boa's hard dick sitting straight up and calling for her juices as the thoughts of her turning him out flooded her mind.

"Come take me there," he said aggressively

"Ask me nicely."

"Come take a nigga there. *Please.*"

She sashayed over to him, leaned on his legs and placed soft kisses all over his face.

Boa closed his eyes and took in deep breaths as her touch

began to ignite his soul. KoKo rested her hands on his shoulders and gave him instructions. "Lean back and relax."

He sat back, full of anxiety, waiting to see what KoKo had in store. She turned her back to him and slowly straddled his lap. Resting her hands on his knees, she ordered, "Make him stand up." Boa gripped his pole firmly in his hand, anticipating her next move.

KoKo half turned her head and looked over her shoulder as she slowly slid down on him, resting her hot, wet pussy on the tip of his dick. She began taking it in inch-by-inch.

"Sssss," Boa moaned as her muscles massaged him just right.

She bounced up and down slowly, gradually picking up speed and continuing to bounce until she heard the change in his breathing. When he was on the edge, she leaned all the way forward placing her hands on the floor and her feet firmly on the wall behind him. She threw that pussy at him fast and hard.

Boa gripped her hips and braced himself for the nut rising fast in the bottom of his stomach. "Oh shit!" he mumbled. Within minutes he began to release and yes his legs did quake. KoKo continued her pace until she had drained him of every drop. Boa pulled her up into his arms and held her tight. "Damn you feel good."

"Don't fuck around and get sleepy. You got some work to put in."

"You gonna make a nigga do overtime on his first day on the job," he joked as he placed soft kisses on her shoulder.

"Who you thought you was fucking with, an amateur?" she

said, releasing his rod. She got up and walked over to the bed.

Boa looked at her sexy body glistening from their sweat. He stood up, removed the plastic, stroked himself back to life and then replaced it with another one. When he climbed onto the bed, he focused on redeeming himself.

"I think she needs a kiss first," KoKo said as she pushed his head toward her waist.

"I've been wanting you to bless my tongue." He put his face in the place and said his grace, giving her orgasm after orgasm.

When Boa woke up, he took a few deep breaths and stretched. He looked around the room for KoKo, who was nowhere in sight. He pulled back the cover from his chiseled body and placed his feet on the floor. Then he heard a knock on the bedroom door. "Who?"

"Mr. Boa. I'm here to work," the female voice with the broken accent came blaring through the door. Boa grabbed the towel off the chair and walked to the door and opened it. "Miss KoKo told me to take care of you." She walked past him and went to open the curtains and then headed to the bathroom to draw him a bath. She moved around the area cleaning and gathering the sheets.

Boa sat down in the chair by the bed as the woman did her job thoroughly. He grabbed his phone and turned it on and thumbed through the messages that popped up one by one. Then he hit KoKo's phone. "Where you at, ma?" he could hear her music bumping in the background.

"You can't keep tabs on what's not yours," KoKo shot back as she whipped her gold Mercedes GLK350 through the streets.

"Oh, it's like that? You talk a lot of shit, but you scared you gonna love all this good dick I got for you," he said, full of confidence.

She paused as his words gave a small ring of truth. "Go enjoy the morning I have set up for you, and I'll see you later." KoKo hung up.

Boa chuckled, set his phone on the nightstand, and did as instructed. He had put in some back work last night, so he was ready to benefit from whatever she had set up. When he looked over at the lady putting together the massage table, he felt like a hungry man at a buffet. He lay down and thought, *Share her throne. Sheeit . . . I'm about to be the boss and she don't even realize it.*

— 22 —
Furious

"Look, Quran," Monique said, pointing to the front of the FAO Schwartz toy store in the heart of New York City.

Quran's little eyes lit up as he saw all the toys. He tried pulling away from her in an attempt to get lose and touch everything. Within two hours Quran had racked up a bill of over $5,000. Whatever Monique couldn't carry out she had shipped to the house in Dubai.

As the chauffeur loaded all the bags in the trunk, Monique picked Quran up so he could look around. She enjoyed the excitement in his eyes as he took in all the sights for the first time. Monique kissed his cheeks and hugged him tight. "You are grandma's life." She tickled him and as he squirmed and giggled in her arms, her heart filled with glee. He was her Kayson all over again.

"You wanna do some more shopping?"

Quran shook his head up and down as he continued to laugh. She put him down, allowing him to climb in the car. He crawled all over the seats as Monique got in and the driver closed the door. They hit almost every kid store in Manhattan. Monique stopped and had their picture taken and then they went to eat. As soon as they reached the limo, Quran was spent. He laid across his grandmother's lap and passed out as she sat rubbing his head on her way to Kayson's house.

Once inside, she laid him in KoKo and Kayson's bed. She covered him up and looked around, smiling as she looked at the pictures of Kayson and KoKo. She grabbed her wrap and put it around her arms and walked into the closet, touching all of Kayson's clothes. Feeling the material of the many shirts, she grabbed one and put it on. Then she sat in his chair, closed her eyes and cried. Once she collected herself, she got up and continued to collect memories of her son. Her moment would have been almost perfect, but KoKo fucked that up.

KoKo came busting in the closet. "Why the fuck you got my son in New York?"

"Calm down, KoKo. I just wanted him to see the lights and attractions. Plus his birthday is coming up. I wanted to take him to the Big Apple."

"Mo, you know good and well it's not safe for him to be here. You ain't even run shit by me." KoKo stood in full rant mode.

"No one knows I'm here. We will be gone in the morning."

"No the fuck you ain't. You have to leave tonight."

"Look, KoKo, just let him sleep through the night. It's been a long day, plus he wants to see his mommy. Let's just get some rest and in the morning after he eats we can go. Please, KoKo."

KoKo was pissed off. She wanted to slap the shit out of Monique. Because she specifically told her not to come back to New York and under no circumstances should she ever bring Quran here.

While the two women swapped words back and forth,

Quran sat up in the bed, rubbing his little eyes.

KoKo was ready to deliver her verdict and send her back on the first thing smoking, but was stopped by the voice of her little prince. "Mommy," his sleepy little voice rang out.

KoKo mustered up a smile and turned around. "Hey mommy's big boy."

He ran to her and she picked him up in her arms and kissed his little lips. He held her face in his hands and kissed her nose and eyes.

"Mommy," he kept saying and hugging her neck.

"You missed mommy?"

"Yeeeessss," he said, and then slithered down to the floor. "Look!" He ran to the bed and got his big truck and ran back to KoKo's side. "See. See, Mommy." He pressed the buttons and lights came on and music played.

"Ohhh . . . Look at that," she said, squatting to his level and touching the buttons with him.

"Truck, Mommy. Vroom. Vroom," he said as he went to the floor and began rolling it back and forth.

"That is so nice, sweetie." KoKo watched as he became engrossed with his toy.

"Mommy, I wanna get in the big tub." Quran pointed to the bathroom.

"Okay. Let me get it ready." She stood up, turned to Monique, and gave her a serious stare down. Then she walked to the bathroom to prepare the tub. On her way past Monique, she said, "One night."

Monique looked at Quran, who was taking his clothes off as fast as he could. "Can I put my truck in, Grandma?"

"No, Quran. But grandma has something else for you." She moved toward the bags.

"Okay." He took off running naked toward the bathroom. Monique giggled because of how much he looked like his dad.

KoKo got in the tub with Quran and laughed and played with the tub toys. When they got out, they got in their pajamas and she had the maid prepare him dinner. After they ate, she got in bed and snuggled up next to him and watched a few movies. KoKo put her face on his and inhaled the aroma of Johnson & Johnson nighttime lotion. His soft skin caressed her face, tickling her nostrils.

"I love you, Mommy."

"I love you too, Quran." She hugged him tight in her arms. He was the only peace she had in her world full of chaos. Even though seeing him brought her so much joy, she could not shake the fact that Monique being in New York was for more than just a shopping spree, and she damn sure was going to find out what she was up to.

— 23 —
Seize the Moment

On a hot, sunny day in August, Curupt and Goldie were cruising down I-285 heading toward his dealership. They had been inseparable ever since the day he came to her house. They pulled into the lot and parked.

"What you about to do?" Curupt asked, looking over at Goldie.

"I was planning on going home, then just relaxing. Why?"

"Nah, I wanted you to hang out with me today."

"Okay, I can do that."

"I need to run in my office. I'll only be a minute. I have to fax some paperwork."

"Okay, can I watch you work?" Goldie asked in her sexy voice.

Curupt watched as she bit down on her bottom lip. "You know I can't say no to you." He rubbed the side of her face. Goldie kissed his hand as he slowly pulled it away. "I got something planned for us tonight," Curupt said as he hit the locks.

"I hope so," she said, giving him that naughty look.

They exited the car and entered the dealership.

"What's up, Mr. Wilson?" his secretary said.

"Any messages?"

The secretary passed him a stack of call back slips.

He thumbed through them. "Thanks, Kim. I'll be in my office." He walked off with Goldie right behind him.

Curupt sat at his desk separating a few documents and then printing out a couple. The secretary brought him a few more, and he put them in stacks. He began faxing them over to several sister companies in various states. After he was done, he got up to go to the bathroom.

Goldie sent a quick text message. She jumped up and began fumbling through the paperwork. Then she stuck a thumb drive into his computer and began downloading all his files. When she heard the toilet flush and the water come on, she put the computer on snooze, walked back around the desk and sat on it.

When he emerged from the bathroom drying his hands, he got a full view of Goldie. Her legs were open. She was wearing no panties.

"So do you think I can get some of what you were going to give me later?" she asked as she put her foot up on the desk exposing herself.

"Why you ain't got no panties on?"

"Easy access, baby."

Curupt slid his hands up her leg, causing her dress to rise to her waist. He then began to place light kisses on her thighs. He placed his face right between her legs and inhaled deeply. Running the tip of his tongue lightly across her clit, he prepared to get his lips glazed. Just as he was ready to take her there, he heard a commotion developing outside his window.

"Fuck you, nigga!" the voice rang through the lot.

"Nigga, I'll take your life right here!"

When Curupt heard that last threat, he jumped up, looked out the window and hurried to his desk. He reached in his top drawer and pulled out his gun and headed outside.

"Stay here," he ordered, leaving the office and shutting the door behind him.

Goldie quickly jumped off the desk and went to finish her mission. With the download completed, she released the drive and slid it in her pocket book and sat down. About fifteen minutes later, Curupt reentered the office breathing hard and sweating.

"What happened?" Goldie came to attention wearing a look of concern.

"Maaaan . . . these two niggas about to make me go to jail."

"Is everything all right?" she asked and went to look through the blinds.

"Yeah, I handled it," he said, placing the gun in his waistband. "Let's get ready to get outta here," he instructed.

"Okay. You know a bitch need you to finish what you started. Let me run in the bathroom real quick." On her way there, she stopped to kiss his lips.

"Oh, I got you. Let me tighten this shit up real quick." Curupt went to his desk, organized the files and put them in the cabinet. Then he shut down his system and waited at the door for Goldie. "You know you got a nigga open, right?" he said as she walked toward him drying her hands.

"I aim to please." She walked to the door. Curupt was right behind her as he closed the door and locked it.

"A'ight, catch you tomorrow. If anything comes up, text me," Curupt told his secretary.

Kim smiled until they hit the door and then she dropped it. She didn't like it when he came through the office with Goldie.

There was something about her, and she was getting ready to put her ear to the street and find out who this bitch really was.

∼ 24 ∼
The Perfect Hit

"Tonight at eleven o'clock, the horrid tale of a car delivery gone wrong. Three trailers full of luxury cars were headed to Baltimore when an ambush took the lives of all three drivers. As of last update, there are no leads on the missing trailers or the assailants. We will keep you updated as more information becomes available."

Andres picked up his remote and turned down the volume. He stared off as he began calculating the money in his mind. He and KoKo stood to make over a hundred thousand dollars on each vehicle, which they were to split sixty-forty in her favor for the risk. He looked at his two business partners and smiled. KoKo had managed to pull off the heist and elude authorities.

"So when do we settle with them?" one of the men asked as they sat in the back of the coffee shop.

"I am set to meet her tomorrow."

"Do you think you can trust her?" the man's voice rang of sarcasm.

"So far, she is a woman of her word. But if I find out she is not, I have no problem with putting two in her pretty little face."

The man took a cigar to his mouth, inhaled, and then blew

out thick smoke. "You better hope so."

Andres said nothing. He began counting the dollars in his head. He knew KoKo was a stand up type female, and the fact that he was sitting across from and working with a man that not only questioned his intellect, but also questioned his judgment, had just upped Andres's portion of the proceeds.

****

Unfortunate events . . .

KoKo had just turned off her television after seeing the broadcast of the Atlanta hit on CNN. She had called for Night, Boa, and Savage to prepare them for the meeting later on with the Russians. As she sat in her chair puffing and reflecting, she heard a knock at the door.

"Come on," she yelled out as they all piled in. Each man took a seat and waited for her to begin the meeting.

"Any reports?" she asked before she passed out her instructions.

"I think we need to send someone down to Virgina to check on Wise and Aldeen. I have been calling them and just getting the machine," Night stated.

"Yeah, I had the same thing happen last week," Savage revealed.

"I spoke to Aldeen a week ago, but the nigga was in a rush. I try not to put a chokehold on them because I know Kayson's motto would be, 'let a nigga get enough rope then hang the shit out of them with it.'" She paused, looking down at her desk for a few seconds. "Let them be for a minute. When we finish this shit I'ma make a trip."

"A'ight," Night responded.

"Anything else?" she asked.

"Nah, we good." He rose to his feet and everyone else followed.

"Boa. You set for tomorrow?" she asked.

Boa chuckled. "You ready for tonight?" he said pausing to look in her direction.

"Have a good evening." KoKo dismissed him.

"Yeah, I thought so. Scary ass," he said heading to the door. "Hit me if you need something," he said walking out and closing the door.

"Yeah, I'ma hit you alright. When you least expect it," She sat back and folded her hands behind her head.

~ 25 ~
Russian Roulette

KoKo, Boa, Savage, and three of Night's bodyguards sat impatiently waiting for the Russians to show. KoKo was past upset. Late was something she didn't do, and with the importance of this meeting, these muthafuckas were displaying the highest form of disrespect. The atomosphere alone told her that shit just might get heated. Just as KoKo was ready to call the whole thing off, in walked Boris, the Russian's cocky ass son, Vladimir and his goons.

"So, this is Boa?" Vladimir asked in his thick Russian accent as he sat across from him and KoKo.

"Yes. I wanted to make the introduction. So we can move to the next level."

"The next level, huh? And this is who you want me to work with?" he asked, watching Boa sit there with his nostrils flared and eyes slightly squinted.

KoKo looked over at Boa thinking, *What the fuck is his problem?*

"Yeah, he's one of my best. Plus I got other shit to handle, and he will be dealing directly with you."

Vladimir stared Boa down and sucked his teeth. Boa grew angrier by the second, thinking, *No this stringy-haired looking cracker is not sitting here sizing me up.* Unable to contain himself, Boa said, "Man, fuck this shit. We got other pokers in the fire." He rose from his seat ready to bounce. It was something he didn't trust about this whole organization.

KoKo looked up at Boa as the crease in her forehead deepened. "Sit the fuck down!" she ordered.

Boa looked down at her. "Nah, ma. I can't do that. I ain't working with this racist muhfucka. Fuck him!" His voice echoed throughout the room, putting everyone on alert. Vladimir's men went for their guns and so did Night and Savage. The whole room was tense. One wrong move could have turned the whole scene into a massacre.

"You expect me to work with this disrespectful individual. What is this shit, KoKo? I have worked with you and Kayson for years. I have *never* experienced such disrespect!" Vladimir yelled, banging on the desk with spit flying from his mouth. KoKo looked at him with a careful eye. Sensing that she was not budging, he also took her silence for disrespect. "Well, if that is how it is, everything is *off*!"

"Hold the fuck up," KoKo said. "Look, me and you have a deal. So regardless of who you work with, that shit better go through because now you're fucking with my money."

"Deal? Deal, you say. Train this monkey and then you come back to me for deal. Let's go!" he yelled to his men who stood with their guns firmly in place.

"I got your monkey, muthafucka," Boa said as he grabbed his nine.

KoKo grabbed his hand.

"Chill the fuck out!" she demanded.

Vladimir began going off in his language while he and his

men backed up toward the exit with their guns still drawn.

When they were gone, KoKo went off. "What the fuck is wrong with you?" She pushed Boa with both hands.

"Fuck that nigga! I don't trust his ass."

"It ain't about him. This shit is business. We ain't in fuckin' kindergarten." KoKo got in Boa's face.

"Well then you handle it because I can't work with that muthafucka."

Night came between them, afraid the tension would rise to an uncontrollable level. "Don't worry, KoKo. I got it. I'll handle this shit."

KoKo stood there ready to take Boa's life. She had groomed him for this position, and within seconds he managed to fuck up months of work.

"KoKo, I'll take care of it," Night repeated.

"Yeah, you do that. Boa, I think you need a break."

"Fuck them niggas. They ain't the only connect. I got some shit lined up."

"How the fuck you gonna go out on your own and set some shit up?" Night looked at Boa with those piercing eyes.

"Fuck is this nigga talking about?" Boa looked at KoKo and chuckled. "I'ma grown fucking man. I ain't on no fucking leash!" He looked at Night, who was still giving him the stare down.

"Y'all niggas be easy," she yelled out. "Night, you come with me. Boa, get at me tomorrow with the details. We done for the night."

"You ain't said shit. I'll see you when I see you." Boa turned and walked away.

KoKo was on fire as she reassessed the whole situation. Had she jumped the gun trying to get him in with the Russians? "You need to get that nigga under control," Night stated to KoKo as he headed for the door.

"I got it."

KoKo wondered if Boa was really the loyal nigga she thought he was? Or was his closeness to her fucking with her judgment? Either way, she needed to handle this shit and quickly.

~ 26 ~
Deception

Goldie walked into Curupt's apartment up on Memorial Drive using her spare key. "Hello?" she announced as she stepped in the dark dwelling. She surveyed the area, and to her surprise things were all out of order. Pizza boxes were piled up on the table, garbage was running over and the smell was terrible. She proceeded to the bedroom where she found Curupt lying in bed with the lights out and flipping the channels. "What's up, baby? Why you not answering the phone?"

"I got a lot of shit on my mind and I would prefer to be alone," he said, lying there in a dirty white T-shirt and a pair of dusty gray sweat pants. His hair was now a small afro, and he was sporting a full beard and mustache.

"What are you talking about? I went to the office and shit vacant and here I find you looking like shit."

Curupt was quiet for a minute and then he said, "My whole shit is fucked up."

"Well, what happened? It can't be that bad."

"They hit my load. All my shit is gone. Creditors on my ass, investigators all in my shit."

"Well, you have insurance for the loss, and the rest of that shit is irrelevant unless you had something to do with it."

Curupt looked at her with one eyebrow raised. "Fuck is you

talking about? Hell no I ain't have nothing to do with that shit. I invested my whole life into this business, and I promise you this, if I find out who did, I'ma sing like a fucking bird."

Goldie looked at him with squinted eyes as anger rose in her gut. "Look, it's all good. Everything will be fine." She walked over to him and sat next to him and rubbed his head. "Why don't you take a shower and I'll clean up this mess. Then maybe I can run my tongue around the tip of your dick until you feel better." She lifted his face to hers and kissed his lips. "Oh yeah, bust that mouth wash open before you do anything else." Curupt brought a smile to his face. Goldie stood up and pulled him from the bed. Curupt stood next to her.

"Thank you, baby." He hugged her tight.

"I got you. Go ahead." She slapped his ass on the way by.

"Yeah, A'ight. Keep it up."

Goldie went on straightening up the room.

Curupt yelled out, "Goldie, come here for a minute." Goldie entered the bathroom. He was standing at the toilet shaking off as he reached for the handle to flush. Goldie put the steel to his head and pulled the trigger. Curupt fell forward hitting his head on the back of the toilet and cracking both the lid and what was left of his head. There he lay in-between the toilet and the wall. "Run tell that. Bitch ass nigga," Goldie said, and then prepared to leave his apartment. She jumped in her car, heading to NY to give KoKo the news right away.

Mind Your Business . . .

Goldie had just got back from New York. She stopped by the club on the way to her apartment to make sure shit was on track. Stepping through the door, her mood was lifted. "Paitiently Waiting" by 50 Cent and Eminem was blaring through the speakers. She eyed the room admiring the crowd, people dancing and laughing and drinks were flowing. Goldie smiled as she headed toward her office. When she got to the elevator, one of her top girls came running up to her.

"Goldie, I need to pull your sleeve about some shit," she said with apparent urgency on her face.

"Alright. Come up with me."

When they got in the office, the woman started spilling her guts. "This girl named Kim came by here twice aking questions about you."

"What did you tell her?"

"I ain't tell that bitch shit."

"A'ight, good looking." Goldie reached in her pocket and pulled out a couple hundred and handed it to her.

*****

"Bitch, we going out tonight. I'm not trying to hear shit." Goldie heard as she stood on the other side of apartment B12. She rang the bell and then waited with her hoodie pulled down over her face.

"Bitch, let me call you back. That's probably Geek. I'ma try to get some of that dick before we go out." Kim disconnected the call and headed to the door in her robe. She reached out and grabbed the knob. "I knew you couldn't stay away," she said as she opened the door.

Goldie clenched her teeth as she slowly lifted her head,

"Somebody said you were looking for me. Here I go." She raised her gun and shot her in the face. Kim fell against the wall and slid to the floor. Goldie kicked her foot from the doorway and pulled the door closed. As she headed to the car she said, "The best business to mind is your own, bitch." She hopped in the car and peeled out.

~ 27 ~
Fuck You

Boa came bopping in the house as if everything was kosher. He hadn't spoken to KoKo since the blow out and really, he didn't give a fuck. He was busy making moves and securing his position on the streets. Even though he wanted to move up closer to the top, he wasn't ready to compromise what he had worked for. He was just going to let shit cool off, and then approach KoKo with an ultimatum.

When the door shut, Latreece went off. "Where the fuck you been for a week?"

"You know where I been," he said, pulling his shirt over his head and heading to his bedroom.

"Awww, hell no. How the fuck you gonna come in here after days of no calls, no show, and just act like shit is all gravy?" She followed him, awaiting his response. Her hair was wild, eyes puffy, and nose bright red. Treece was on edge. Not only had he not been home, but he had not touched her in weeks.

Boa kept on walking to the closet. He took the lid off the hamper, put his shirt inside, and emptied his pockets. He placed his money on the top shelf and his gun next to it, and then took off his jeans. Treece stood behind him with her hands on her hips still waiting. "Watch out," Boa said as he looked her up and down on his way by and kept going toward

155

his big comfy bed. "Wake me up in two hours." Boa lay across the bed in his boxers.

"Wake you up? You ain't getting no sleep up in this bitch tonight." Latreece walked over to the bed and grabbed the pillow from under his head.

Boa jumped up. "Fuck is wrong with you?" he said, getting all up in her face.

Latreece held the pillow in one hand and made a full fist with the other. Boa was nose-to-nose with her, neither one of them backing down.

"For real, Boa? That bitch got you cursing at me?"

"I'm tired as hell. I'm not in the mood for this shit." He snatched the pillow out her hand.

"What did I tell you would happen if I suspected that you were cheating, Boa?" she said in a low tone, teeth clenched together.

"Don't fucking threaten me. *I* make the rules up in this bitch. I'ma tell your ass for the last time, ain't shit going on. I'm out here trying to make this money."

"Yeah, and making your way between that bitch's legs."

"What the fuck is you talking about?"

"You know exactly what I'm talking about. I saw your punk ass all over her," she lied, unable to control her emotions.

"Maan . . . go 'head with all that," Boa said as he lay back down. It had just come to him what KoKo meant about being cautious when he was touching all over her outside the office.

"Yeah, now you ain't got shit to say."

"Come lay down."

"Fuck you! *You* lay down! You done made a fool outta me for the last time. I don't deserve this shit." She turned around with tears in her eyes, ready to walk away from everything.

"Don't play with me." He turned to see her in a full rage, pulling shit out.

Treece went to the dresser and began frantically snatching her clothes out the drawers. She rushed over to the closet and grabbed her Gucci duffel bag and began stuffing it. Boa rushed over to where she was and grabbed the bag out her hand. Treece reached for it in an attempt to snatch it back.

"Stop, Boa! I got to go," she said as they tussled over her bag.

"You ain't going nowhere," he said. Boa threw the bag in the closet and slammed it shut. Standing in front of it, he had his face all balled up.

Latreece stood there looking at him as tears formed in her eyes. "Why do you enjoy making a fool outta me?"

"I love you, ma. I just gotta handle some shit. Ain't nothing changed between us."

"Everything has changed, Boa. You don't see that?" she pleaded with him.

"Has this changed?" He put his finger between her breasts. The silence in the room became suffocating as she searched his piercing eyes for the Boa she loved. After a few seconds, she nodded her head back and forth. "That's all I needed to know. Don't nobody else exist in our world, Treece. Come here." He took her in his arms and hugged her.

"Boa, this shit gotta change. I can't live like this," she cried as she melted in his arms.

"Don't worry, it will all be over in a minute. Just stick with me. I promise I'ma make you happy. Just a little longer. Don't give up on me, Treece." He picked her up and carried her to his bed and did what it took to ease her mind.

As Boa stroked deep inside her, Treece surrendered her body, but her heart could not feel him. Her mind couldn't release the truth that Boa was no longer her's, and KoKo was the bitch to blame.

— 28 —
Disrespectful Ass Nigga

Once Treece was asleep, Boa got up, dressed, and headed to the game room. His mind was heavy. He needed to get around his boys and clear his head.

"That nigga is disrespectful," China said to his boy loud enough for Boa to hear him. China was the cat who KoKo allowed to have a piece of the meth sales in the Bronx. He got the name due to his chinky eyes that only accented his chocolate skin and deep waves. His muscular frame made him sometimes think he could strong arm niggas, but Boa was not that nigga.

"What the fuck you say?" Boa responded, looking up from his hand.

"Nigga, ain't nobody scared of you. You heard me loud and clear."

Boa stood up, slamming his cards on the table and everyone became alert. "You think I'm disrespectful? Straighten me the fuck out then." He walked up to China, breathing all in his face. Boa knew what he was getting ready to do was a violation, but he wasn't the type of nigga to get chumped.

"You don't want none of this, playboy." China stood firm.

159

Savage jumped up from the card table and moved through the crowd like an angry bull. "Y'all niggas better go 'head with all this bullshit."

"Nah, this pretty nigga think he in charge. I earned my bones just like he did. I don't give a fuck about him," China yelled.

Boa's nostrils flared as he envisioned putting this nigga on his ass. "Yeah. A'ight, you got it." He maintained eye contact with China.

"Y'all niggas know KoKo ain't going for no bullshit up in here. We got too much at stake right now. Y'all better peace this shit out and get back to business."

"Y'all better teach that nigga some manners," China taunted, not knowing he was only shortening Boa's fuse and an explosion was inevitable.

Boa nodded up and down and then he turned and walked out the door. His silence was both unpredictable and scary. He moved swiftly past everyone and slammed the door on his way out.

China went to the bar and ordered a drink. "Hit everybody up on me," he yelled across the bar, feeling like King Kong.

"You need to calm your ass down," Savage warned as he walked back to the table to finish his hand.

"Fuck that nigga!" he said, taking swigs of his drink.

Within minutes, Boa reentered the game room. He spotted China at the end of the bar whispering in some female's ear as she giggled. Boa dropped the bat from the sleeve of his jacket and moved double time in China's direction. By the time Savage looked up it was too late. Boa cracked China over the head with the bat and went to swinging at a rapid pace. Mugsy jumped up, almost knocking his shorty to the ground. Savage pushed through the crowd, almost knocking three people over on his way to where they were. Savage and Mugsy grabbed Boa's arms and pulled as China lay there with his face busted open. He had a hole in his head almost the size of a grapefruit.

"Boa!" Savage yelled out as they tried to restrain him.

"Get the fuck off me!" He snatched away, breathing heavily. "I got his fucking manners! Pussy ass nigga. Talk shit now!" Boa yelled. "I guess you can't with your shit all fucked up." Boa slowly walked away with China's blood and pieces of his skull on his bat. When the door slammed, Mugsy bent down to feel for a pulse on China. It was there but faint.

"We gonna have to handle this nigga. He outta control," Mugsy said to Savage, looking up from China's side.

"I know. KoKo trying to work with this nigga, but this nigga too loose. Let me hit Night, so we can handle this shit," Savage responded.

"Chuck, come help me with this nigga."

China lay there gurgling up blood and struggling to breathe.

Mugsy stood up, walked over to the bar shaking his head. He grabbed the towel off the bar and wiped his hands. "Fill me up with something strong." Mugsy braced himself to give KoKo the news.

Later that night . . .

"Boa, you fucking up," she said as she tried to remain calm. KoKo sat in her big office chair across from Boa and Night.

161

"I had to teach that nigga a lesson."

"*I* teach the fucking lessons around here, not you!" KoKo yelled.

"Look, you handle your shit, and I'll handle mine."

KoKo got ready to say something then Night cut in. "Let me take him with me, KoKo."

"Wait, hold up." She sat up in her chair. "What the fuck is that supposed to mean?"

"Ain't nothing hidden in my words. They clear," Boa spat.

KoKo paused, ready to go off some more. China was laid up in the hospital, leaving his spot vulnerable. And to top it off, Boa was sitting in her face talking shit instead of trying to make shit right. "You know what? You right. Your shit loud and clear." KoKo and Boa's eyes locked and tension was high. Neither one was backing down.

As he stood up he said, "Let's go. Hard-headed ass nigga." Night could see shit was getting ready to escalate.

"I'm coming. Let me holler at you for a minute in private, KoKo," Boa said.

KoKo just stared at him.

Night looked back and forth between them, and for the first time he could see that KoKo was giving too much power to Boa, and that shit was not sitting well with Night. He looked at KoKo for approval. KoKo nodded. "I'll meet you downstairs," he said to Boa.

Boa sat, looking at KoKo. He rose from his seat, walking to her side. He stood over her.

"What do you want, Boa?"

"I need to make love to you tonight."

"Are you serious? What the fuck is you smoking? You just put a worker out of commission? You better run me my money."

"I got you. Stand up and let me get a handful of that juicy."

KoKo got out her chair, preparing to leave. Just as she began to walk past him, Boa forcefully grabbed her into his arms. "Boa, don't play with me. Let me go," she said while trying to struggle. With every futile move, Boa squeezed harder.

"Why you always acting all fucking hard?" Boa asked as he grabbed a handful of that ass.

KoKo gave him an icy stare as she reached around her back and attempted to remove his hands. Boa took the opportunity to grab her wrist behind her back with one hand and grab a handful of her hair with the other, pulling her head back. He began to kiss and suck on her neck, nibbling on her chin while talking shit. "You know you want me to make this pussy act up."

"I want you to let me go," she stated as her body began heating up.

"Gimme a kiss and I'll let you go," Boa asked, towering over her.

"You can kiss my ass."

"I wanna kiss that too."

"Boa. Let me go."

"Either you gonna give or I'ma take." He continued to squeeze her tight and suck that hot spot on her neck.

Needing him to stop before shit got outta control, she submitted. KoKo turned her face to his and allowed his lips to find hers. Boa kissed her deep and passionately. When he heard a small moan come from her mouth, he slowly released her hands and began rubbing her breasts. KoKo rested her hands on his chest as he began to slide his hand between her legs.

Just as things seemed to be going his way, KoKo backed up. "You got what you asked for and then some. Now get out my office before I change my mind about my plan A."

"What? You was going to put a toe tag on a nigga?" he asked then chuckled, looking at her like he wanted to eat her up.

"Maybe."

"I got something you can hang something on."

"Run a bitch her money. Until then, beat that shit," she said, looking down at his bulging print. Then she walked off.

Boa chuckled. He loved KoKo's attitude and damn sure knew what to do with it.

"I'ma run something all right." He walked out her office. To carry out her request, he figured he would go with Night and redeem himself by making the Boss's pockets swell. He knew he had to make shit right and he knew just how to do it.

*****

"I wish you would have come to me months ago," Andres said to Boa as he offered him a cigar.

"No thank you," Boa said, looking around the coffee shop. He felt like he was stuck in a godfather movie. Everybody had on suits and pinky rings.

"So Boa. Do you think you can talk to KoKo about letting you join us?" He sat, pulling on his cigar.

"I'm my own man."

"Good. I think it will be worth your while." He waved over a husky man dressed in all black. The man set a bag in front of Boa.

"I will say this. It's not KoKo you need to be worried about. It's those greasy ass Russians."

"Don't worry about them. I have a little plan for Vladimir."

Boa looked at all the neatly stacked bills inside. "This is good for a start." He zipped it up, stood and prepared to leave.

"Don't cross me," Andres warned.

"Don't cross me," Boa responded. "If you keep your word, I won't break mine."

"We will see," Andres said as he continued to puff.

Boa headed to his car with the first leg of his plan in action.

— 29 —
Let's Play

KoKo had just gotten out the shower, put on her pajama set, and laid across her bed. She had been running for weeks, and the comfort of her pillow top mattress felt like heaven. She closed her eyes, took a few deep breaths, and began dozing off. Just as sleep began to settle in, her phone vibrated on the nightstand. She started not to even move, but with all the shit that had been going on, she figured she should at least check the ID. She grabbed the phone and looked at the screen. "Shit!" It was Boa. She reluctantly answered, still upset with him for that bullshit he had been pulling.

"Yes," she said drowsily into the phone.

"Get dressed. I'm about to come get you."

KoKo could hear his car radio playing like it was the middle of the afternoon. From what she could guess, he was close. "Boa. I'm sleepy. Let me get at you tomorrow."

"Nah, ma. I need to see you. I got that package."

"Boa, tomorrow."

"It ain't up for discussion. I'll be there in a minute." He hung up.

KoKo looked at the phone, threw it across the bed, and laid her head down. Closing her eyes, she started to let that nigga come over for nothing. But as the seconds ticked on, she thought, *fuck it!* She jumped up and put on a short skirt, a T-shirt, and a pair of Pajar boots. She tucked her gun in the gun holster in the small of her back. Then she combed her hair, brushed her teeth, grabbed a wad of money and headed to the door. When she reached the living room, her cell started vibrating. "I'm coming," she stated in the phone with a slight attitude.

"Hurry up," he shot back and then hung up.

"This muthafucka love to hang up on people," she said and opened the door.

When she emerged from the building, Boa was sitting in his car, music bumping and pulling on a blunt, looking sexy as usual.

KoKo stood by the car and looked at him. Boa turned slowly toward the window, looked her up and down and then hit the locks.

"Why the fuck you ain't open the door?" she blurted as she slid in the seat and slammed the door.

"Don't be slamming my shit. Learn to have some patience," Boa said.

"Look, you called me out in the middle of the fucking night. I could have been in my bed."

"I'ma make it worth your while." He smiled at her as he looked down at those sexy legs. Before he pulled off, he reached in his glove box and handed her an envelope full of money. KoKo took it and laid it on her lap. Boa gave her that sneaky grin, and shifted the gear into drive and pulled off, tires screeching.

As they drove block after block, KoKo sat back and

relaxed. She took in all the New York nightlife. People were still scurrying back and forth, and so were the many cars and taxi's speeding and blowing their horns. She thought, *There's always something to see in the city that never sleeps.* Boa passed KoKo the blunt. They smoked and talked and laughed for over an hour. When they got to Chinatown, silence fell over the car once again. They both enjoyed the lights. After crossing the bridge approaching Flatbush Avenue, KoKo yelled out, "Oh shit! Junior's! I need some cheesecake."

"Later. I need something else sweet on my tongue," Boa said as his mouth started to water at the thought of KoKo's pussy dancing on the tip of his tongue.

KoKo looked over at him and her thoughts were confirmed. This nigga had her out in the middle of the night to get some pussy.

He drove to Lafayette, turned left, and then made a few turns and was at the opening of Greenview Park. He pulled into a parking space and got out. When he opened her door and extended his hand, she looked at him like he was crazy.

"What?" she said, all indignant with her arms folded and head tilted to the side.

"Come on. I got you."

KoKo looked around at the trees. "I don't do parks."

"Stop being so fucking tough and come on." He took her by the wrist.

"I'ma come, but if you got some bullshit up your sleeve, I'ma put something hot in that ass."

"Oh, you will cum. I promise you that," Boa stated with his deep, sexy voice as he pulled her from the car and into his arms. Placing light kisses on her neck and caressing her back, he hit the alarm and released her from his grip. He took her hand and walked her to his destination. When they reached the swings, he sat down and pulled her between his legs.

"You brought me out here in the middle of the night to play on the swings."

"Shhhh . . . you talk too much." Boa grabbed KoKo and held her tightly in his arms. It had been days since he had had a good dose of her. KoKo wrapped her arms around his neck as he placed soft wet kisses along her neck and collarbone. His hands moved strategically along her back and butt, finding their way between her thighs. When he realized she didn't have on any panties, his dick got rock instantly. "Let me find out you out here in the middle of the night without no panties on."

"A real bitch stay ready," she shot back as she began to heat up.

"That's what the fuck I'm talking about. Put your foot here. Let me show you why they really call me Boa," he commanded.

KoKo placed her foot on the side of Boa. He grabbed her other leg, pulling her up to stand over him. Her pussy was at face level. She held onto the chains as he reached under her skirt and placed his face between her legs and inhaled. KoKo looked down at him, savoring her scent and became wetter by the second. Boa reached up, placing his arms around the chains and palmed her ass with both hands. Then he placed his hot mouth right on her clit and began to suck gently. With KoKo right where he wanted her, he kicked off with his feet causing the swing to rock. She held on tight as he sucked harder. Boa picked up speed while giving her some wicked tongue action.

The more she moaned, the harder he sucked and the faster he swung. When the contractions came on, KoKo gripped the chains tighter. It felt as if her hands had become one with them. "I'm about to cum, Boa," she moaned as he continued to take her higher.

When she could take no more, she began to cum long and hard. Boa licked and sucked as her juices rained all over his mouth. She felt like she had risen out of her body. As Boa brought the swing to a stop, he removed his hands from her butt and opened his pants, releasing the dragon. KoKo laid her head on her arm, closed her eyes and enjoyed the warm breeze on her skin and the moonlight that beamed through the trees.

Boa placed his feet firmly to the ground. He pulled KoKo down, placing her legs behind him as he slid up in her wetness. As he guided her up and down on that steel, he began whispering in her ear, "I'm falling in love with you. I need you in my life."

"Loving me is dangerous," she whispered in his ear.

"And not having you is impossible."

KoKo just rode that dick in search for her spot. Boa pushed off again sending the swing cruising back and forth. She held on tightly to his neck as he grinded deep inside her.

"Ahhh . . . ssss . . . " she moaned as the intensity of her pleasure heightened.

He held her firmly in place as he played with her spot. "I need you, baby. I need you," he whispered.

"I'm about to cum," she whispered in his ear and then bit into his neck. She sucked, causing Boa to bounce her faster on his dick bringing her orgasm on strong. They swung back and forth, panting until they both released.

KoKo heaved in and out trying to catch her breath as Boa placed passionate kisses all over her face.

"You know I'm not letting you go," he confessed.

KoKo didn't respond. She was high as hell, just enjoying their moment together. After a few more minutes, Boa lifted her, allowing her to stand up. He placed himself back in his pants and stood as well.

Boa stared at KoKo's half opened eyes. He wrapped his arms around her and said, "So you like the park now?"

"That shit was boss."

"Let's get the fuck outta here so I can go put those sexy ass legs over my shoulder. I want to get to the bottom of some shit."

"That's what the fuck I'm talking about. Come on and let me show you why they really call me the Boss."

Boa chuckled, grabbing KoKo by the waist and walking her back to the car.

*****

Around six in the morning, Boa was awakened from his sleep by KoKo moaning out Kayson's name and tossing and turning back and forth. He quickly turned on the light and began shaking her from her nightmare, "Baby. Baby. Wake up."

KoKo jumped out of her sleep and wrestled around, looking both confused and fearful. Sweat dripped down her forehead and temples. She panted, breathing hard.

As she tried to calm herself down, she put her hands up to her face and wiped sweat from her brow. "I'm fine," she said, getting off the bed and heading toward the bathroom. Once inside, she turned on the water and sat on the side of the tub as she ran the memories through her mind. Once she calmed down, she ran water over her face and then exited the bathroom. She moved around Boa's room, gathering her things.

"Hold up, ma. Where you going?"

She put on her skirt and one of Boa's T-shirts and her boots. "I'll hit you later," she said as she headed to the door.

"You gotta stop letting that nigga haunt you, KoKo," Boa yelled as he grabbed the blanket and threw it up on the bed. He lay back, wondering if chasing KoKo was really worth it.

~ 30 ~
Pit Stop

The next day KoKo was back on the road. Running from her demons had become the order of the day. After KoKo ran through the trap spots, she headed to the club, pleased at how successful Golden Paradise turned out. The club was always packed, and the girls were turning niggas over for money every night.

At twelve midnight, KoKo pulled up to the club. Her usual routine was in and out. She would check in once a week on any given night and just look around, receive messages, and give orders. This particular night she felt funny. All night she kept getting sinking sensations in her stomach, so she decided to meet Goldie in her office to get the intel she needed. She gave her ten thousand dollars to hit the girls, Zori, Porsha, and Shameezah with a bonus because she had been hearing good things. After she concluded the conversation, she planned on moving out, but remembered something she needed to impress upon Goldie.

"Yo, make sure you let them bitches know this is an increase for 'your effort pay', not vacation pay. So don't make me have to go back on my good will and put my foot up somebody's ass."

"Oh shit." Goldie laughed." You crazy as hell, KoKo."

"Let them bitches start slippin' and they'll see crazy.

Sheeit. . . I don't play with two things."

Goldie cut in. "What's that, KoKo?"

"My money and my man. Don't fuck with my pockets or slide on my dick, and we good."

"I. Hear. That," Goldie said and slapped KoKo's hand three times.

"Look, I'm about to bounce. I got some shit to handle." She stood to leave.

"A'ight. Can you roast a stem with a bitch first? I got some of that Hawaiian gold already rolled."

"Shit, don't threaten me with a good time. You are exhaling when you should be inhaling. Like Goodie Mob said, 'Put some fire to the ass end of that weed'."

Goldie burst out laughing. "Girl, you better not ever change." She grabbed the blunt, lit it up, and they hit it until it was all ash."

KoKo grabbed a bottle of water off the wet bar and took a couple swigs. "Good lookin', I'll get at you tomorrow." She headed to the door.

"Cool," Goldie responded as she watched KoKo walk out her office. She jumped up, stretched, and said, "Let me go watch these bitches, so you won't have to give me some foot work."

KoKo chuckled as she headed down the steps and for the exit. When she reached the front door, some chick was posted up looking her squarely in the eyes. KoKo quickly took inventory of all the bitch's features and noticed a tattoo on her foot in Chinese writing and a white leather watch with rubies and diamonds in the face that looked like the Michelle watch she had at home. KoKo moved to the door, thinking, *Let me hold onto that info. I might need that for something.* She proceeded out the door. On her way to her car, she whispered two words to the bouncer and then slapped his ass.

"Keep that up and I'm going to have to take you home with me."

"And where yo' bitch gonna sleep?" KoKo shot back, causing the first couple of girls on line to ooohh and laugh.

"You got that," Chico yelled as she moved past the crowd.

KoKo was done entertaining, so she just smoothed off to her car. She looked around and then jumped in her car, which was always parked a few spots back from the door. In her mind, she went over the conversation she had with Rock the other day and how she should deal with him wanting more than a friendship. KoKo popped the trunk and grabbed a pair of sneakers. Then she slammed the trunk closed.

Once positioned in the driver's seat, she started the engine. While adjusting the mirror, a small SUV pulled up behind her with lights bright as hell. She couldn't make out the car or the driver. But shit didn't sit right, so she cracked the door slightly and slid her shoes off. Kayson's warning came to her as if he sat right next to her. *If you see danger prepare for war.* She kept her eyes on the rearview mirror and slowly reached for her nine and took off the safety.

As she prepared to go hard with whomever it was, two figures approached from each side of the rear of the car.

She eased her left leg up so it was in her seat. KoKo said, "These muthafuckas must think I'm a fucking fool. Well, they got to bring some ass to get some." One of the nigga's moved on her passenger side, running fast and the other guy crept toward her driver side window. Both dudes wore hoodies, so she couldn't get a good look at their faces. She put her hand on the passenger seat, maintaining a firm grip on the gun. Then she heard the nigga on her side speak.

"Yo, bitch, you KoKo?" a deep voice asked.

"In the flesh, muthafucka." She kicked the door open, hitting him and causing him to fall back. His gun went off striking KoKo in the side. At the same time, she let off several rounds at the other guy, hitting him in the stomach. He fired off three bullets before he hit the ground and his slugs hit the window inches from KoKo's face.

The shots alerted the bouncer who came running to her car, guns out blasting.

The nigga driving the truck quickly backed up and tried to pull off, but her boys were right on his ass, sending bullets flying through the front window, hitting everything moving.

KoKo grabbed the Carbine 15 from the console and jumped out the car. The nigga she hit with the door was getting up from between the two cars where he hid from the rain of bullets. He tried to run, but made it only a few inches. KoKo pumped three of those 223s in him, blowing holes in his back and sending his guts flying out the front and onto the car in front of her. He slid down the car and then hit the ground all dismantled.

Chico said, "KoKo, you're bleeding, ma. Let us get you inside."

She said, "Check the truck. Make sure the only air that's flowing through it is wind and not breath."

When they got close to the truck, the back passenger door opened. A dude jumped out and took off running past KoKo's car. She broke right behind him, pulled the Carbon and then blasted, hitting him in his right leg. He went down instantly. The crew was right on her heels. When they caught up to her, she was bent over the nigga in full question mode.

"Your boss must be a bitch. He sent all y'all out here for little ol' me? Sheeit, you had a better chance at running up in a gay bar bent over with KY in your ass and not getting fucked than you had at hitting me." She stood up and spit on him. "Who sent you?" she asked.

"Fuck you, bitch. I ain't telling you nothing!" he yelled out in apparent pain.

"Is that right? We'll see about that."

"Just kill me 'cause I ain't got shit for you."

"That might be true. You probably don't got shit to say. But I bet you on your mother, father, any siblings, your bitch, and your kids' grave, that you'll be singing like a fucking canary by the end of the night."

KoKo could hear the faint sound of sirens in the background. KoKo turned to her crew and gave her orders, "Hurry up and get this muthafucka outta here. Take him where you got to take him and do what you got to do, and don't stop until I get back to you."

They dragged his ass around the corner and were gone. Chico stayed with KoKo as they headed to her car, and then Goldie came running up to her.

"What the fuck happened?"

KoKo snapped. "Your concern is inside, not outside." She

gave her the look of death. That was the first time she had seen KoKo's full dark side.

Goldie looked down and saw blood on KoKo's shirt. Goldie wanted to say something else, but turned and walked back inside.

"Go grab the tapes from the camera and spread some money around the crowd because none of those muthafuckas saw shit. Get rid of my shit and I'll call you."

KoKo limped over to her car, went into her trunk and grabbed her boots. She put them on, and then looked at her side. The gaping wound was bleeding profusely. She snatched up the towel she normally used to wipe off her car and pressed it against her injury. Then she got a jacket and put it on. Now that the adrenaline was wearing off, the gunshot wound throbbed and ached with an intense burning.

"KoKo, let me take you where you need to go," Chico said, wearing a worried look and trying to persuade her once more. Just then, a light rain began to fall.

"Do what I told you." KoKo tossed him her keys and limped off. Just as she hit the corner, the police were all over the scene. Chico threw the keys to one of the bouncers, and he jumped in her car and drove off. Thank God the niggas in the truck had tried to back out of the street in reverse, blocking the cops from getting too close, giving Chico time to regroup. Chico turned to say one more thing to KoKo, but she was gone. He sent D-Rod inside to instruct Ralphie to erase and alter the surveillance equipment. One of the other bouncers subtly passed out hundreds as they let people in the club.

"You ain't see shit, right?" D-Rod asked each patron. All

he heard was, "Hell no." and "What was there to see?"

After the cops roped off and assessed the immediate scene, they walked down to the club to see if there were any witnesses, but no one was talking. They then turned their questions to Chico.

Chico said, "I don't really know what happened, officer. The truck pulled up and the driver was talking to some guys in a black Honda, and then they started to exchange fire. At that point, I just had all our customers get down on the ground."

"Does your establishment have cameras?"

"Yes, sir."

"Can we see them?"

"Sure. Let me get the manager so she can take you to the office."

"Thank you."

"No problem. Shit. We just want our patrons to be safe."

Thank God KoKo had everything covered. Her computer technician, Ralphie, whom she brought down to the 'A' from Jersey, had set up fake ass loops with different cars and people specifically for the cameras just in case shit like this ever happened.

When KoKo had gotten around the corner, she hailed a cab and jumped in. "Take me to Buckhead." Once she sat down, she had a chance to get a better look at her injury. It was still bleeding and appeared to need a couple stitches. Her wound hurt like a muthafucka, but she applied pressure to it and tried to relax. The rain dripped softly at first, but thirty seconds later, the rain violently began to pour. Relief consumed KoKo for the moment. What little evidence that remained at the scene would begin washing away. As they approached their destination, KoKo reached in her bra and pulled out ten one-hundred dollar bills. "You never saw me, *right*?" she affirmed to the cabbie.

"I'm on my way to the airport to drop off a tall white kid with a black hoodie and blue jeans." He picked up his radio and called it in.

"Roger that 0479," came back across the radio.

"Are you going to be all right?"

"Hell yeah. But if you run your mouth you won't be 0479," she said, reaching over and grabbing the door handle with her sleeve and proceeded out. She headed down the street and the familiar dizzy feeling started to come over her. She held her side with one hand and the Carbine in the other. It took the last of her energy to make it down the street and around the corner.

*****

At 2 a.m. the cleansing rain fell hard as hell. Rock had just gotten out the shower and put on his silk pajama pants. He went into the living room and poured himself a drink. Grabbing the remote, he turned on his 62-inch plasma flat screen to ESPN to catch the sports highlights. He wanted to just relax, but he couldn't shake the conversation he had with KoKo, and the fact that she had his head all fucked up and hadn't even given him any pussy yet.

All he could think was, *what is it about this woman that's got me so hazy?* He sat for about thirty minutes sipping his drink and watching TV. Then he stood up and hit the remote and was heading to his room when his doorbell rang. He turned to look at the wall clock and said, "Who the fuck could

be ringing my shit at this hour? It better be important as hell."
When he got to the door, his eyes popped open. "What the
fuck?"

KoKo stood there drenched from head to toe. Her hair was
stringy and she looked a mess. Then he saw the Carbine 15 in
her right hand. That threw him all the way off.

KoKo looked him in the eyes and said, "Nigga, if it was
your day, all that shit you tossing around in your head would
be a one-on-one with God." She always blew his mind with
the shit she said, so he just looked at her like she was crazy.
KoKo had no more strength left to fight, so she said in a calm
voice, "Can you let a sistah in?"

Rock looked at her other hand at her side and saw blood
dripping from it, so he reached out for her just as she went to
one knee. He quickly grabbed her, and as she fell into his arms
he picked her up and carried her to the bathroom. Rock placed
her in the tub, looked her over and then he ran and got his cell
phone. He made sure the door was locked and peeked out the
blinds to make sure no one was following her.

"Yo, Sandra, you up?"

"Yeah. Why? What's good?"

"Go get me a milkshake and some fries. I'm hungry as hell
and hurry up." That was his code for a gunshot victim.

"All right, I'll be right over." Sandra was a nurse who had
been his friend for years. She had everything needed for all
occasions.

Rock went back in the bathroom and started to undress
KoKo so he could see what they were working with. The
bullet had gone right through the flesh of her side. It was

"That's what I'm afraid of," Rock said, releasing a chuckle.

The doorbell rang just in time. It was Sandra. He left KoKo in the room and let her in. When Sandra walked in the room and looked at the way Rock attended to KoKo, she became very jealous. She had never had to help him with a female before, and the fact that it appeared that he was feeling her, put Sandra in a bad mood. She walked over to her and removed KoKo's IV and checked and changed her bandages. Once done, she passed KoKo a Prada sweatsuit, a bra, panties, and a pair of sneakers along with the weed and a blunt. KoKo looked at the clothes and turned up her nose. She dropped the robe right in front of them, popped the tags and put the clothes on.

"We would have left out and gave you some privacy," Sandra said, trying to make light of the situation as she packed her things back in the bag.

KoKo turned and said, "For what? You got a pussy, and if he ain't seen one by now then something is wrong." She went to the nightstand, grabbed her money, and put it in her pocket. She sat on the bed and quickly rolled a blunt and then took it to the head. Rock and Sandra just stood there looking at her.

KoKo picked up the pre-pay and called a cab. Then she turned to Rock, who was still trying to recover from her last statement. "Thank you so much, baby. Believe me when I tell you I got you. Sheeit . . . You betta be glad a bitch came up in here fucked up, or you'd be laid out sucking your thumb right about now."

"You got jokes."

She limped over to him and kissed his lips again. At the same time, she took some money out her pocket and passed it to Sandra. "I appreciate your help."

Sandra looked at her and then at Rock. "You don't have to pay me. Rock will handle me," she stated dryly.

Rock looked at Sandra with a wrinkled brow because he wasn't used to her catching feelings. KoKo chuckled as she looked into Rock's eyes and said, "Hook her up real good, so I can have even more to thank you for." Seeing that old girl was catching feelings, KoKo gave her a reason to really be upset, and allowed her hand to roam up and down Rock's semi-hard dick. She ran the tip of her tongue between his lips.

Rock enjoyed the two ladies' little fight over him.

KoKo pulled him to her, placing his dick right at the base of her pussy and said, "Yo, Sandra. You got anything in that bag for swelling?"

Rock shook his head and smiled. Sandra frowned as she continued to pack her bag.

"Can I have my steel?"

"Anytime you want it," he responded.

"I know that, but I need the bitch I walked in here with. I'm going to bust yours off later."

Rock went to the closet, got the bag with her gun in it, and handed it to her. They heard the cab blowing the horn.

"Walk me to the door." They left out the room as she yelled, "Bye, Sandra."

— *31* —
Interrogation

"Who sent you, muthafucka?" Night yelled and smacked Junior with his gun. Blood spurted out his mouth. He was fucked up and exhausted and on the brink of giving up everybody. The crew had been giving him a severe ass whipping for over eight hours. After KoKo got shot, her crew began putting extreme pressure on the 'A' for answers. Junior's name went to the top of the list.

On his knees with his hands tied behind his back, he lifted his head. With his right eye slightly open, he saw KoKo trailed by three guys coming toward him.

"He talking yet?" she asked.

"Nah, this nigga holding strong," Night responded.

KoKo pulled out her gun, rested it at her side, and then shot him in the shoulder. His screams filled the room. KoKo pulled a bottle of gin from her back pocket, took a swig, and then poured it on his wound.

"Ahhhhh!" Junior yelled out again as the pain coursed through his body.

"You feel like talking now?"

"Fuck you, bitch!" he barked as he leaned over in pain.

"I figured you'd say that." She smiled and then waved her hand at Savage.

He left and brought back a hooded female. Savage snatched the hood off the woman and pushed her to the ground.

Junior's eyes widened when he saw his wife lying at KoKo's feet. Junior swallowed his spit and raised his head with a grimace on his face. "I don't give a fuck about her or you," he growled,

Tears streamed down his wife's face as she began to weep hysterically. KoKo smiled and said, "Chucky, let me get part two." Chucky left and returned with a small boy and brought him to KoKo.

She rested her hand with the gun on his shoulder.

Junior put his head down and shook it from side to side. Tears ran down his face.

"Noooo . . ." his wife made a bone-chilling scream at the sight of the gun now resting against her son's chest. She glared at Junior with hatred in her eyes. "You tell them, you sorry son-of-a bitch!" she bellowed.'

Junior kept his head down as he heard his son' cry. "I don't want to die," the small boy whimpered as he looked at his dad.

Junior raised his head, tightened his lips, and then said, "I'll make another one."

His wife looked at him with narrowed eyes and blurted, "Kemo!" The hair on KoKo's neck stood up. Then she shot Junior in the chest.

"Oh my God! No! No! Noooooo!" his wife shrieked as she cried and shook uncontrollably.

"See, your dad gave his life for you," KoKo whispered in the little boy's ear. She pointed the gun at the wife and shot her in the head. Her body slammed to the ground. She looked down at his son and said, "Your mother too."

"Mommy!" the little boy yelled and dropped to his knees at his mom's side. He shook her but got no response.

"See that he gets dropped off at his grandmother's house." KoKo squeezed her gun tight, her breathing quickened as her thoughts went to Diablo.

Chucky scooped him up as he kicked and screamed for his parents.

"Let's move on them niggas," KoKo said. She and Night rolled out while the rest of the crew did their clean up.

Later that night . . .

KoKo and her death squad pulled up to Diablo's motorcycle shop five trucks deep. They jumped out wearing all black, looked around and walked to the entrance of the shop. Diablo's security looked her up and down and then let them in. They were led to a wall that opened up to a staircase. They walked down the stairs and into an underground room the size of half of a football field. They walked to Diablo's desk, strapped and all. Searching wasn't in the program today. Diablo believed in fair fighting ground. If death was meant for either side, it would have to work hard for it.

"You got something you want to tell me?" KoKo got straight to the point.

Diablo pulled hard on a cigar and blew the smoke out before responding in a deep, raspy voice. "Speak what's on your mind. Don't slow stroke me."

"A man's dying wish was that I tell you hello."

Diablo nodded and waved at a nearby gunman who brought a limping man over to the desk who was thrown at KoKo's feet. "I believe this is who that dying man wanted you to holla at. I held onto him until you got here."

"What the fuck is this? Some kind of joke?"

"Nah. This ambitious young man thought it wise to start a little war, unaware of the fact that you are one of my number one people. Isn't that right, about to be dead ass muhfucka?" Diablo yelled at Kemo.

He shook uncontrollably. "Diablo, I'm sorry. We didn't know," he cried as he realized that his hour had come.

"I bet you know now," Diablo said as he blew a hole in the back of Kemo's head. Brain matter and blood flew to the floor and his head followed.

As he hit the ground, KoKo pulled out her gun and put two more in the empty spaces for good measure and then stuck it back in its place. "Our business is complete," KoKo said as she turned to walk away.

"Fair enough. But, can I talk to you in private right quick?" Diablo asked.

"Sure," KoKo responded.

"Y'all niggas hang back a little so we can talk business," Diablo ordered.

Every one moved back to the other side of the room except Diablo's most trusted and Night, KoKo's most trusted.

"Something to smoke?" Diablo offered KoKo and Night.

"No thank you," KoKo said, remaining professional.

"Let me ask you something. What does the name Scarie mean to you?"

"Scarie?" KoKo sat for a minute running names through her mental database. "I don't know anything about Scarie. Should I?"

"I don't know if you should. But he damn sure wants to meet you."

"Is that right? What gives you that impression?"

Diablo took a long pull on the blunt and blew out a thick cloud of smoke into the air. "You're the type that likes to smoke out your own information, and I plan on letting you do that. But I will tell you this." Diablo paused for a minute. "This nigga Scarie is a monster. No loyalty. I don't trust that nigga when I'm looking at him and damn sure not outta my sight. He wants you bad. Be careful," Diablo warned.

"Is that it?"

"For now."

KoKo stood up and Diablo made one last statement, "We do business, so it's always give and take on fair ground. But I trust you, so you have my word I won't roll on you. But I won't ever risk my own for your safety, so watch your back."

"Indeed," KoKo shot back as she looked Diablo over.

"You need to stop playing and let me find out why niggas like to taste KoKo."

"Nah, I'm good. I like bones in my fish," KoKo shot back not breaking her stride.

Diablo just smiled.

It was always hard for her to deal with Diablo because her appearance threw KoKo off. Here was a 5'10", 200-pound muscular beast with a deep voice, full beard and mustache and face tatted up. But under all that deep husky voice, thuggish attitude and gangsta power, was a pussy and a pair of tits. *Unbelievable*. KoKo shook her head as she headed for the exit. She was now on another search for a ghost in the darkness.

~ 32 ~
Gather The Troops

Chico was on KoKo's phone going off in a combination of English and Spanish.

"Calm the fuck down," KoKo said into the phone.

"I don't like niggas playing in my back yard," he barked into the phone.

Once Boa had found out what happened to KoKo he went down to the A and turned shit up. Things had gotten real hot very fast, making it hard for niggas to handle their business. Chico was pissed.

"I got it, Chico. Just keep shit stable. I'm going to call for a meeting."

"Yeah. Okay," Chico said with a little hesitation in his voice

"Am I clear about my orders?" KoKo barked.

"Yeah, you clear."

"Alright. Wait for my next call." She hung up and took a deep breath.

"Your boy fucked up again?" Night asked.

"We need to have a big meeting. I'm pulling people in the circle and everybody needs to know who's who so we don't have mass violation."

"You ready to do a big party?" Night asked with concern in

194

his voice.

"I'll be all right." KoKo sat thinking about the last big party thrown, the night Kayson was killed. She had been avoiding having the function, but she realized the parties were a part of Kayson's method of making sure the major players in the organization were aquainted, and therefore no one would step on each others' toes. "Start gathering everyone up. The party will be this weekend." Night nodded and got up to leave her office.

KoKo called in a favor from Diablo. A sit down with Chico and the leader of MT7 was set and a compromise was met. When big money lay on the table, fuck ups needed identifying and all bullshit required elimination in order to keep business moving.

*****

When Saturday came, KoKo still felt conflicted about the whole event. Even though everything was in place and they had security out the ass, the pain of the evening hovered over her like a black evil cloud.

KoKo stood in her walk-in closet in her bra and panties looking at her dress and shoes. After a few more hits of her blunt and swigs of her drink, she was ready. She slid her feet into her shoes and then pulled her dress over her head. Once completely dressed, she stood in the full-length mirror and looked herself over. "All right bitch, pull it together. We got shit to do," she said aloud. She grabbed her clutch and headed out the door.

*****

The evening was warm yet comfortable. Around ten

o'clock everyone began pulling up to the rented mansion for the all red affair. Everyone stepped out their cars sharp as hell dressed in different variations of red, from deep dark red to bright red accented with either gold or silver.

The room was huge, decorated with high ceilings and crystal chandaliers. Silver coffee and end tables sat next to dark red couches with big black fluffy pillows. Silver ice buckets with expensive champagne were positioned in several areas throughout the room. The one fixture that set the center of the room off was the crystal circular bar that served nothing but the finest libations at the guest's request.

As the members entered the house, the servers began passing out glasses of champagne. The DJ had set the mode going from one hot hit to the next. As everyone started to mingle and talk, the evening had officially started. Night, Mugsy, Boa, Chucky and Savage arrived around 11 p.m. with their wives on their arms.

"It's live up in here," Chucky said as they made their way into the room.

"I'm about to get fucked up," Mugsy said as he took a glass from the tray in front of him.

"Hell yeah," Savage said, grabbing one also.

After everyone had a glass, they put them together and Night made a toast. "To the future," he said as each glass touched and smiles came across their faces.

"It is so nice in here," Latreece said as she squeezed Boa's arm." She was so happy to be out with him. Boa looked down at her and nodded. He had been quiet since he got there. He had one woman on his arm and another one on the way. With all the shit going on, he hadn't had any time with KoKo and his mind was scheming on how he was going to steal a moment alone with her.

By twelve o'clock, the room was buzzing with conversation. KoKo came through the door wearing a sheer, body-hugging, knee-length dark red off the shoulder dress. The silver four-inch heels strapped around her ankle were accented with Swarovski crystals. Her hair was swept to one side, which gave a full view of her dangling diamond earrings and matching necklace.

All eyes were on her as she moved through the room. Boa's mouth watered at the sight of all that chocolate skin covered by that sexy red dress.

"Gotdamn!" Savage said as he hit Mugsy with his elbow.

When Mugs looked up, he felt his dick jump at the sight of that dress clinging to KoKo's perfect ass. "Damn, Boss Lady," he mumbled under his breath.

"Y'all niggas better fall the fuck back," Boa barked.

"Nigga, fuck you. We ain't trippin'. Just enjoying the view," Savage shot back.

The closer KoKo approached, Boa could feel his heart beating faster. She stopped a few feet away from them and briefly addressed a few issues with Wadoo from Cali. Giggling and tossing her hair, she touched his arm and then whispered in his ear-causing Boa to get a slight attitude.

The crew was caught up in gazing at KoKo when the wives returned with their drinks. "Damn, take a picture it will last longer," Latreece said as she shoved Boa's drink in his hand.

"Go ahead with all that." He took the drink and shot her a

dirty look.

Lynn, Clarisah, and Rain just stood back and watched the little quarrel going on and shook their heads. They had been on the team for a while and knew their place. One thing was for sure, nobody wanted a beef with KoKo.

"Good evening ladies and gentlemen," KoKo said as she approached.

"What's up, Boss lady?" Savage said and leaned in to give her a hug.

"You killing that dress, ma," Mugsy said as he also gave her a hug.

"You know how we do," she said, looking Latreece in the eyes. "Boa, get everybody ready. We need to meet in the office on the left in fifteen minutes.

"Enjoy the evening, ladies," she said to the women and then turned and walked off.

Fifteen minutes later, almost half the room cleared out to attend the meeting. Latreece stared at the doors as they closed shut.

"You gotta stop tripping, ma. This is how your man handles his business. Either you can be down or spend your life being pissed off and miserable," Clarisah, Chucky's wife said as she sipped her drink.

"I can't get used to this shit. Ever since he moved up closer to her, he has not been the same," Latreece said as she kept looking at the door.

"I don't care what Mugsy do anymore. A bitch is rich and comfortable," Lynn said as she sat down and crossed her legs. Rain didn't even respond. She had her run-ins with KoKo in the past, and she already knew where Night's loyalty lied. Latreece sat there feeling sick to her stomach. She couldn't understand how the women in the organization accepted infidelity in exchange for money and power.

After an hour, everyone began to emerge from the room. Boa was one of the last people to exit with a big smile on his face. KoKo came out after him. Night was right behind her.

Boa and Night headed to where the ladies were sitting, and KoKo mingled a little more. The DJ slowed the music down and couples began to get their slow grind on. When the ladies excused themselves to the bathroom, Boa made his move.

"I'll be right back. Watch my back," he said and moved toward KoKo's direction.

"That nigga sprung," Mugsy said, shaking his head.

"Nah, that muhfucka in love," Savage said as he headed to make a few more connections.

KoKo was posted up by the patio talking to Gwen. Gwen's mouth was moving at the pace of a jackhammer. She moved from one subject to the next. However, KoKo couldn't pay attention if she wanted to because the heat that was beaming from Boa's eye sockets had her pussy tingling. He walked right up to her, grabbed her hand, and pulled her onto the patio with him.

"Well damn," Gwen said and then walked off.

"What are you doing?" KoKo asked.

"You sexy as hell in this dress," Boa said, ignoring her question.

"I look sexy in everything."

"I don't want to fight with you," he said as he moved

closer.

"If you would do what I tell you we wouldn't fight," KoKo said, looking up at him.

"I need you tonight," he said as he kissed her cheek.

"You better go check on your girl," KoKo said as his hands rested on her waist.

"She straight. I need to make sure everything is good with us."

"You need to let me be in charge and stop doing shit that makes me have to justify why your head is still attached to your shoulders."

"You know you need my head," he said, licking his lips and looking at her through the slits of his eyes. Boa moved closer pinning her against the conrete railing.

"Seriously, Boa. You gotta stop all this reckless activity," KoKo said as he began to place soft sensual kisses on her shoulder.

"I hear you." He placed his hand under her chin and kissed her lips. "Let me taste your chocolate," he said as his hands caressed her hips.

"Your girl is looking for you," KoKo said, looking past Boa and into the room through the curtain.

"Well then, I better hurry up." He lowered himself to her waist and took a deep breath enjoying KoKo's scent as his fingertips firmly eased up her thighs. Grabbing her panties, he pulled them to her ankles. KoKo stepped out of them as he placed her leg over his shoulder. KoKo rested her hands on the top of his head as he began to tickle her clit with the tip of his tongue.

KoKo's eyes rotated between open and closed as Boa caused her body to move in response to his touch. "Damn, boy," she mumbled.

Boa was in his glory. He began sucking her clit softly, waiting to hear the sensual moans that started to leave her lips. When he felt her leg tremble, he sucked harder.

"Ssss . . . mmm . . . Boa," KoKo whispered as she gripped his head tighter. She looked down at him handling his business and then back at the curtain. She could see Latreece looking for Boa and getting closer. "Boa, hurry up," she moaned.

Boa stopped to run his tongue between her slippery wet lips sending chills through her body. "Mmmm . . . hurry up, Boa."

"You still mad at me?" he asked, looking up into her glossy eyes.

KoKo shook her head back and forth then said, "Make me cum, Boa."

With that, he licked and sucked until her contractions came on strong. KoKo threw her head back and gripped the edge of the rail.

"Did you see Boa?" they heard Latreece ask as she planted herself right by the patio doors.

KoKo opened her eyes as she released all over Boa's mouth. Boa slid his tongue in her jucies, savoring her taste.

Latreece stood there with her arms folded in panic mode. "Boa, stop," KoKo whispered.

Boa rose, dick hard and ready. "Boa, no." KoKo grabbed his hand.

"Shhhh . . . they gonna hear you," he whispered as he pulled her up to his waist and slid in.

"Damn, you feel good."

"Boa, wait," she pleaded.

Boa moved deep and fast.

"Night, did you see Boa," Latreece asked as she turned to the side and continued to look around.

"Nah. But he should turn up soon," Night said and then moved on.

KoKo held on tight as she felt another orgasm coming on.

"You gotta let that bitch go, Boa," KoKo whispered.

"Ssss . . . It's all about you KoKo," Boa hissed as he too began to cum.

KoKo watched the curtain as Latreece turned to face where they were. Boa stroked faster as her wetness became crippling. The intensity of the moment caused Boa and KoKo to cum hard just as Latreece reached her hand out to open the curtain.

"Treece!" Rain yelled out.

Latreece turned quickly in Joveeda's direction.

Panting and sweating, Boa rested up against KoKo and then let her down.

"You know I'm addicted to this pussy, right?" Boa whispered in her ear.

"Do what I tell you, Boa, and you can have it whenever you want it," KoKo said as she walked toward the steps leading off the patio. Boa straightened his clothes as he watched her walk down the small trail leading toward the front of the building.

"Boa!" Latreece said as she walked onto the patio looking in all directions. "I have been looking for you," she said as she looked him up and down.

"What's up?" he asked, all relaxed.

"What were you doing?" she asked with her hands on her hips.

"I was wrapping some shit up."

"What's wrong with your clothes?" Latreece asked hands on her hips, nostrils flared and eyes squinted.

"Stop asking me all these questions." He glared at her, slightly agitated.

Latreece paused, looking in his eyes. "I don't even know who you are anymore."

"Whatever. Come on," he said as he exited the patio.

"Boa!" she called out, but he kept on going. She realized then that her relationship with Boa was over.

— 33 —
Bitch Bye

KoKo sat in the VIP section of a local New York nightclub, enjoying a drink and watching the action. Over the last couple days, she had been having shit thrown in her lap left and right. She needed to sit and regroup. KoKo was just getting to a point of mental comfort when Chucky came to the door and knocked as he entered. KoKo gave him that look that said, "I wasn't trying to be bothered."

"Excuse me, KoKo, but Boa's wife is out here trying to see you."

"Who?" KoKo said as she took a pull on her blunt.

"Latreece. And she's drunk and upset." Chucky stood waiting for his instructions.

KoKo paused, took another pull and blew out smoke. "Bring her to me." Chucky left the room and returned ten minutes later with Latreece marching behind him. The two security guards frisked her before entering, and then led Latreece into the room.

"What can I do for you?"

"How do you sleep at night knowing you're a homewrecker?" she asked with a slightly drunken slur.

KoKo maintained her calm demeanor. "Well, after Boa finishes eating my pussy I sleep like a baby," KoKo responded.

Latreece sneered at KoKo through blood shot eyes full of disgust and pain. "You're a hateful bitch. I should have known the whole time you were after my man."

"First of all, if I'm a bitch, I'm the baddest bitch you will ever meet." KoKo stood up, grabbing her gun.

Latreece's eyes grew wide.

"Oh, now you quiet?" KoKo walked toward her. When she got right up on her, she put the gun under her chin, pushing her head all the way back.

Tears slid down the sides of Latreece's eyes.

KoKo leaned in and whispered," Let me share three things with you right quick. One, can't no bitch take what's yours. Second, never confront the other bitch. It could be hazardous to your health. And three, tonight when Boa is deep up in this good kitty, and he whispers, 'KoKo, let me taste you,' I'ma lay back and throw these sexy chocolate legs over his shoulders. And as the tip of his tongue dances up and down my pussy, and I feel the urge to cum, I'ma arch my back, reach around the back of his head, and call out your name."

Latreece and her falling tears didn't move KoKo's emotions one centimeter. "Who are you again?" She chuckled. "Oh yeah, you don't fucking exist in my world." KoKo backed up. "Get this bitch outta my face before I change my mind." Slowly, she put the gun in her waist and moved toward the table.

Chucky came to Latreece's side and took her by the arm. The anguished look on her face made him feel her pain.

Back in her seat, KoKo watched Chucky escort Latreece

out the room. "Bitch, you better be lucky I already met my killing quota for the week, or you'd be having niggas saying nice shit over you." She crossed her legs and grabbed her drink.

As Latreece reached the main door, shame and betrayal trumped her emotional state.

KoKo relit her blunt and smirked. "Fuck outta here." She took a long pull, blowing smoke in the air. "This is my world. And every fucking thing in it." Those spoken words bounced off the walls. Her heart sank at the thought that just a few years ago, she was the wife of a boss. And now she had turned into the very bitch she would kill over her man. The painful reality caused her to pour drink after drink until she no longer gave a fuck.

You Have a Collect Call From. . .

The middle of the summer meant 'hot as hell' in Rikers Island prison, which made for dangerous conditions behind those wretched walls. Baseem was working the routine he set for himself, to keep busy and avoid killing a nigga. He had just returned to his cell from the yard, face pouring with sweat after running sixteen miles and a strenuous routine of pushups, sit-ups and pull-ups. When he hit his cell he got an instant attitude. A new inmate was put in his room, and after being in there alone for a month he wasn't feeling having a roommate again.

"What's up, Ak? I'm Curt."

Baseem looked at his hand and replied, "What's up?"

Baseem went past him and grabbed his towel and sweatpants and T-shirt from his locker.

Curt felt a little uneasy because Baseem was moving around quietly and with an apparent attitude. He looked up from where he was hanging his pictures and was about to say something when Baseem asked, "Where you from?"

"Cali," Curt responded.

"Well, just a quick intro. I've been in here too long for bullshit. I'm a loner and I don't talk much, so you don't have to bother trying to find shit to talk about, I'm good." He pulled his shirt over his head.

"That's cool. I feel the same," he responded, not really knowing how to receive Baseem.

As Baseem turned to walk out the cell, a photo caught his eye. A group of cats were inside a club holding up bottles. He honed in on the one guy in the middle as he said to himself, *What the fuck?*

Two hours later . . .

"You have a call from a correctional facility. You will not be charged for this this call. This call is from, 'Baseem.' To accept this call dial five now," the operator's voice came through KoKo's phone.

KoKo pressed five and was connected. "Yooo!" she said into the receiver. It was a pleasant surprise.

"What's good, sis?" Baseem said with a smile.

"You good? Everything okay?" KoKo asked, growing a little concern as it was not his habit to call her directly.

"Yeah, I'm good. I need you to come see me." He paused, letting her know that it was important. Baseem never asked for a visit.

"All right. When is the next visiting day?"

"Tomorrow at 9 a.m."

"I'll be there."

"See you then."

KoKo hung up, wondering what could have taken place that he needed to see her all of a sudden. Whatever it was, she was on her way to finding out.

The Visit . . .

"Dawkins!" the fat white correction officer yelled out, looking over his glasses at the inmates with coldness. KoKo rose up from her chair. All eyes were on her as she walked to the desk in her tight white skinny jeans, matching tanktop and all white high-heeled open toe sandals. Her feet and nails were perfectly manicured. She put her I.D. on the counter and signed the book. A husky female guard waved her along toward the metal detector. As soon as she got close, the detector sounded its beeping. KoKo looked at the butch-looking officer who yelled out, "Go back through." She complied and the detector beeped again.

"Again!" she yelled and sucked her teeth with attitude all in her voice.

KoKo leered at her like she wanted to smack her, but instead she walked through again.

"Lieutenant!" the white guard said to the young black

guard who was filling out forms. He took his time and then stood up, grabbed the wand, and headed toward KoKo.

"Can you put your arms out?" he said in a flirtatious tone.

KoKo extended her arms and opened her legs. The officer ran the wand over her arms and up and down her legs and back up. When his eyes met with KoKo's, she said, "It feels good to pull out something long and hard in front of a bad bitch, huh?" Then she smiled.

The officer flashed a nervous smile and then let her go. KoKo winked at the female guard, grabbed her money and moved toward the doors. After being marched through several sets of doors that slammed hard every time the last person passed through, she was then led to the visit hall. The women behind her started to rush for seats and then to the machines like high school girls. They wore all kinds of skirts and tight ass jeans. KoKo stood back and watched. "I could never get used to this shit," she said, going to the back of the hall where the last of the seats were. She found one in the middle, took off her jacket, and placed it on the chair.

KoKo looked around a minute more, and proceeded to the machines and got two apple juices and a sandwich for Baseem. As she walked back to her seat, inmates were emerging from a door near the corner, and all eyes were on her. She sashayed past the wondering eyes and walked to her seat. As she sat back down, she watched the children run into their father's arms and the women followed, waiting for the wandering hands and sloppy kisses.

Next to her, a full make out session had started. She just shook her head. After about fifteen minutes, Baseem emerged from the back of the line. He had that familiar grimace on his face, bopping hard and giving no love. A few niggas shouted him out. He nodded slightly and kept on moving. When he got to KoKo he saluted her. KoKo returned it and then he picked her up and hugged her tight.

"Stop, Bas. You play too much," KoKo said, giggling.

"Sheeeit . . . I miss the hell outta you," he said, releasing her from his grip."

KoKo hit his arm. "I miss you too, but I don't need my spine rearranged."

"Stop being so mean." He smiled.

KoKo smiled also. "It's good to see you, Bas."

"Yeah, a nigga doing what he gotta do."

"Loyalty can't be brought," KoKo responded.

"I know. It's earned."

"Indeed. Did ya mom get everything?"

"Yeah, she straight. Thank you."

As they sat in their seats, KoKo went right to business. "So what do I owe the pleasure of this visit?"

"I saw your boy."

"Is that right?"

"Yeah, Aldeen took a vacation."

"Really?"

"Yeah, to Cali."

KoKo gave him a raised eyebrow.

"Yeah, my thoughts exactly. Nigga was all posted up in pics and shit."

"What else do we know?" KoKo asked.

"Little of this, little of that. I'm trying not to press too hard."

"Okay, don't. When a nigga is proud of his work he signs his own contract."

Baseem nodded in agreement.

KoKo looked over to her right and a couple was getting it in.

"Damn, it's like that?" she said to Baseem.

"That ain't nothing. Sometimes I'm in charge of taking the pictures out here. Niggas be fucking bitches all up against the wall and shit," Baseem added as he opened his drink and began taking sips.

"See, I can't be with no nigga locked up. I need to go to sleep and wake up with that shit in my hand."

Baseem snickered while trying to keep juice from coming out his mouth. "You so crazy. Sheeeit . . . I wish I could sneak me some pussy. Nigga got two years strong in this muthafucka." He put his hand between his legs and rocked his knees back and forth.

"Don't worry, KoKo got you. Check it. In a couple week's, a counselor will be here. Fine ass redbone. She is going to send for you and I want you to encourage your boy to seek the same counselor." KoKo gave him that look. Baseem again nodded in agreement. KoKo rose to her feet. "Don't get fucked up." She laughed.

"Sheeit . . . I'ma be a counseling getting muhfucka." He hugged KoKo tight and then released her.

"Let me know if you need anything."

"Will do. Oh, yeah, thanks for everything." He looked in her eyes, getting serious.

KoKo smiled. "Just make the appointment and thank a bitch when you balls deep."

Baseem laughed and then put back on his grimace as KoKo headed to the doors to exit the visit hall.

~ 34 ~
Road Trip

KoKo pulled into the projects on Benning Road in D.C. She had taken a trip to Wise and Aldeen's house in Virginia, only to find out that no one was home. So she headed to the trap spot out there in D.C.

When she pulled in the lot, she looked around to check her surroundings. After securing her guns, she got out and walked up to the entrance of the apartment building that she was told they would be in. Then she walked up to the second floor. KoKo rapped on the door and waited. She stood in full murder mode, ready to kill or be killed. After a few minutes of no answer, she knocked again. She pulled her gun and removed the safety. Just as she brought her arm up to knock again she heard someone.

"Who is it?"

She paused and waited for the voice to get closer.

"Who the fuck is it?" the voice rang out again, sounding eerily familiar, yet she wasn't sure who it was.

"Is Wise here?" she asked.

After a few seconds, she heard the chains being removed from the door and the locks opening. When the door cracked, the smell of garbage and basin hit her nose. She scrunched her nose and wrinkled her brow with her finger firmly on the trigger, prepared for whatever. As the door opened more, she was met with the grotesque sight of Wise.

He looked at her with a little shock. His face told it all. Sunken cheeks sleep-deprived eyes, and sweat beads covered his face like he had been running a country mile. The classic look of a basehead who was up all night. "What's good, sis?" he slurred and reached out to hug her.

Repulsed by the whole scene, KoKo allowed him a half embrace but quickly pulled back. "What took you so long to open the door? And why the fuck you ain't letting me in?"

"Oh, my fault. Come in," he said, inching back. KoKo squeezed past him as he locked the door. "Excuse the apartment. We just run a little shit outta here," he said, following KoKo into the living room. He tried to pick up a few bottles and cans on his way to the kitchen.

"So what you been up to, Wise?" KoKo asked, even though it was apparent. He had lost mad weight. His skin was dark and his clothes dusty. He was definitely not the Wise she once knew.

"Ahhhh, man, you know how we do. Me and Al just trying to keep D.C. on the map," he said, taking a seat. "You want something to drink?" He stood up quickly on his way to the refrigerator.

KoKo looked back at the dishes piled up in the sink with food stuck all on them. "Nah, I'm good."

"Oh a'ight," he said, sitting back down. "So what brings the Queen down here to see the little people?" he asked sarcastically.

"Just checking on my brothers."

"Humph. I see. Well, it took you long enough. I thought you forgot about a nigga."

"How can I forget about you, Wise?"

"It's funny because muhfuckas are around here doing all kinds of shit that I would never expect," he said, joining eyes with KoKo.

"Where is Aldeen?" She got straight to the point.

Wise chuckled. "'Doin' him, I guess." He pulled out a cigarette and lit it.

"You guess? What the fuck is that supposed to mean?"

"Like I said. He doin' him. That's a grown man. You need to ask him what he's up to."

"What the fuck is you talking about?" KoKo was getting agitated. "I sent you two muthafuckas down here together. How the fuck you don't know what's going on?"

"The same way you don't."

KoKo was getting ready to go in when a woman emerged from a door by the living room. "Wise, come tie me off," the woman yelled like she was asking for butter or some shit.

"Go back in the fucking room!" Wise yelled.

The woman wore a dirty gown and her hair was all over her head. "Come on, Wise, I need you," she whined and anxiously scratched her arm.

"Get the fuck back in the room. I'll be right there!" he said, feeling ashamed.

KoKo looked the woman over. Through all the trauma apparent in her appearance, KoKo could tell the woman was Wise's side piece from back in the day who drove the red Jag. She couldn't believe this high-post bitch that always had the

215

best, was now strung the fuck out.

The woman stared at KoKo and squinted. "KoKo, is that you?" she slurred with a half-smile.

Too disgusted, KoKo didn't even answer. "You need to get the fuck back in that room like he told you before I put you out of your dirty ass misery."

The smile dropped from her face as she looked over at Wise. She walked back in the room and slammed the door.

"What the fuck is going on up in here? You done got down here and turned into a fucking junkie? Aldeen's ass running around 'doing him', as you so eloquently put it, and you don't know shit. Y'all muthafucka's done lost y'all mind."

"It's your fucking fault!" Wise stood up and cut in. "You don't give a fuck about us!" He was breathing hard, and it appeared that a tear had welled up in his eye. "You let that nigga Night come in and take over, snatch our status, and put us in the fucking outskirts while you run around building shit. When was the last time you came down here? I haven't seen your ass in months." He paused and then went on. "We built this shit with you." Wise pounded his chest as his voice vibrated through the living room.

Wise's words had struck a chord in KoKo. She could see the pain in his face, but she had no real sympathy. He was a grown ass man, and he was getting ready to feel some real pain. "Nigga, man the fuck up. I ain't your fucking mother. Your black ass ain't going through nothing that nobody else ain't going through. Look what the fuck I lost. You don't see me putting shit in my veins and sucking glass dicks. And why the fuck you ain't reach out? That bitch, Ma Bell, runs both ways. You wasn't on the other end of my line."

"Fuck you, KoKo. You only care about yourself." His words again bounced loudly off the apartment walls.

KoKo gripped her gun handle tight as she rationalized the severity of his words. Part of her wanted to feel for him, but the other parts said 'kill this nigga.' KoKo raised her gun. "Fuck me?" she said with her arm extended, gun firmly in hand, and finger-hugging the trigger.

Wise dropped to his knees in front of KoKo as tears fell from his eyes. "I don't give a fuck. I ain't got shit to live for. I failed you. I failed Kayson and I failed myself. Kill me. Shit, it's better than living the life of a fucking junkie." He locked eyes with KoKo, arms stretched out and awaiting his verdict.

"I love you, Wise," KoKo said. She grabbed him by the back of his head and pulled it to her waist. Wise wrapped his arms around KoKo like she was his mother and cried.

"I'm sorry," he repeated.

KoKo stood over him and allowed him to release the guilt plaguing his soul. "I'm sorry, too," KoKo confessed as a single tear streamed from her eye. Before the tear reached the bottom of her chin, she put the gun to his head and ended what was left of his life. Wise fell back, arms stretched out, and legs to the side. KoKo took a deep breath as more tears threatened to leave her eyes. She held back as she remembered she had one more kill to make. KoKo stepped over Wise, heading for the door where Asia had went moments ago.

When she opened the door, Asia lay slumped over in the bed with a rubberband tied around her arm and needle in her hand. Foam oozed out of her mouth. KoKo moved to her side and felt her neck. There was no pulse.

"Shit. Better safe than sorry," KoKo said, putting two in her head. She scanned the room with a quick eye. A phone sat next to a small stack of money and a little bag of brown powder. She grabbed the phone figuring it may have a few clues on it and then she moved out just as quietly as she entered.

When KoKo got to her car, she threw it in drive and peeled out, heading toward I-95. She needed to get back up top as soon as possible to get with the crew and start her killing session.

You Ain't Going to Believe this Shit...

KoKo rode in her car thinking about what Baseem had revealed, and the fact that she had just took Wise's life. Then she started putting together a plan. First, she had to send Zori into the prison and then set things into motion. She was sick at the thought that Aldeen was in bed with some Cali niggas, and to what extent? She had him down in Virginia letting him run his shit without a lot of interference. But was her leniency producing disloyalty, or was this muthafucka already a snake?

As she continued to ride, her mind went from event to event, and anger rose up in her gut. Then she flashed back to the night Kayson got killed. Her mind set on every face in the crowd and how distraught Aldeen was. To find out he may be one of the major players caused her to feel sick. Knowing that the closest ones to her were the ones to betray her made her heart cold. Revenge was an understatement to describe what she was going to do when she found out who set all the shit in motion. Then her phone rang. She started not to answer, but saw that it was Gwen from Cali. She hit the speaker button on the steering wheel and said, "Hello?"

"Hey KoKo," Gwen's voice came blaring through the speakers.

"What's up, ma?" KoKo wasn't really in the mood for Gwen's hyper personality, but she figured she'd listen for two minutes.

"Girl, you ain't going to believe what I just witnessed."

KoKo sat straight up in her seat. Gwen now had all her attention. "What?"

"Well, let me start from the beginning. You know Thursday is my massage and kitty lick day."

"I don't need that part," KoKo quickly shot back.

Gwen laughed. "My bad. Anyway, I was standing in the lobby of the hotel chopping it up with my girl at the reception desk. So we in the middle of our conversation when this bitch walks up and plops her bag on the counter with major attitude trying to pay her little bill or whatever. It was something about her. I looked at her, ready to check the bitch, 'cause you know I don't play that shit. And just as I was about to go in, I looked the bitch up and down giving her a checklist. She had that out of town look. The chick was on point, but that wasn't what stopped a bitch in her tracks."

KoKo was listening with both ears. "Yeah and?"

"I looked at her wrist and she was wearing one of those watches that the wives of your lieutenants' wear."

"Bitch, get to the point?" KoKo was very familiar with the

watch. She handpicked each one, but she was ready to scream because this bitch could never get to the damn point.

"'A'ight, damn. I don't want you to miss shit. Anyway, the bitch paid then threw her little bag over her shoulder and headed to the door. I turned to see where the bitch was going and what I saw next almost made a bitch faint."

"Gwen!" KoKo yelled into the phone. Gwen started rambling information off in high speed.

"Giiirrrll. She was with Aldeen. They had bags and shit— holding hands and snuggling and kissing. They stood there waiting for their car, I assumed. So I quickly turned to my girl and said, 'Who is that bitch?' She talked with no coercion. She said that she had been coming here for over a year with the same guy. They spend a week or so every month, and drop a couple grand. She really don't leave the room much except to shop, and she comes right back. But he comes and goes all hours of the night. So I was like, 'Pull that bitch up, so I can see who she is.' And when she said 'Vanessa' I almost lost it. When I turned around again, they had stepped out the door and were loading the car with the bags. I slid out the door, got a cab, and followed them. And guess where they pulled up?"

KoKo waited for the other shoe to drop. "Those projects Terrance used to hang out at," Gwen finally said.

KoKo's head started swimming. It couldn't have been. What the fuck was Aldeen doing in Cali? And fucking Wise's wife? It had been going on for over a year nonetheless, and then they pulled into where Terrance used to hustle. "A'ight Gwen, good looking. I'll see you in a couple days. Check your account tomorrow morning."

"A'ight boss. Try to enjoy the rest of your day." They hung up. Gwen was smiling from ear to ear. She loved it when she could stun KoKo with good information, and her bank account loved it too.

KoKo gripped the steering wheel as she drove in silence. Anger rose in her gut as all the information began to process in her mind. By the time she pulled up to her driveway the anger had turned into rage. Somebody's ass was about to die.

— 35 —
Rest in Peace

KoKo stood in the back of the funeral parlor up against the wall with Night and Savage. Posted outside were three cars of security strategically placed just in case niggas wanted to act up. She watched as people piled in and went to the casket and falling to their knees crying, and his mother periodically yelling out, "Not my baby!" while most others just sat around watching the show.

KoKo thought, *Where were all these fake ass nigga's when he was sucking that glass ass?* It always puzzled her how a nigga can't show you love until you don't even know that they giving it to you. You could spend years with people and never hear I love you, but when you going into the dirt, niggas got mad loyalty. "Ain't that a bitch?" she mumbled and prepared for the wait. Everything was going well until she heard, "Haaay, KoKo." One of Wise's ex-girlfriends came up to her, giving her a fake ass hug.

KoKo looked her up and down. *What the fuck she got on? This bitch at a funeral dressed like she going to the club. Tight ass dress all up her ass. Big ass shades and shit.* "What's up?" KoKo asked as she returned the greeting.

"I'm holding up. You all right? I know how much you loved your brother."

"I'm maintaining. Go ahead and get you a seat. Niggas pouring up in here like it's free before eleven." KoKo faked a smile.

"All right. If you need me I'm here."

KoKo nodded. As the woman turned, KoKo gave her a disgruntled stare. Her nostrils flared. *What the fuck she got that I need? This is the same bitch that killed four of his babies, and she got the nerve to come up in here like she the first lady. Bitch please!*

Night glanced all around waiting for the man of the hour, and his patience would pay off. When he looked up, Aldeen entered with Wise's wife, Vanessa on his arm like he was comforting her. She walked a few paces and halted like each step was painful. She looked down the aisle at the coffin and went to her knees. KoKo wanted to hand that bitch an Oscar.

"Get the fuck outta here!" KoKo said in disbelief, unable to hold it in. She looked on as Night's lips twisted to the side. Savage just put his head down. He wanted to burst out laughing, but he didn't want to have to smack anybody if they said something.

Aldeen helped her back to her feet as her legs wobbled. He walked her to the front and sat her next to Wise's mother. She hugged her tight, crying hard and saying "why" over and over. Aldeen stood there for a minute rubbing and patting her back. He whispered in her ear and then walked back toward KoKo.

"Damn, that was the realest nigga," he said as he leaned in and hugged KoKo. She hugged him back as the surge of heat coursed through her veins. She wanted to make that shit a two for one and lay his ass right next to Wise, but she needed to remain calm, so she could collect the rest of the pieces.

"How you been?" KoKo asked, searching his face for guilt and deception.

"Feel like I lost my left arm," he responded, avoiding eye contact.

KoKo thought carefully before she spoke her next words. "He will be missed." She said the only civil words she could muster. Then she went straight to business. "I need to see you tonight."

Aldeen looked up, trying to formulate an excuse. "Well, I was going to try and get back down that way. I don't want niggas to get outta pocket now that Wise is gone. You know how that is?"

"Oh, you ain't got to worry about that. I already sent a crew down. So I'll see you at 10 p.m. at my office," she said and then turned the conversation to Night. "Stay with him until it's time." She gave Night a look and then walked off headed toward Wise's mother.

When she arrived at her side, she placed a hand on her shoulder. The heart-broken mother looked up with watery eyes. "Anything you need you just call me," KoKo said.

"Thank you, sweetheart." She took KoKo's hand and rubbed it against her face. "He loved you," she stated. KoKo stood there hearing her words, but feeling no validity in them. For KoKo, this was only a formality. The Wise she knew had died years ago.

*****

Later that night KoKo had Night bring Aldeen to the pool

hall. When Aldeen walked into the dimly lit back room, his heart seemed to beat outside his chest. Savage, Mugsy, and Chucky were all posted up, and he could see death in their eyes. KoKo sat comfortably at a small table in the center of the room.

"What's up, sis?" Aldeen said as he walked to her and bent over to kiss her forehead.

"Just checking my traps," she responded. "Take a seat."

Aldeen sat down as he continued to look around the room at the stone faces staring back at him. Night dragged a chair over to them and sat it down hard. Aldeen jumped at the sound.

"Fuck you jumping for, nigga? You nervous?"

"What the fuck I gotta be nervous about?"

Night didn't respond. He just stared at him.

KoKo pulled out a blunt, lit it up, and passed it to Aldeen.

"So what you got for me?"

"What you mean?" he asked, taking a deep inhale.

"You mean to tell me your brother just got killed and you don't have that city in an uproar?"

Aldeen passed the blunt back as he searched his mind for an answer. Spit developed in his mouth as he could feel heat coming from Night's eyes as he glared at the side of Aldeen's face. "You know how it is. I got my eyes and ears out there. But that ain't our town. 'It's going to take a minute before shit come to the surface," he nervously stated.

"No, I don't know how it is. Because when I want to know something I find out," she said, looking in his eyes and pulling hard on the blunt.

"You have my word. When I get back I'ma find out everything."

"Yeah, you do that." KoKo grabbed a bag from under the table and passed it to Aldeen.

"What's this?" He opened it and looked inside. His eyes bucked when he saw the stacks of money. "What's this for?" he asked, puzzled at the amount.

"Just a little something. Ain't nothing."

Aldeen looked up at KoKo and a calm came over him. In his mind, he was over. She hadn't brought out any of his skeletons, and she gave him a grip. He grinned. "You know I'ma turn this shit over and have your cut in no time," he said, full of pride.

"Take your time. I trust you," she said without changing her facial expression. "If there's nothing else, you can leave."

Aldeen stood and turned his back as he prepared to leave. "I'll hit you when I get back down bottom."

"Aldeen." He turned back in her direction. "You don't have nothing to tell me? Nothing at all?"

Aldeen blinked and clutched the bag tightly. He swallowed hard before saying, "Nah. I ain't got nothing."

"Okay. Work with that team I set up. I'll be in touch." She rose to her feet.

"A'ight." He gave her a half hug and was out.

"Why you let that nigga go, KoKo?" Savage asked, apparently agitated.

"Be patient, Savage. I got this. I learned if you want to catch your prey you have to carefully bait the hook." She walked toward the door. Savage smiled. He had to respect her

226

gangsta.

Counseling . . .

"Baseem, you have a pass to see the counselor," the guard said into the cell.

"A'ight," Bassem said as he got up and took a look in the mirror and then headed out his cell. As he walked down the long hall heading toward the offices, he tried to imagine what KoKo had set up for him. When he got to the area of offices, he looked for the door with her name on it. Taking a seat in the chair right outside the door, he watched different counselors call other inmates who were waiting their turn.

"Benton?" Zori called out while standing in the door of her office. Baseem rose from his seat and headed in her direction, taking note of her knee-length fitted tan skirt, white silky sheer blouse, and tan four-inch heels. "Have a seat please." She went to her desk and sat down. "I'm Mrs. Hamilton. You were reassigned to me, so you will need to update your file and I will need to see you at least twice a week to familiarize myself with your case," she stated while looking down at the folder.

Baseem saw her mouth moving but focused on the plumpness of her breasts and how they sat up in her blouse. She looked up from his file as he brought his eyes up to meet her eyes.

"What were you saying?" he asked smoothly.

Zori smiled and her pretty white teeth emerged between a pair of lips that looked suckable. Zori walked to the door, gave the lieutenant 'the look' and then closed the door. She came and stood by Baseem. His eyes met her waist and wandered all over her curves.

"Turn around," he instructed.

Zori twirled around and Baseem's eyes rested on her fat ass. His dick came to full attention. He grabbed her by the waist and sat her up on the desk. Wasting no time, he unzipped his pants and stood between her silky thighs. Zori began kissing and sucking his lips. Baseem reached under her skirt and pulled her panties from under her butt and then down her legs until they hit the floor.

Zori broke the kiss to say, "KoKo told me to give it to you however you want it." She lightly bit her bottom lip and looked at him with glossy eyes.

"I need you to make sure you break that nigga. We need Curt talking." Baseem began to coach Zori about her mission, as he planted tender kisses on her lips and neck.

"Yess . . ." she moaned as his hands roamed up her skirt, finding their way to her wetness. When his fingers slid deep inside her, she gripped him tight.

"You have one month. Then you gotta kill 'im," he said as he placed the head of his dick at her opening.

"Yess . . ." she moaned as he began to part her lips with that steel. "Let me make you cum," she whined as he eased in deeper.

"Handle your business," he said and pushed himself all the way inside her.

With that, the conversation was done. Baseem struggled to hold back as her tight walls careesed every inch of him. Her wetness was damn near crippling. He wanted to enjoy it, but knowing his time was limited, he went in deep and stroked fast. Breathing heavily and squeezing her ass tight, he hit the bottom until he busted long and hard. He leaned up against her, out of breath and satisfied. Zori held him tight in her arms. Baseem took in all that sexy for a few more minutes. He then slid out of her wetness and put his dick back in his pants and fixed his clothes. "You said twice a week, right?"

"Yes." She looked at him with starry eyes.

"Keep it right for me." He backed up and then turned toward the door. Zori eased off the desk, bent over, and picked up her panties. She stood up and crossed her legs at the ankle to keep Baseem's warm seed from flowing down her leg. With the first part of her mission complete, she watched this big, black sexy man walk out her door, and all she could say was, "Damn."

— 36 —
Long Over Due

Boa had been deep in the streets making some serious moves. His crew was tight and held shit down, giving him the opportunity to make some major moves. In the last couple weeks, KoKo had put him in charge of all street level business in all five boroughs. Niggas were a little resistant, but Boa was not to be fucked with. Mugsy, Chucky, and Boa were putting the city in a chokehold, making firm examples out of any opposition and forcing niggas to get in line. Once Boa settled in his apartment, he sat on the couch and grabbed the remote. Turning on the television, he then grabbed his cell phone to check on KoKo.

"Hello."

"Hey beautiful."

"Hey Boa."

"You miss me?" he asked.

"Not really."

"Oh, it's like that?" he said and then chuckled.

"What's up, Boa?"

"I need you in my bed tonight." Boa got right to the point.

"Is that right?"

"Hell yeah. I was talking to little Boa today, and the little nigga was getting hostile wondering why he hasn't been able to get between those chocolate thighs."

KoKo was silent. "Yeah, well, I don't think it's going to happen."

Boa picked up on her slight attitude. "What up? What's with all that attitude?"

"Your bitch came to see me. And on a humble I let her live. But I told you I don't share dick. Plus I got shit to do. I'll holla at you," she said and disconnected the call.

"Shit!" Boa said as he tried to call KoKo back, but there was no answer. He threw the phone on the table and sat back and wondered how he was going to fix it.

*****

Rock stood in his office wrapping up a deal and preparing to leave for the night. He had been on several dinner dates with KoKo, and tonight he was planning on making a move.

"So Mr. Lambert, I will have everything ready for you to sign tomorrow, just meet my assistant at the bank to finalize everything and pick up your check," Rock said as he reached out to shake his client's hand.

"Thank you for all your help, kind sir," the older southern gentleman said as he rose from his seat. Just as Rock was about to see the man to the door, his phone rang. He decided to answer it.

"Hello."

"KoKo is on line 2033," his secretary informed him.

"Okay, put her through." He sat back down. "Please excuse me, Mr. Lambert. Amy will see you out. I have to take this call. He picked up the line and put the call through.

"Miss KoKo," he said in his deep sexy tone.

"Hey Rock."

"I hope you're getting ready for our date." He looked at his watch.

"I'm running late. I was going to ask for a rain check." KoKo was only in town to check on some shit before she had to get back up top.

"You're not getting off that easy. What time do you think you will be free?"

"Around eleven o'clock."

"Alright, I'll cook for us. You just bring all that sexy with you and I'll take care of the rest."

"Okay. I'll see you then." She disconnected the call and continued her meeting.

Rock sat back in his chair and kicked his feet up on his desk as he began thinking of the evening he was going to have with KoKo.

Rock had carefully planned and waited for this moment for months, and now it was here. He lit the candles sitting on the dining room table, and then headed back to the kitchen to complete his meal.

It was now eleven-thirty on the dot. KoKo rang the bell just as Rock was turning off the last pan. He walked over to the door, looked through the peephole and then opened it with a smile. KoKo stood there in her three-piece suit looking beautiful as usual. He opened the door and looked her up and down. A smile came across her face.

"Well, are you going to let me in or just stare at me?" KoKo asked.

"My bad. Come in." Rock moved to the side allowing her

to pass.

As he shut the door, he announced what he had planned, "I hope you're hungry. I hooked up a little sumthin, sumthin."

"What we got?" she asked, walking into the kitchen and looking in the pots.

"I hooked up a little steamed shrimp, some yellow rice and some string beans and a nice wine chilling over there." He pointed in the dining room at the perfectly set table.

"I see your work. Let me find out you can cook," she said, turning in his direction.

"I have a lot of talent you're about to find out about." He walked up on her, grabbed her around the waist and kissed her lips.

"I wanna freshen up real quick so I can join you. I've been running all day."

"Don't make me come and get you."

"I'll be right back," she responded as she squeezed past Rock. KoKo walked down the long hallway and into the master bedroom and stripped down, hopped in the shower making sure to wash everything thoroughly, including her hair.

Thirty minutes later, she stepped out and applied lotion and then walked over to Rock's closet and found something to put on. As Rock put the finishing touches on their plates, KoKo emerged from his room. He looked up to see KoKo wearing one of his dress shirts half buttoned with cleavage and her bare, sexy brown legs on display. "You ready?"

"More than you know." He took her hand and led her to the dining room. Rock pulled out her chair and kissed her forehead. KoKo smiled as she sat down, loving how attentive Rock was.

He walked to the kitchen and then brought back the plates and placed them on the table. Rock sat across from KoKo. They ate, talked, and laughed. When they were done, he cleared the table and went to load the dishwasher. KoKo went to the bathroom to freshen up. She returned and stood in the doorway watching him clean up.

"Thanks for dinner," she said, looking him up and down and admiring his dick print in his loose fitting pants.

"I'm glad you enjoyed it." He closed the dishwasher and washed his hands. Rock turned to face her.

"Is that why they call you Rock?" KoKo said, reaching out and sliding her hand along his stiffness.

"You can answer that for yourself in the morning."

"I don't do spend the night." KoKo stared into his eyes while continuing to massage him.

"I haven't met a woman yet that has been able to walk away from my bed." He stared back at her, enjoying her hand action.

"You must be fucking with those rookie type bitches."

"And you must be a woman that's just used to getting fucked." He stood calculating everything he was getting ready to do to her. *She don't know who she fucking with.*

For the first time KoKo was quiet and intrigued. Rock took that silence as a slight fear and made his move. He pulled her close and snatched the shirt open. The buttons popped off, exposing her perfect breasts and neatly shaved kitty. KoKo inhaled deeply and released his dick from her hand. Rock placed his hands on her breasts and gently squeezed her nipples as he walked her backwards to his room, kissing her neck and face and nibbling on her collarbone, without another word. Once at the foot of his bed, he slowly eased the shirt off her shoulders and watched it hit the floor. Rock took a minute to look at her body. KoKo didn't know how to receive him. One minute he was calm, and the next minute he was tearing her clothes off.

"Get up on the bed," he ordered.

KoKo did exactly as told. Rock undressed and stood there with all of his splendor on full display. KoKo lay back on her elbows with her pretty pussy staring him in the face. She admired his body and the way he stroked that rod to full potential. Rock strapped up and prepared to do damage.

His first thought was to taste her sweet nectar. Then he thought, *Nah, I need to break that ass down first, and then I'll bless her with this tongue.*

Rock climbed between her legs and placed his dick right at her opening. Then he placed his mouth on her nipple and sucked lightly, tickling it with the tip of his tongue. Pulling back a little, he released it from his mouth and gave the other one the same attention, taking time to nibble all around her breasts. He then licked everything he could get his mouth on. KoKo was on fire. Rock stared into her lustrous eyes as he began planting soft kisses all over her face, stopping to slide only an inch of himself into her at a time.

KoKo's breathing increased. She was ready to feel all that steel he was slinging. She pushed upward with her waist in an attempt to get him to go deeper, but every time she pushed up, he pulled back. Rock grabbed one of her legs and placed it in the crook of his arm to keep her from wrapping her legs around him, so he could continue his tease. KoKo was ready to scream. She wanted to feel him inside her. Her heart was racing as the words left her mouth.

"Do it to me," she whispered, kissing and sucking his neck. Rock slid in a few inches. "Ahhh . . ." she moaned, trying to grind on him and inviting him to go farther. And just as she thought he was going to go full throttle, he pulled back.

"Rooock . . ." she whined and repeated, "Do it to me."

Rock was enjoying every minute. KoKo had been giving him the chase of a lifetime, and he was glad he had all the control. In a matter of minutes she was helpless, vulnerable, and begging.

When he saw a little frustration set in, he made his move, pushing himself all the way in until he hit the bottom. "Ohhhh…" KoKo moaned as she began riding him from the bottom. Just as she was finding her spot, he pulled back. KoKo grabbed him around his neck, "You better not," she said firmly in his ear.

"You're in my playground now. You gotta fuck by my rules." He gave her a serious look and then threw her leg up on his shoulder and went in deep again and grinding slow.

"Mmmm . . . Right there," KoKo moaned.

Rock buried himself deep and close inside her, stroking with precision. The deep penetration and pressure on her clit was bringing on a strong orgasm.

"Ahhh. . ." she moaned. *Damn, this nigga is doing his thing!* A powerful sequence of contractions came one after another. "Oh my god!" she said as her head dug deep into the pillow and thrust back and forth. While holding on tight to Rock she instructed, "Right there . . . ohhh . . . Right there," she managed to get out as a paralyzing orgasm rocked her soul.

Rock continued to grind deeply as KoKo tried to recover. Out of breath, her stomach heaved. She closed her eyes and decided to enjoy the feeling. Little did she know he was just getting started.

As Rock quickened his rhythm hitting it from all angles, he looked down at her and smiled. All that tough shit went out the window. He threw the other leg on his shoulder and put some speed on that push. Once she had come several times back to back, Rock released one of his own. He then pulled out, stood up, and walked over to the big suede ottoman across the room. He pulled off the magnum and grabbed another one as he stroked himself back to full capacity.

"Come over here," he gave his next order.

KoKo looked at him stroking his dick back to life as she tried to sit up. Once she managed to get to the edge of the bed, she planted her feet on the floor and then walked over to him.

"Bend over," he said as he slid his stiffness into another condom.

KoKo got on all fours. Rock stood behind her caressing her butt. KoKo watched him in the mirrors strategically placed right in front of the ottoman. Rock kneeled behind her and pushed inside her inch by inch. KoKo dropped her head as he rationed out those inches, and again she found herself craving him. He teased and teased, pulling her into him until her ass cheeks smacked against his thighs. "Mmmm . . . Damn, you feel good," she moaned.

"I know. I'm surgical with this muthafucka." He pulled back, going from side to side faster and faster. KoKo enjoyed every stroke, and within minutes she came hard, panting and moaning. Rock pulled her up so her back was in his chest.

"Open your eyes," he told her. KoKo tried to look through her small slits as she watched his thick dick disappear in and out of her wetness. Rock began rubbing his fingers up and down her pussy lips and flicked his finger back and forth over her clit. "See how good I make you feel?"

KoKo matched each stroke with a downward thrust. Rock wrapped his arm around her waist, pulling her firmly into him. "Yes. Yes. Yes." She placed her head on his shoulder as she rode that dick well. Rock watched in the mirror, enjoying every second.

He pulled her legs farther apart so he could get a better view of her popping that coochie. In minutes, they were both cumming and breathing hard, and he wasn't done. He pushed her forward and gave her deep doggie for about an hour. When KoKo's legs started to give, he pulled out and took her back to the bed and showed no mercy.

When morning rolled around, KoKo woke up and looked around. Rock was nowhere in sight. She managed to sit up and get out the bed. She walked her naked, sexy ass to the bathroom and sat on the toilet and had to laugh to herself. *I talked all that shit and ended up getting some dangerous dick, spending the night and waking up with my kitty purring.* KoKo flushed the toilet and washed her hands and then her face. She looked in his medicine cabinet and found a toothbrush and mouthwash.

After getting her breath and face right, she hopped in the shower. Forty minutes later, she walked out the bathroom butt naked and just air dried. She grabbed her purse and retrieved the small bag with a thong, bra, and a small bottle of lotion and deodorant. Once her skin was scented, she grabbed her pants and shirt and put them on. She gathered her things and then walked out the room. Rock stood at the stove making some eggs. Orange juice and fruit cut up in a bowl sat on the counter.

"Thanks for last night. I needed that."

"Did you sleep well?" he asked in his smooth, relaxed tone.

"Too well," she confessed. "Everything looks good. I wish I could stay for breakfast, but a sistah got some appointments." She kissed his cheek.

"When will I see you again?" he turned and pulled her in his arms.

"Don't worry. You will see me soon." She kissed his lips and then pulled away.

KoKo then turned to the counter and picked up the juice.

Rock watched her sip the orange juice and bite into a strawberry. He reveled in his glory, knowing he had handled that pussy thoroughly. As she sashayed to the door, he thought, *I got that ass.*

KoKo was also thinking, *Damn, that nigga dick game is on point. I might have to double back for some more of that.*

— 37 —
Building an Empire

"So what's on the table?" Night asked KoKo as they cruised through midtown. It was that time of year in New York that most people regretted . . . summer was ending. Soon, the trees' green leaves would turn orange, red, yellow, or brown, and the warm air would become breezy and cool.

"I have that meeting with the Russian tomorrow. I plan to execute the final stage of my plan," KoKo replied.

"Why don't you let me handle that?"

"Nah, I got it," she stated firmly.

Approching the red light, Night looked over at her.

"What?" She turned her head in his direction.

"Ain't nothing. I'll just do what I do best—make sure the crew is on point."

"Yeah, that's what I'm paying you for." She turned her eyes back to the road.

"I don't work for you. I work *with* you," he said with a small attitude.

"Well, who do you work for?" KoKo looked at him with a wrinkled brow.

"What the fuck is that supposed to mean?" Night asked.

"Look, we're building an empire. Somebody gotta lead, and somebody gotta fucking follow," she stated. "At the end of the day you're following what Kayson told you to do, and that was follow what I say. *Right*?" KoKo asked, looking at the side of his face.

Night drove in silence. KoKo's little smart ass mouth could sometimes be very aggravating.

"It's okay. You don't have to answer. As long as we on the same fucking page." She paused. "I don't even know why we are having this conversation." She looked forward. "Turn in here." She pointed at the corner. KoKo got out and shut the door. Leaning in she said, "Relax. Stop letting shit get you all bent. Trust me. I got this. Yo ass all uptight and shit. Go home and get your dick sucked or something."

"Fuck you, KoKo," Night shot back.

"No, go home and fuck your bitch. Get that nut up off ya back." She stepped back as he pulled off.

Bragging Rights . . .

Curt was on cloud nine, hustling for Baseem, and earning a better name for himself and gaining respect. Plus, with him getting a once a week pussy regimen, he felt like prison royalty.

"Damn, nigga. You look like you just won the lottery," Baseem said, looking up from reading *Payback Ain't Enough* by Wahida Clark.

"I feel like I just won the lottery," Curt said, moving through the cell.

"Yo. Let me ask you something. Who are those dudes in that picture? Is that your crew?"

"Those niggas are my brothers." He got the picture off the

wall and sat on his bunk across from Baseem. "This right here is Shorty. He got killed, leaving behind a wife and a baby. And this is Terrance, he put me on. He got killed a little before I got knocked. This nigga right here was the truth." He pointed at a big fat dude that stood next to Aldeen.

"Yeah. What happened to him?"

"I don't really know. He got into business with some grimy ass niggas from NY. No disrespect."

"None taken."

"Yeah, but he got knocked and then got jumped in the yard. They stabbed him over fifty times."

"Damn. Who is this cat right here?"

"Oh him? That's Aldeen. He came to the city flashing money and grouping niggas. He rolled in town with some gun-toting beast ass niggas. He called all the shots, but I could tell he wasn't in charge."

"What you mean?"

"One time my man Terrance was having a meeting with somebody that he said was the head of Aldeen's whole organization, and they was plotting on this nigga named Kay something, I can't remember . . . Anyway, the door was cracked. I was ear hustling hard, but couldn't really catch everything and never got a chance to see who he was talking to. But the thing that stuck with me the most was when Terrance said, 'If this nigga is so hard to get to, how do you expect me to hit him?' And the voice responded in a cold, malicious tone, 'If you know a nigga's weakness it's easy to kill 'im.'" Curt paused, staring off for a minute as if he were reliving the moment. "I heard their chairs moving, so I got away from the door and went downstairs. She caused the downfall of the whole organization." He stood up and put the picture back in its place.

"Damn, that's fucked up. Hold up. Did I hear you say she?"

"Hell yeah. And if I ever find out who that cold-hearted bitch is, I'ma kill her slow." He got up and walked out the cell.

Baseem sat up in his bed. His head was spinning as he said to himself, "A woman? KoKo? Nah, can't be." He continued to turn it over in his mind and then he headed to the phones.

*****

KoKo sat across from Andres in his coffee shop as he laid out his plan for trying to make peace and better business relations with the Russians.

"KoKo, I have dealt with you for a lot of years, and we have made each other a lot of money."

KoKo stayed quiet.

"There is a lot of tension between us and the Russians." He paused and took a long pull on his cigarette. "You and your people are close to the streets. That is why I am coming to you. I need you to help me settle this problem."

KoKo sat listening to him trying to be eloquent when in actuality he was being the total opposite. *He must think I am some kind of fool,* she thought. "What's in it for me?"

"Oh plenty. I'm ready to cut you in on that deal with the Columbians."

KoKo had to chuckle inside. She was already in on the deal with the Columbians. But fuck it, she might as well hear him out.

"I'm prepared to give you twenty percent of the weekly take if you can remove the Russians and help me move the product."

"Forty."

He laughed then looked at his partner. "Twenty-five."

"Thirty and I take care of pick up and distribution."

He thought for a minute, looking in her eyes for any sign of unsurety. There was none. KoKo was focused. "We have a deal." He reached out and shook her hand.

KoKo rose to her feet. "I'll call you in a week. In the meantime, tell your people to keep their nose clean. If I have to clean up someone else's mess the deal will be forty." She turned to walk away.

"That woman has too much power," the man sitting next to Andres stated.

"It's okay. I am just allowing her to get in so deep she has no choice but to fall under us or die."

Trustworthy . . .

Boa walked in the restaurant and went straight to the hostess and asked for Night. The woman walked him to the back of the restaurant to Night's table and placed a menu at his spot. She took his drink order and then disappeared.

"What's up, my nigga?" he asked as he shook hands with Night and took a seat.

"It's all about you. Or so I hear." He gave a half smile.

"Sheeiit . . . If I had your money I'd be all right." They both smiled.

Night went right into business mode. "So, is everything going well with that shopping center?" Night spit the code for pick up.

"Everything is on schedule." Boa looked up as the waitress returned with his drink.

"Are you ready to order?" she asked with a smile.

"Yeah, let me have the hot wings and an order of fries."

"Six or twelve?"

"Twelve." He closed his menu and handed it to her. She wrote everything down, took his menu and disappeared. Boa checked out that ass in her skirt as she walked away.

"Let me ask you this. What are your intentions toward KoKo?"

"Did you ask her what her intentions toward me were?"

"Nah, I trust her intentions."

"Uhm," Boa said, grabbing his drink. He took a swig and then set it down. "Whatever my intentions are, that's between me and that woman. However, what's it to you anyway?" He folded his hands, sat straight up and made eye contact with Night.

"I have two duties that I hold very sacred. One of them is none of your fucking business and the other one is KoKo. And I put my life on them both, and not you or God himself is going to interfere with me carrying those duties out. Do you understand?"

Boa chuckled. "It sounds to me like you're a man that's mad he didn't get to the pussy first."

"You young and you dumb. And you so blinded by pride

that you don't even recognize the danger that's staring you right in the face."

"Look, nigga. I don't owe you shit. My loyalty is to KoKo. She trusts me. Therefore, I don't give a fuck whether you do or not. But if there is a problem, speak it." Boa's nostrils flared and his heart beat fast.

"I'm cool until she says I'm not. However, at any point you give me the impression that your ass needs to be no longer breathing, nothing KoKo can say will keep me off you."

"You threatening me?"

"Nah, muthafucka! I'm promising you that if at any point I have the slightest inclination that you foul, you a dead man."

"Let me explain something to you on my way outta this mufucka because I'm trying real hard to remain calm. Stay the fuck outta my business. You got something to say to me. Pass that shit through somebody, because the next time I see you we might have to let some lead speak. Excuse me. I just lost my fuckin' appetite." He stood up, bumping the table, causing his drink to rock and spill almost tipping over.

Night stared at him, not even blinking. As Boa walked away, he thought to just turn around and empty on that nigga. But too much was at stake. He needed to get to KoKo and check that ass for having this nigga all in his face.

— 38 —
Frustrated

"Why the fuck is Night breathing down my throat?" Boa barged in KoKo's office and slammed the door behind him. The mirror on the back of her door shattered and crashed to the floor.

"What the fuck is wrong with you?" KoKo jumped out of her seat, slamming the phone down, hanging up on whomever she was talking to.

Boa walked over to her and got right in her face. "You sent that muthafucka after me?" He pointed in her face.

"First of all, calm yo' black ass down. Second, what the fuck is you talking about?" KoKo raised her voice as the line in her forehead deepened. She was ready to go ham.

Boa stared at her, breathing hard as he tried to calm down. "Your little babysitter confronted me about us, and I almost sent him to join his boy," Boa said with venom in his voice.

KoKo's anger level exceeded Boa's. She was probably going to regret everything that came out of her mouth next, but she didn't give a fuck. "Nigga, you don't fucking question me. You on payroll just like he is. I ain't the fucking guidance counselor. If you got a problem with that man and you ain't settling it, then that's your bad." KoKo pointed at him. "Coming up in here slamming shit, acting like a fucking fool."

Just then the phone started to ring. KoKo and Boa were in a

standoff, neither one wanting to stand down. The phone stopped ringing and started again. KoKo grabbed it. "Hello!" she yelled into the receiver. "Send him up." She looked at Boa and said, "Anything else?"

"Nah. I think you said everything you needed to say." He nodded back and forth. "When you end up one man short I hope me and you don't have no problems."

"I don't take no shorts because I don't wear none. But if you fuck with my family or my money, we definitely gonna have problems."

"Well then, get ready for the fall out." He turned to walk away.

Just as he reached the door, KoKo looked at the broken mirror. "Get somebody to clean that shit up."

Boa reached in his pocket, pulled out a wad of money, and dropped it on the floor. "Nah, you get somebody to clean it up. I don't work for you no more." Then he exited her office, again slamming the door hard on his way out.

"Shit!" KoKo yelled and threw the glass ball sitting on her desk. It hit the wall and then crashed to the floor. Savage and Mugsy came rushing into her office.

"What the fuck is going on?" They came in sliding on broken glass and in kill mode.

"Nothing. Did you see Boa on your way in?" KoKo stood behind her desk, hands on her waist and fire in her eyes.

"Yeah, that nigga pulled outta here like he was on a mission."

"Take that money and get somebody to clean this shit up. Then y'all go find Boa and call me when you got him in a

good mood. Y'all hold down the meeting for me. I'll be back."
KoKo picked up her gun, tucked it in her waist, threw on her
jacket and headed for the door. She needed to see Night and
quick. She had all kinds of business pending, and Boa was at
the center of it all. She could not afford to let shit fall apart
now.

Back the Fuck Up . . .

Buzz. Buzz. Buzz.
"Who the fuck is it?" he yelled through his intercom.
"A pissed off bitch!" KoKo yelled back. Then she heard the
buzzer release the lock. She reached for the door and swung it
open and headed for the steps. She was so pissed she didn't
give a fuck that he lived on the 8th floor. KoKo ran all the way
up taking two and three steps at a time. When she reached his
floor she was in full kick-ass mode. She came bopping down
the hall headed to his door while running through her mind
how pissed Boa was and all the shit that was at risk if he
decided to act the fuck up.

"Bang. Bang. Bang." KoKo rained hard knocks on Night's
door.

After about seven, the door came open. Night's little so-
called girlfriend stood there. "Hey KoKo," she said, all
cheesed up. She was always trying to get on KoKo's good
side.

"Bitch move!" KoKo said, moving swiftly past her.

Rain twisted her lips and sucked her teeth as she watched
KoKo head toward Night's room.

When she didn't see him she busted right in the bathroom without her usual greeting. She went right for his neck. "So what the fuck? We ain't running shit past each other anymore?" KoKo held her hands out to the side, anticipating his answer.

Night sat in his black Jacuzzi, staring at KoKo like she had lost her mind.

"I don't see your mouth moving," KoKo said.

Night continued to ignore her and stood up, allowing the water to run off his sexy frame. He slowly walked up the steps and out the tub, dick swinging and all. "Pass me that towel," he said in his deep, calm voice.

KoKo turned and picked it up off the counter and threw it at him.

Night caught it in mid-air and then began drying himself off. "Now, what is it that you were talking about?" he said as he moved around naked. He went over to the counter and began to apply lotion to his skin while KoKo stood there looking at him like he was crazy.

"Night, don't play with me. You know good and well what the fuck we talking about."

"What? That little nigga came crying to you?"

"Let me explain something to you. My personal business ain't got shit to do with you. Don't go behind my back no fucking more." She was ready to get out of his presence. His, 'I don't give a fuck' attitude had her ready to stab his ass.

"I'ma tell you like I told him. I don't trust his ass. And all your business is my business," he said as he continued to groom himself.

KoKo took a deep breath. "Look, I know you made Kayson a promise. I love and respect that you're a man of your word. But you got to trust me and know that I got this." KoKo paused, trying to carefully choose her next words. "I need Boa right now. I can't afford for you to fuck up what I'm working on."

Night looked up in the mirror at KoKo to gauge her mood. "Like I said, I'ma hold up my end. Just don't fuck up your part."

"Fuck up my part? Fuck is you talking about? All this shit is mine. You, work for me. I call the shots around this muthafucka. Kayson ain't here no more. I'm here and I need you to stay the fuck outta me and Boa's business."

"Fuck that nigga!" Night yelled, causing the walls to vibrate as he turned and moved toward KoKo. "You in charge? Get the fuck outta here. We in this shit together. My loyalty is proven. I love you to death, but if you ever side with that nigga over me again . . ." He paused as thoughts of his promise to his boy came to his mind. His breathing was heavy as he struggled with his anger, but he had to admit he couldn't let it cloud his judgment and stand in the way of business. He could also see KoKo wasn't backing down.

"You right. You the boss. Set up a meeting so I can peace this shit out with this nigga." Night quickly calmed down. "I'ma tell you this though. If I find out later he foul, I'm killing him."

"Fair enough. But remember this—I'm the bitch that gets to make that call."

Night nodded his head, turned and went back to the sink.

"We done?" he asked.

"For now," KoKo responded. "I still love you." She threw on a little half-smile and turned to walk away.

"I love you too. With your crazy ass." He turned and gave her the same half smile.

KoKo turned back and said, "Yeah, and put that shit away. That's why that bitch be acting up."

"Sheeit . . . This is why she act *right*."

KoKo chuckled, shook her head, and left the bathroom. Walking past Rain, she said, "Bitch, you blessed. Don't fuck up."

Rain just glazed at her with wrinkled brows.

KoKo left the apartment, headed to find out what was up with Boa. She needed to make this shit right between them.

*****

"KoKo, you have a visitor," Chucky announced as he came into the back room of the pool hall.

KoKo looked up from the blunt she was rolling and asked. "Who is it?"

"The Russian."

KoKo paused for a minute. "Bring him in the back," she instructed, taking a seat.

Chucky, Mugsy, and three other members of the crew came in with the Russian and his three bodyguards. KoKo sat at a table in the middle of the room with her legs crossed.

"KoKo, thank you for seeing me."

"Anytime. Please have a seat," she said as she lit up her blunt. "What can I do for you?"

"I need your help," Boris said as he reached in his pocket

and pulled out a cigarette. "Oh, excuse me. May I?"

"Please. Make yourself at home."

"I have not seen my son in a week. He has been having a little beef with the Italians." He paused and pulled on his cigarette. "I know that you have a relationship with them, and I am asking that you please speak on my son's behalf."

KoKo listened to the man's request. She looked around the room and then locked eyes with the Russian. "I have my own family. I try not to get into other people's business."

"I would forever be in your debt, KoKo. He is my only son," he said in his thick accent.

"What is in it for me?"

"I know you want to renegotiate with the Colombians. I can cut you in on my deal with a ten percent profit."

"You want something from me, but you treating me like the fucking help," KoKo stated smoothly.

"Fifteen," Boris offered.

"Thirty," she countered.

"Twenty-five. Anything more and I would be cutting off my own hand."

KoKo sat puffing and blowing out smoke for a few seconds. She knew she had his ass. In actuality she would have done it for fifteen, but since his son was so fucking disrespectful she drove up the prices. "Twenty-five it is. And you will have to transport."

"Thank you, KoKo. I believe I can sleep easy with this deal." Boris reached out and shook her hand.

"So you want me to go with you to talk to the Italians?" Mugsy asked.

"Nah, the Russian's fate is already sealed."

"Why you let that nigga go through all that shit?"

"Fuck him. He don't respect me. He's like most niggas. They think the only way a woman should be on top is if she's riding their dick. I earned every bit of the repesct I got. And ain't no nigga gonna take it from me. They gonna have to kill me."

Moving On . . .

It took days for Savage to calm Boa down. He was ready to blow up the world. Even Latreece couldn't get him into a good mood. It was like they were roommates. They hadn't had sex in weeks, and everytime she tried to talk to him they would argue, so she decided to move out.

Boa turned his key in the lock. When he opened the door, Latreece stood there holding three suitcases. He paused. "So what's this supposed to mean?"

"It's not supposed to mean anything. I just can't live like this anymore. I love you, no doubt, but I love me more." She stared at him.

He could see the relationship was taking a toll on her. Latreece had lost weight and bags were underneath her eyes. "I told you that you didn't have to leave. This place is for you. I'ma move my things out as soon as possible." He walked over to the small table by the door and checked the mail.

"No, it's okay. I have a place. I want to start all over, and being haunted by what we had and what we lost by looking at these walls is not going to help." She picked up her bag and raised the handle of the other one to pull it on its wheels. "Let me run this downstairs, and I'll be right back." She walked past him as he kept his back turned. Once she loaded the bags in the car, she came back to retrieve the last of her things. When she opened the door, Boa was coming out the room with a small, brown leather bag.

"Here." He handed it to her.

She took it and then unzipped it. Her eyes grew big at the sight of its contents. "What is this for?" Latreece looked up at him.

"Look. I never intended to hurt you. We are just going in two very different directions. I still love and care about you, but the shit that I am moving into has no room for us." He looked into her eyes that were now welling up with tears. He wiped away the one that had fallen down her cheek. "Don't cry. You deserve better than I can give you."

She chuckled. "So what's this, a buyout?" she asked, her voice dripping with pain.

"Nah. Nothing like that. I want you to be comfortable. The car is paid for and you in a new place. So this is just a little something to hold you over."

"Hold me over? How much is it?"

"Five hundred thousand. And if you ever need anything, I'm here."

"Five hundred thousand? I can't take this." She pushed the bag back toward him.

He gently pushed it back toward her. "You can and you will. Give me a hug and take care of yourself. Make a nigga give you what you deserve." He reached out and hugged her tight.

Latreece hugged him even tighter like this would be the last time she would see him. After the long embrace, he walked her to the car and placed the last of her bags inside. Closing her door, he leaned in and kissed her lightly on the lips.

"Call me when you get in. If I don't answer, leave me a message. I just want to know you're safe."

She nodded up and down, put the car in gear and pulled off. Boa watched as she drove away. He was feeling fucked up over the events that ended their relationship, but he knew there was no way he would be able to keep her safe with all the shit that was about to go down.

∼ 39 ∼
Killer Instinct

Boa stood in the open field looking down at Vladimir, the Russian's son. He was fast asleep from the ass whipping Boa had put on him. Boa unzipped his pants and began pissing in Vladimir's face. Slowly, he came to and attempted to open his eyes. "Rise and shine, muhfucka," Boa said with evil dripping from his lips.

"What the fu—" Vladimir tried to say as he struggled with the ropes that bound his hands and feet.

"Your daddy, Boris has been a very bad boy. And guess what? You're going to pay for it." Boa walked over to a box that sat on a chair

"What is that bitch paying you? I promise my dad will double it," he yelled.

"You see. That's where you should have done your homework. Because what she uses to pay me, I can't get from no nigga." Boa smiled as he untied the moving bag.

"Wait! Please. I can fix this," Vladimir pleaded.

Boa stood over him and released five death adders, one of the world's most venomous snakes.

Vladamir's eyes widened in fear.

Boa took out his gun and fired two shots quickening Vladamir's movement. The snakes attacked. Over and over they sank their sharp venom-infused fangs into his skin as he screamed for mercy, which only quenched Boa's thirst for murder.

Boa pulled out a blunt and lit it up as he watched the man's skin blister and swell. "Another successful day on the job," Boa said as he hopped in his car and headed back to the city.

*****

KoKo was seated comfortably on her private jet on the way from Miami when Sarah brought her the emergency phone.

"Ma, when will you be here?" Night asked with urgency.

KoKo looked at her watch. "We should be landing in about thirty minutes. Why?"

"A meeting has been called for heads of the families. They want you to make peace."

"Make the spot neutral. I'll call you when I touch the ground."

"A'ight." Night hung up.

KoKo crossed her legs and gazed out the window, staring at the clouds. Her plan was coming together step by step.

*****

KoKo was the last to arrive at the meeting at Ink48 in Manhattan, and the tension was already at a critical level. Night had everyone strategically seated. The Italians were on one side of the table and the Russians were on the other. Two of the top guys from the Columbians' camp were seated at the very end. KoKo took her seat at the head of the table and the meeting began. Each side voiced their concern as KoKo sat listening and looking back and forth. Everything was going well until Andres insulted the Russian.

"See KoKo, this is what the fuck I speak of. There's no compromise in this bullheaded fuck," Boris said in his thick accent.

"You speak past me to her!" Andres yelled out.

The men again went at it. "Hold the fuck up!" KoKo yelled, bringing silence to the room. "I didn't come out here for this shit. We're trying to make money. Y'all gotta squash this petty shit.

"It's hard to talk reason with a snake," Andres said.

"You call me snake! You call me snake!" the Russian yelled as he rose to his feet. "I'll see that your mother burns in hell!" Boris and his crew got up and stormed to the door.

"I can't work like this, KoKo," Juan, the representative for the Columbians said as he got up and headed for the door.

KoKo got up. "I will fix it."

"I hope so. This is very bad for business," Juan stated as he exited the room.

Andres and his team walked over to KoKo. He placed his hand on her shoulder. "Thanks, little princess. But the only thing that will settle this is blood." They walked out leaving KoKo and the crew behind.

"What the fuck was that?" Mugsy asked.

"The beginning," KoKo said as she headed for the door.

Close Call . . .

KoKo left instructions with Night to send Boa to Las Vegas to meet with Mr. Lu. It was time to make a payment, and with all the new shit popping she was able to give him double.

When Boa got back from Vegas, shit on the streets was quiet. He called KoKo to schedule a meeting, but could not catch up with her. He scouted the area for Mugsy and Savage, and they too were hard to catch. Boa felt some heavy shit was going on. He needed to regroup and hit his spots to see what was biting. Pulling into his driveway, he flashed back on his birthday gift from KoKo. It immediately brought back all the good feelings he had when he drove to his apartment.

"I'ma have to thank her real good when I catch up with her," he mumbled as he parked his car, hopped out, and headed inside.

Boa unlocked the door to his apartment and went inside. He was feeling good as hell. He then went into the kitchen and checked the refrigerator for something to drink. "Damn, a nigga need to stop by the store." He took off his shirt and then hit the stereo. Jay-Z came on. Boa whistled to the beat as he walked to the bathroom. He unzipped and started to take a piss, but noticed something on the floor out the corner of his eyes. A stream of crimson-colored liquid led from the tub to his feet.

"What the fuck?" He shook off, put away the steel, washed his hands, and headed to the tub. He snatched back the curtain. "Oh shit!" He grabbed Latreece, who was lying in the tub in her bra and panties with both wrists slit from one end to the other. He grabbed her out of the tub and placed her on the floor. Then he ran to the closet and got some towels and rushed back to Latreece lying on the floor. He began wrapping her wrists. Reaching in his pocket to get his phone, he dialed 911.

"Hello, I need an ambulance to 1344 Baldwin Drive. Hurry please." As he tried to divide his attention between the woman on the phone and Treece, he used his freehand to lightly pop her face. "Come on, baby. Don't do this to me." She had a pulse, but it was very faint. "Stay with me, baby. Hold on."

"What is your emergency?"

"My girl slit her wrists. Send somebody!"

"Sir. Sir? Is she breathing?"

"Yes. But hurry up. I don't know how long she's been like this. She lost a lot of blood," he said with tears in his eyes.

"Just keep talking to her. They are on their way."

"Hurry the fuck up!" he yelled into the phone.

"Just try to stay calm and keep talking to her. I'll stay on the phone until they get there," the woman stated in a calm voice.

"Come on, baby. Stay with me." He frantically shook her and checked for a pulse. Five minutes later, the bell started to ring. He released her and ran for the door. The paramedics rushed past him as he pointed them in the direction of the bathroom. Once inside, they put her on oxygen and stabilized the wounds. The paramedics placed her on a stretcher and moved swiftly to get her to the ambulance.

Boa grabbed his coat and keys, jumped in his car, and then followed them to the hospital.

*****

Two hours later, the doctor entered the hospital waiting area accompanied by two police officers. He greeted Boa and updated him on Latreece's health. "She is stable and asleep. She has been placed under twenty-four hour suicide watch.

We would like to contact her next of kin if you can provide us with that information."

"Yeah, I'll give you her mother's number. But she is on a cruise with her two sisters. I placed a call, and I'm waiting for them to get back to me. So as of right nowf, I'm all she's got."

"Very well. We will keep you posted, and when she wakes up we will let you know." The doctor walked out the room, leaving him with the officers.

"Can you tell us how you know Miss Simmons?"

"We used to date."

"Can you tell us why she would want to kill herself?"

"Your guess is as good as mine."

"Look, sir. We are just trying to do our job. It seems a little suspicious that your ex-girlfriend would come to your house and try to kill herself."

"My thoughts exactly."

"Are you sure there isn't anything you want to tell us, son? We just want to help."

"Look, I got enough shit fucking with my head for one day. So if I'm not under arrest, leave me the fuck alone. I ain't got shit else to say." He stood up with blood all over his clothes and walked out the room.

"Don't leave town," one cop yelled out.

Boa didn't even bother to respond. He just kept on walking.

Three days later . . .

Boa sat in his car with soft jazz playing in the background. He had been at the hospital by Treece's side day and night. The doctors said they thought it wise for Latreece to go into a psychiatric hospital for a few weeks. Boa found a nice facility in Connecticut. As he drove, he looked over at Latreece, who sat staring out the window with her head against the headrest.

"You all right?" he asked.

She nodded and pulled her feet up into the seat. "Thank you for saving my life," she spoke very soft words.

"No thanks necessary," he firmly responded. His heart was breaking seeing her like this. Knowing he was the cause was killing him.

"Why couldn't you just love me, Boa?" she asked, still staring out the window.

"I do love you, Treece."

"But not more than you love KoKo," she said as tears ran down her face. She wiped her eyes with her sleeve as the pain of her words pierced her heart.

Boa sat quietly, trying to choose the right words. He didn't want to escalate the situation. "Let's just wory about getting you well. We can talk about all that other shit another time."

Latreece didn't respond, but she continued to stare out the window.

Boa pulled into the driveway and parked. He got out and walked to her side, opened the door and helped her out. A psychologist and an orderly pushing a wheel chair greeted them. As she was rolled up the ramp, she reached out and grabbed his hand. Boa squeezed her hand tight in an attempt to comfort her. "Everything will be fine, Miss Simmons. You're in good hands," the middle aged, thin doctor stated.

Latreece gave a semi-smile and then looked ahead. Once inside, they went straight to the doctor's office and were given the rundown on the treatment plan. Boa felt confident that she would get the help she needed. Once the doctor was done, they were escorted to her room, which was laid out like an expensive hotel room.

She got out of the wheelchair and sat in the soft, suede chair with an ottoman. The orderly got a blanket and covered her legs and then left.

"Boa, don't leave me here," Latreece said.

Boa sat down on the ottoman and grabbed her hand. "It's okay. They are going to help you get better and in a couple weeks I can take you home."

"I love you, Boa." A tear ran down her face.

"I know. I love you too," he stated, trying to do as the doctor ordered and not say anything to upset her. He had love for her, but he was no longer in love with her. And hopes of them being together were nonexistent. "Just worry about getting well."

She brought his hand to her face, closed her eyes and took a deep breath. "Thank you."

Boa kissed her forehead. "Let me go get your things from the car. I'll be right back." He got up and headed to the door. When he left out, a short, white woman came in her room and sat down. She still had to be on watch.

Boa got to the car, opened the trunk, and retrieved two bags. He had gotten her all new clothes and sleepwear. In his heart he had done everything he needed to do and was setting her on the road to recovery. Her mom and sisters were to return the next day to be by her side.

Boa walked back inside and the doctor checked the bags to

make sure everything was safe to give to her. There were several pairs of jeans, a few jogging suits, and T-shirts and sneakers. Toiletries, pajamas, and slippers. Everything was cleared and he was sent to her room.

When Boa got to the end of the hall, he looked into the sitting area at the residents gathering for social hour. Everyone seemed to be dressed alike and moving about the room slowly. But one woman, who appeared to be wearing rather expensive attire in what he considered a crazy house, caught his eye. She also had on several pieces of high-end jewelry, diamonds to be exact. He made a mental note and kept on walking. When he got outside Treece's room, he noticed a very sexy woman at the nurses' station eyeing him hard and smiling. Boa threw her a little smile and kept on walking.

He unpacked Treece's bags and hung up all her clothes. The doctor overseeing the unpacking had Boa remove the laces from her sneakers and lock her closet. By the time they finished putting everything away, she had come out the shower, got into her pajamas and laid down. Whatever medication they had given her had taken over and she gave in to it. Boa kissed her and promised to see her in a couple days. He rubbed her hair as she dozed off, and then he exited the room.

"Don't worry, she will be fine," the doctor assured him.

"Thank you for everything. If she needs anything just give me a call." He shook the doctor's hand, walked over to the nurse's desk and introduced himself. "I'm Boa, and you are?" he asked and extended his hand.

Filled with giggles, she said, "I'm Nona." She firmly shook

his hand.

"They got you working all hard. When do you get a break?"

"Unfortunately, I just came on duty," she said, unable to control her smile.

"You dealing with somebody?"

"No," she happily answered.

"Let me get your number, and I can call you when I'm on my way back up here."

The woman quickly grabbed a pen and scribbled her number on a pink post-it.

"I hope it's soon," the naive woman said in a shy voice.

"Me too. Let me ask you something. What do you do?"

"I'm an LPN. I give out medication and schedule appointments for treatment."

"That's what's up." He paused and then got right to the point. "So the people in that room"—he pointed—"are they less dangerous than others?"

"They are our permanent residents. Most of them have lived here for many years."

"Oh, okay, I was wondering, because I saw a lady in there who looks like she is very comfortable and very well off."

"Who?" She stood up and looked down the hall.

"Her right there." He pointed in the woman's direction.

"Oh, her? That is our Lourdes as we call her."

"Why y'all call her that?"

"Well, I don't know if I should be telling you this—" She lowered her voice and looked around.

"I won't tell if you won't tell," he said in a shy voice.

Nona looked at those sexy eyes and submitted. "Well, Lourdes doesn't just live here. She has a little house on the grounds with her own cooks and everything. She has the most expensive clothes and jewels, but she never gets any visits. A huge check comes in every month to pay for not only her care, but also to fund a couple programs on site."

"Damn, it's like that?" he said, trying to sound intrigued.

"Yep. She's a sweetheart. She doesn't really talk. She just sits and looks out the window. She comes up here three times a week for her treatment and then she goes back to her house," she said, sitting back down in her chair.

"Wow. Okay. Now back to me and you. Can I take you out to eat when I come back?"

"Sure can. Just call me so I can be ready."

"If anything goes wrong you call me first." He reached in his pocket and pulled out five hundred dollars. As he reached to shake her hand, he slid the money to her. "I'm the emergency contact in Latreece Simmons' file. If anything happens, call me." Nona smiled and flirted with her eyes, but the intercom interrupted her.

"Nona Giles. Report to the second floor med. room. Nona Giles, report to the second floor med. room."

"I have to go. See you in a couple days."

"Sounds good," Boa said as he watched her switch toward the elevator.

When Nona stepped onto the elevator, he dropped his smile and went to work. He walked into the recreation room and walked over to the lady who sat looking out the window.

"Hello," he said and kneeled down in front of her."

267

"Hi," she said and smiled. She was even more beautiful up close.

"Are you enjoying the view?" Boa asked.

"Yes, I am. Thank you." She looked him over, searching for familiarity. "Do I know you?" the woman asked.

"No, ma'am, I was just caught by your beauty."

"Oh, how sweet." The woman patted Boa on the head. "You're such a nice young man. Maybe I should introduce you to my daughter."

"Oh, you have a daughter? Is she as pretty as you?" Boa asked and then watched the woman blush.

"Even prettier," she said, reaching for the locket on her chain. She opened it up and pointed to the left. Boa almost lost his breath.

He mustered up a smile. "Yes, she is." He took her hand and kissed it. "You enjoy the rest of the day."

"Thank you, young man. I will be sure to tell my daughter about the fine young man I met today."

Boa rose to his feet and gave her another smile. "I look forward to meeting her."

"Excuse me, sir. But you are not supposed to be in here," a male voice rang out, breaking his train of thought.

"Oh, my bad. I was just talking to the nice lady." He turned to walk out, leaving the woman sitting in the chair staring out the window. The man came in and stood next to her. Boa didn't even look back. His thoughts were all over the place as he quickly rushed to his car, jumped in and hit the highway. Boa had some dirt he needed to dig up, and he knew just the place to start digging.

— 40 —

Investigation

Rock sat at his desk going over some paperwork. He looked up from his desk and tensed up when he saw three black undercover cars pull up in front of his real estate company. He hit the intercom and said, "Jackie, call my lawyer and tell him to get his ass down here." He rose from his desk and prepared for the worst.

Within seconds, the authorities were barging into his office flashing badges and yelling out demands. In minutes, he was being escorted to the station.

Rock sat in an interrogation room surrounded by two-way mirrors. He had been sitting there for an hour without any explanation. His mind was racing, thinking about why he had been hauled down there.

A few minutes later, in walked two detectives in suits. "Hello, Mr. Davis. We are agents Malone and Sanders from the Federal Bureau of Investigations. We need to ask you a few questions." They flashed their badges and sat down.

"Is my lawyer here yet?" Rock asked and folded his hands.

"Not yet. But if things go the way we think they will you won't need one," the black agent said as he pulled out a folder and slid it in front of Rock. The white agent folded his hands and sat up in his seat.

"What the fuck is this?"

"This is what we're hoping you can help us out with." The black agent opened the folder, revealing a photo of KoKo. "Do you know this woman?"

"I might."

"How about now?" He flipped through the folder, stopping at a picture of Rock and KoKo together. Rock looked up and then back down. The agent continued to show him pictures of KoKo coming and going to his office, house, and several other spots around the city, mostly her club.

"I sell her property. Is that a crime?" he asked, trying to remain calm.

"Yeah, it's a crime. Did you know that all the houses she brought are with fraudulent information and fictitious paperwork?"

"So what does that have to do with me? I'm a businessman. I sell houses. If the paperwork checks out, then I put the deal through. I don't have shit to do with what people do with it after I sell it to them."

"Really? Well, you might want to look at these." He pulled out another file that had all the checks KoKo collected and signed with his signature and all mortgages with his name listed as the co-signer.

"I don't know anything about this. I can't help you, and I ain't got shit to tell you. My lawyer will be here in a minute and I'll walk. Y'all ain't got shit on me."

"How about murder?"

"Murder? I ain't saying shit else. I need to see my attorney."

"I figured you would say that. Look, the house fraud is enough to get her on. However, we want her bad. She has been slipping through the cracks for years, and this paper trail is what we need to put her away for a long time. Now, you can either help us or become an accomplice to murder."

The agents stood up and Malone said, "We're going to leave you alone with your thoughts for a little while." Then they both exited the room, leaving Rock sitting there with all the photos and paperwork. Rock started to go through everything, keeping in mind that he was being watched. He couldn't believe how KoKo had all the paperwork hooked up. His name was on everything. He closed the folder and then went through the one with the photos. The evidence was overwhelming. Not only did they have her and him, they had pictures of him doing business with other clients that he was keeping under wraps. KoKo was bringing heat on his hustle. Rock started to close the folder when he saw an envelope behind the pictures. He opened it up and was floored. Pictures of that cat named Boa, whom Rock had seen at Golden Paradise showed Boa meeting up with some foreign-looking guy. In a few photos, money exchanged hands and documents were being signed. Rock didn't know what it was about, but he easily figured out that the Feds had some major shit on KoKo and Boa.

As soon as Rock closed the folder, in walked his lawyer and the two agents. Rock thought about the murder and fraud and then those pictures. The fact that he stood to be tied into it all had him ready to see what deal was on the table.

It's Our Anniversary . . .

"Where is KoKo?" Savage questioned Boa as he walked into the basement of the pool hall.

"I don't know. I haven't seen or heard from her in days," Boa answered.

"I've been calling her phone and no answer." Savage looked at the monitor, walked to the intercom, and buzzed in Mugsy.

When Mugsy walked in, Savage sat back down and started the same line of questioning that he had just put on Boa's lap. "You seen the Boss?"

"Nah," he answered as he hit fists with Boa and then reached out to Savage. "I talked to her about three days ago. She sent me to take care of something, but that was the last time. I figured she was outta town." He took a seat next to Boa. Savage turned in his seat, propping his fist under his chin and putting on a serious thinking cap.

"Boa, I need you to go to this address." He wrote something on a small piece of paper and handed it to him. Then he reached in his pocket, grabbed his keys, and handed him a single key. "Hit me when you know something."

Boa stood up, ready to carry out his mission. He picked up the paper and the key.

"Nah, memorize the address and leave the paper," Savage instructed.

Boa looked it over for a few seconds and then bounced. Savage picked up the paper, grabbed his lighter and set it on fire. "Go make the rounds," he said to Mugsy, not even

272

looking in his direction. He was focused on KoKo.

Boa hopped on I-280 West toward the Poconos and followed the directions he was given until he reached exit 277. He pulled off and stopped in McDonald's to use the bathroom. Then he hopped back in his car, steering onto the Pennsylvania turnpike, and driving about another twenty minutes. When he got to exit 105, he got off and pulled through the tollbooth and continued down the winding mountain road. Arriving at his destination in Dallas, Pennsylvania, he pulled into a long driveway and next to a silver Infiniti. He grabbed his gun out of the hidden compartment, checked the bullets, deaded the engine and stepped out the car heading for the door.

The house was huge. He looked through the window and saw no movement, just flickers of light. Boa put the key in the lock and turned the doorknob slowly. He pushed the door open and adjusted his eyes to the darkness, and then proceeded inside. As Boa moved through the house, what he saw was unsettling. Drawing his gun and stepping carefully over the shattered glass, he followed the trail of clothes that were certainly KoKo's. Moving alongside the wall, heading in the direction of the room with the flickering light, he stood at the cracked door and peeked inside. Hearing music and very low mumbling, he slightly pushed the door open.

Sitting on the floor up against the bottom of the bed in her bra and panties, Koko held a tall bottle of Absolute Vodka. She looked up at him, but didn't say a word.

"You a'ight, KoKo?" Boa asked, squatting beside her and taking inventory. His first motive was to see if she was all right. All he could see was that she was fucked up and had been crying, as there were tissues all around her. Upon a closer look, he saw a picture of her and Kayson and then one of a baby. KoKo slowly moved the pictures behind her.

"What are you doing here?" she asked, wiping her nose.

"Savage was worried. He sent me up here to check on you."

"Well, you checked. You can leave now," she said, taking the bottle to her mouth.

"I'm not leaving you here like this, ma."

A single tear fell from her eye. She caught it with the back of her hand. "I need to be alone right now," she slurred.

"I understand, but I'm not leaving."

KoKo chuckled. "You don't understand."

"Make me understand."

KoKo ran her hands through her hair and slowly rocked back and forth, thinking about all the shit she had been through, accompanied by the things she had done, the worst being taking her sister's life. "I did some shit that I will be paying for, for the rest of my life." She looked at Boa like a hurt child. He pulled her into his arms.

"Let me have some of that pain tonight." Boa held her tight and rocked her in his arms. "Come on, let me get you straight." He stood and then picked her up from the floor, taking her to the bathroom. Boa placed KoKo in the shower and washed her from head to toe. He dried her off, got her dressed, and put her in the bed.

"Thank you, Boa," she whispered.

"No thanks necessary, Boss," he said, playfully. KoKo

cracked a smile.

"I'll be back." He left her and called Savage to confirm she was good. Then he proceeded to clean up the mess. Once he was done, he ran out to his car and grabbed his little black bag. He took a shower and changed and then sat in the chair across from her bed and lit up. Taking deep pulls and watching KoKo sleep, he wondered what the fuck was haunting her soul.

Right Place . . . Right Time . . .

Baseem emerged from the search area, panning the room and walking past the many rows of visitors heading to the back of the visit hall. When he got to KoKo, he went straight to business.

"I see you looking real relaxed," KoKo said with a little smile on her face.

"I'm good," he said as they sat down.

"Whatever. Just watch yourself. New pussy makes niggas act crazy."

"I got this."

"Give me the math," she said, taking a seat.

"That nigga over the edge. Everytime he come back from seeing old girl, he run his mouth. I found out that a female helped out with the hit."

KoKo's brow wrinkled. "What you mean?"

"Like I said . . .   "

"Did he see who it was?"

"Nah. But he said she had a slick tongue and before she left she said, "If you know a man's weakness you can do anything you want to him." Baseem watched KoKo carefully to see if any guilt arose in her face or body language. "So what you think?" he asked.

"Nothing yet. I got some homework to do." KoKo got up. "Anything else?"

"Not right now," Baseem stated, maintaining eye contact. Just as he got ready to say something else, he rose to his feet and gave KoKo a hug. As he leaned in, KoKo whispered in his ear. "Pull that nigga's plug." Baseem nodded and let her go.

He watched KoKo exit the visit hall, praying that she was not the one behind Kayson's death. He vowed right there that she was living on borrowed time.

****

It took three days for Baseem to get everything lined up. Once it was straight, there was no turning back.

"What we eating tonight?" Curt asked Baseem as he laced up his boots.

"I don't know yet. We can plan it when we get back from counseling."

"Yeah, we should be good and hungry when we get back. She'll work a nigga's appetite into overdrive," he stated with a sneaky grin on his face.

Baseem just nodded in agreement. As they walked the halls toward the offices, Baseem thought over the plan. He knew everything needed to be calculated right up to the second. They walked up to the desk, signed their names, and took a seat.

After about five minutes, she called Curt into the office. "Did you miss me?" she asked as she closed the door.

"Hell yeah," he responded, looking at her ass as she switched to the other side of her desk.

Curt followed and took his position right between her legs.

Zori began to kiss and suck on his lips as she released his dick from his pants. "I've been thinking about you all day."

Curt grabbed her by the waist and sat her up on the desk. "I want you to make a nigga cum hard," he said as he eased inside her.

"No problem," Zori said as she began to squeeze her muscles around his dick.

Curt hissed with every thrust. Zori continued to squeeze as she grabbed his ass, pulling him in deeper. "Gotdamn!" he moaned.

He closed his eyes and enjoyed her wetness. Within minutes, he was ready to bust, picking up speed as he bit down into her shoulder.

When Zori heard the series of moans Curt would make right before he came, she slowly reached for the razor Baseem made for her. Curt was breathing heavily and pumping faster, and just as he released, Zori grabbed him by the back of his head and slit his throat. He grabbed his neck and fell up against the wall. She jumped up and put a few more lashes on his chest and arms. He slid down the wall, gasping for air, looking utterly confused.

Zori cut open her blouse, making a small incision on her chest. She then slightly cut her hands and forearms. Lying on the floor, she pulled him on top of her and began to scream for help.

Baseem burst into the office, grabbed Curt, and stabbed

him twice in the chest before the guards came and wrestled him to the floor.

"No. Wait! He was helping me," she pleaded.

The guards pulled Baseem to his feet and handcuffed him. Three more guards rushed in checking Curt and then Zori. "Are you okay Miss?"

"I think so. I don't know what happened. We were talking and then he attacked me," she said as she burst out in tears.

"I need a medic in the counselor's office," one of the guards radioed in as the other guard lifted Zori off the floor and placed into her chair. Baseem was hauled off for questioning. Zori watched as Curt leaked blood all over the floor. Tears of joy rolled down her face as she thought, *Mission accomplished.*

— 41 —
I Got Your Back

KoKo cruised the city looking at all her old spots and reminiscing about the good times when she, Wise, and Aldeen used to hurt the streets during a time when all she had to worry about was making sure the count was right. Those times were a distant memory, however, it felt good to her spirit to recall those days when hustling was what she lived for. Then she got a phone call from Rock, interrupting her nostalgia.

"I need to see you," his harmonious voice rang through her phone.

"I won't be back down there for a couple of days. Can it wait?"

"I'm in the city. When can I meet you?"

"I will be in my office in about an hour. I have to meet with a few people, but then I will be free. Is six good for you?"

"Is it the office I came to before?"

"Yes."

"Okay, I'll see you at six." He hung up and handed the woman at the counter his credit card to pay for his room at the Aloft hotel in Harlem. After getting his keys, he headed up to his room to get ready to have this sit down with the woman whom the FBI called *'The Boss.'*

Six O'clock . . .

"A'ight, y'all gotta put the squeeze on them niggas. I have to meet with someone." KoKo looked at her watch, ready to dismiss the crew when she looked at her monitor and saw Rock exiting a cab and heading to the door. He walked up and hit the buzzer. KoKo buzzed him in and watched him enter the building and then the elevator. "Anything else?"

"Nah, we good," Night said as he rose from his seat.

"I need to holla at you," Boa replied.

"It will have to be later. I have to handle some business real quick." Just as she finished her sentence, a few taps came on the door. She buzzed Rock in the room and everyone greeted each other, except Boa. He didn't even speak. KoKo watched as frustration set in on Boa's face.

"Good evening, gentlemen," Rock said as he put his hand out to greet each man in attendance. Boa turned his back and walked to the wet bar. Rock ignored his banter and moved on to KoKo. "Hey sexy." Rock walked over to her and kissed her on the cheek.

"Hello, Mr. Davis," KoKo responded. "So what's up?"

"I need a private moment of your time," he said, looking KoKo up and down.

"I'll see y'all later." KoKo dismissed everyone except Rock.

Each person nodded in agreement and began exiting the room. Boa tossed back his drink, gave KoKo a cold stare, and shook his head and then headed to the door.

"I'm going outta town. I'll catch up with you in a couple of days," he spat.

KoKo watched Boa leave the office with evil in his eyes. She wanted to check him, but she had other business at hand.

"So, what's so important?"

Rock took a seat and started his spiel. "Some people came to see me."

"Is that right? What did they want?" she asked, but already knew from the tone of his words.

"They think they have something on you. Mostly property shit. But I think some dirty shit went on, and they want to tie it in to build a case. But I know you will do your research."

"What role do you play in all this?"

"I'm good. You ain't got to worry about me. But I think you need to check your boy."

"Which one?"

"The one with the attitude—they got more shit on him than Al Capone."

"Fact or fiction?"

"Real fact in color."

KoKo processed his words. She knew exactly what was going on, and she was going to do more than research. "I thank you for coming to see me in person."

"You know by now that I got you." Rock stood up and KoKo followed suit. He walked over to her side of the desk and looked into her eyes.

"You know we need to cut ties, right?" KoKo advised.

"Look, I care about you, no doubt. But I am no fool. I knew what type of person you were the day you walked in my office. I loved every minute we spent together, and if the circumstances were different I would make you my wife.

However, our paths crossed in war time." He smiled and KoKo returned the gesture. "You have my word. I will protect you at any cost. If you ever need me for anything—anything, I'm here." Rock pulled her into his arms and hugged her tight.

"Thank you," she said as they stood for a few more seconds in their embrace.

"Now, can a man at least get a meal out the deal?" he asked, pulling back.

"Hell yeah, you just saved a bitch a whole lot of footwork. That's the least I can do."

Rock and KoKo exited her office for what would be their last time together. On the way to the elevator, KoKo's mind raced. She now had to make sure Rock was a friend and not an enemy.

Night on the Town . . .

KoKo had Boa meet her on the side of the Hudson River. He pulled up next to her car and got out. She exited her car and leaned up against it with folded arms.

"You got something to tell me?" KoKo asked.

"No. Why?" Boa replied.

"It's too much shit going on, and I don't know what the fuck you doin'," she stated.

"Good!" Boa replied.

"What the fuck is that supposed to mean?" KoKo went on the defensive.

"It means I'm a grown fucking man. I don't need you to be checking on what I'm doin'."

"What? You smoked some bad shit this morning? I'm in charge of this shit!" KoKo said, hitting her fist in her hand.

Boa paused. The sound of cars going by and horns blowing filled the space when their words did not. Then he finally spoke. "You're so used to being in charge that you can't let a man handle shit. Well, I ain't your bitch." KoKo looked at him sideways as the words left his mouth. "I'ma do what I gotta do to make shit happen. Either you trust me or you don't. Either way, don't fucking question me no more." He turned and walked to his car and pulled off.

"No this muthafucka didn't." She placed her hands on her hips and then got in her car, thinking, *This nigga gonna make me kill him.*

*****

"Come on, KoKo. It's just one night," Savage pleaded. The crew had been trying to get her to spend time with them for weeks, and with her running from one state to the next it was almost impossible to catch up with her.

"I'm not in a party mood, Savage. I just got in the city and I just want to soak in a hot tub and give my pillow some head." KoKo had just returned from Atlanta, kicking ass and covering shit it up.

Savage chuckled. "Fuck is you? An old lady? Throw on that hot shit and let's go."

KoKo thought for a minute. She wanted to hang up, but she could hear the sincerity in his voice. "Where y'all want me to meet y'all?"

"Nah, sis. We coming to get that ass."

KoKo chuckled. "A'ight, give me the time and get off my

phone so I can get my shit together."

"See you at eleven." He hung up.

KoKo looked at the clock, which read 9:30 p.m. Taking a deep breath, she yawned and stretched with her hands over her head. She headed toward her closet and looked at all the clothes color-coordinated in rows. KoKo picked a color for the night and then walked to the row filled with jeans, selected a pair and a shirt to match. Since she wanted to be fly yet comfortable, she chose a pair of two-inch shoe boots. Laying everything on the bed, she then picked out her earrings, chain, and a bracelet. KoKo headed to the bathroom, ran a hot bath, and poured in some scented bubbles.

Forty minutes later, she emerged from the tub and took a quick shower. She got dressed, grabbed two guns, and put them in place.

As soon as she reached her bedroom door, her phone vibrated. "I'm coming," she said into the receiver and hung up.

*****

Everybody was seated at the bar in KoKo's basement. Savage turned up the radio as he announced, "Line 'em up. She'll be down in a minute."

Mugsy grabbed a bottle of Ciroc and filled some shot glasses.

KoKo emerged from the elevator with a solemn look as she approached Night.

"Stop being so fucking serious." He pushed her as she passed him.

"Keep it up, and I'ma be sending your bitch some

condolences." She picked up a glass.

"You always talking shit." Everyone laughed as they moved closer around the bar and reached in for their glasses as well.

"Hold 'em up," Night instructed. Everyone raised their glasses. "To life, love, wealth and loyalty." The clinking glasses chimed throughout the room. Each drink was taken to the head and empty glasses hit the bar one by one.

After four rounds, they headed to the garage and hopped in three different trucks. Savage, Chucky, and Mugsy rode in the front vehicle. KoKo and Night in the middle. And Velour, a cat from their Jersey crew and Pete, brought up the rear.

Cruising through the streets, Night wanted to use his time alone with KoKo to pull her coattail. He turned the music down a little. "So you got a handle on all this shit popping up. What's good?"

Everything is butter. Just keep your crew in order. I can handle everything else," KoKo said smoothly.

"I'm worried about you, KoK."

"Don't be. Shit is what it is. We have done what we had to do to maintain the throne. At some point, some muthafucka greedier than us will try to collect."

Night looked over at KoKo and admired her calm in the middle of the shit-storm they were in. He had to respect her. She had been through the death of the only man she had ever loved. KoKo was taking care of his mother and his child, plus maintaining and building on everything he'd left her. And she had gotten shot twice, and was still beasting in the streets with no fear.

KoKo turned the music back up, grabbed the blunt from the ashtray and lit it. She puffed all the way to the spot. They pulled next to three parking spots, which were blocked by orange cones a quarter-block from the door.

Night flashed his high beams at security, and one of the guys ran over and moved the cones so they could park. Everyone got out of their cars, straightened their clothes, and checked their guns. They hit the alarms and then headed to the entrance. As they walked, they laughed and joked, forming a fort around KoKo. They all treated her like she was a precious gem, each one with their own reason for their loyalty.

They approached the door and the security team greeted them and, lifted the velvet rope to allow them entrance to the club. They hit fists and proceeded through the doors. Once inside, all eyes were on them. Females were smiling and tapping each other, displaying girlish giggles. They were escorted to the VIP area. Their hostess moved quickly into the room, set three bottles down on the table and moved to the bar. She grabbed a few glasses, set them down next to the bottles, and dimmed the lights. When she went to close the curtains, KoKo ordered, "Nah, leave them open." The woman turned to look in her direction, raising her eyebrows and nodding in agreement.

"Do you need anything else?" the woman asked.

"Just keep the drinks coming. Only closed bottles," Mugsy yelled.

The woman nodded and exited the room, closing the door behind her. Chucky went to the wet bar and started popping bottles. Savage began rolling that green. They relaxed, enjoying the music.

"All y'all niggas is worth living for and dying for. A bitch respect your hustle and sacrifice. Know that," KoKo announced, creating a serious moment.

"Real recognize real. I ain't got no regrets, ma. I'd do that shit all over again," Chucky responded.

"We live by the gun. And we'll die by that muthafucka," Pete said as he raised his glass to salute.

"What the fuck? Y'all niggas 'bout to pull out tissue and shit," Velour yelled.

"Nigga, fuck you," Savage said as they all burst out laughing.

"Tell 'em, Savage. Remember when this nigga first busted his gun? He came back to the spot all shook and shit. Fuck outta here with all that bullshit," KoKo said.

Everybody looked at Velour awaiting a response, and as usual he didn't let them down. "Y'all niggas know I be needing a hug," he said. Everybody cracked up laughing.

Night looked on and smiled. It made his heart feel good to see KoKo having a good time.

For hours they laughed and reminisced. Then Chucky, Savage, and Mugsy left out and made their rounds through the club, pinning down some dick play for later.

A short time later, the entourage exited the club. The night air hit their skin, forcing a bit of sobriety. "Damn, I'm hungry as hell," Savage announced.

"I second that shit," Mugsy chimed in, rubbing his stomach."

"So what y'all niggas wanna do?" KoKo asked.

"It's your night. What you wanna do?" Night asked.

"Let's hit that spot Uptown."

"A'ight." They agreed and headed toward their cars.

As they were about to cross the street, a few figures appeared from behind three parked cars. KoKo was the first to spot the shiny object and go for her gun. "Watch out!" she yelled. It was too late. Within seconds, bullets were flying. The first ones hit Savage in the neck, Chucky in the leg, and KoKo in the chest. They all scattered, busting back as Savage hit the ground holding his neck. Night grabbed Savage and Chucky by the back of their jackets, pulling them toward the car that shielded him from the onslaught of bullets.

"KoKo, you a'ight?" Night yelled, pulling open her jacket.

KoKo grabbed her chest, breathing heavily as the pain coursed through her body. "Get this shit off me!" she yelled as the heat from the vest burned her chest.

Night quickly unstrapped her vest. KoKo looked down to see if everything was intact. It was, except her dad's medallion, which took some of the force of the bullet.

KoKo crawled over and ducked between two cars, reaching up to bust off as bullets passed back and forth, hitting metal and shattering glass. Night, Velour, and Pete ducked behind some nearby trees and cars, exchanging rounds. KoKo blasted until she was out. A brief moment of silence interrupted the small war in the streets.

Night peeked out and saw men moving in KoKo's direction. He stepped from behind the tree, gun in each hand, blasting. "KoKoooo!" he yelled as his voice vibrated in KoKo's eardrum. Velour and Pete stepped out from behind the trees and let their steel bark. Velour hit three of their guys, laying them down, but not before taking one to the shoulder.

"Night, I'm out!" Pete shouted as he ducked back down.

KoKo remained between two cars as the direction of the bullets became impossible to pinpoint. She flipped over on her hands and knees in an attempt to look under the cars to see where the shots were coming from. When she looked over, the footsteps were right at her head.

KoKo paused as adrenaline rushed through her body. "Yeah, bitch. Move and I'll blow your fucking brains out," the voice barked down at her as he held the gun in place over her head.

"Fuck you, nigga! Do what you gotta do," KoKo barked as she tried to remain calm.

"Even with death staring you in the face you still try to act tough. All these niggas following you. Sheeeit . . . you ain't nothing but a bitch that came up on some rich dick. I'm in charge of New York now, bitch. Tell Kayson I said I'm the Boss now!" He clicked back the hammer, ready to squeeze.

KoKo braced herself for the inevitable. She closed her eyes and said a prayer. All she was focused on was Quran.

Then.

Boom. Boom. Boom. Shots rang out.

Silence filled the atmosphere, and then it was as if time didn't exist. Even the air was void. As KoKo tried to open her eyes to see the repercussion of the hateful blast, the shooter fell to his knees in front of her. She met eyes with the assassain whose brains oozed from his head and onto the cold concrete.

KoKo grabbed the gun from his hand, stood up and pointed in all directions. There wasn't a man standing.

"KoK!" she heard Night yell out.

KoKo ran to his side to assess the wounds. Everyone had taken at least one shot except Night, who was now holding Savage, trying to keep him alert. KoKo heard the sirens approaching fast.

"Get outta here, KoKo!" Night ordered.

"I'm not leaving y'all," KoKo declared full of anger.

"I got this shit. Go! Now!"

KoKo rose up, making eye contact with him and seeing that he wasn't taking no for an answer.

"Hurry up, them blues gonna be all over this place in a minute."

KoKo turned, stepped quickly into Night's truck and hopped in and peeled out. As she drove, she became overwhelmed with emotion. Tears ran down her face as she dodged through cars while running lights and stop signs. When she was a fair enough distance away, she slowed down.

"Shit, shit, shit!" she yelled as she pounded on the steering wheel. She drove, thinking that within minutes the same men who had put their life on the line was now fighting for it. Anger, regret, and fear rumbled in her gut as she toiled with the reality that once again she faced losing the only family she had.

Somebody was about to feel her rage.

— 42 —
Rage

Boa was on high alert. The news about the hit on his crew had him flying through the streets in full killer mode on his way to check on KoKo. Winter was in full effect as he pulled his jacket up to his ears on the way out of his car. A cool mist of breath left his mouth as he double-timed it to KoKo's building.

"Baby, you all right?" Boa said as KoKo opened the door to her apartment.

"Yes, I'm fine, Boa," she stated as she walked to the living room. "What's going on at the hospital?" KoKo took a seat on the couch.

"It's crazy over there. All their wives and family over there crying and shit. I had to get up outta there."

"What about Night?"

"They had him at the precinct all night. I just dropped him off. He told me to come straight over here and check on you."

"Shit is fucked up, Boa." She put her head in her hands.

Boa walked over and sat next to her. "We got this shit. You need to fall back and let us handle it."

"Fall back? You know I can't do that."

"Fuck you mean, you can't do that?"

"I built this shit. And if it's gonna crumble, I got to be right there with it."

"You talking crazy as hell. That's why you got goons. I'm not asking you. I'm telling you. Fall the fuck back!" He rose to his feet.

KoKo jumped up beside him. "So what am I supposed to do? Run and hide?" she yelled.

"You do what you gotta do. But I don't want to see your ass on these streets," Boa angrily stated and then walked out.

*****

Over the next week, the whole organization was on high alert. Savage was still in critical condition, but everyone else was stable and preparing to be released from the hospital. KoKo had every ear to the street in a strong effort to pinpoint who was behind the hit. So far the whole situation had China's name all over it. KoKo was furious because she had been pleading with Boa to watch his temper and handle shit with a cooler head. Now his bullshit had put everyone's life at risk.

Since that shit happened, she was forced to close a few spots and relocate their meeting. KoKo was lucky to find a small office space in Hoboken. She filled the room with a few couches, a desk, and a small bar and pool table. "So did we cover everything?" KoKo asked, walking around her desk after giving everyone their orders.

"Nah. But I need to holla at you," Boa interjected.

KoKo looked over at him and then around the room. "Anybody else?"

Night stood up and the six new guys he brought in followed. "That's it for now. We have a big week ahead of us. Everybody needs to stay focused." There was a strong consensus throughout the room and then they moved out.

"We'll meet you downstairs in five minutes," Night directed his order at Boa with a stern look. Night had reached his limit with Boa, and he was ready to violate the promise he made to KoKo and kill this reckless nigga.

"A'ight," Boa responded as he watched Night and the crew move out.

When Boa was sure that they were gone he asked KoKo, "So did you think about what we talked about?"

KoKo didn't even look up. "What are you talking about?" She continued to go through her mail.

"So I guess all that shit we talked about was just procedure?" Boa had requested a little more control. He was ready to be in charge, but the only thing missing was KoKo's blessing.

"Boa, it's so much shit going on, I haven't had time to think."

Boa got ready to respond and the intercom went off. "Miss KoKo, you have an important call on line two," Lori's voice came through the speaker.

KoKo hit the button. "Thank you." She turned her attention to the caller. "Hey, Miss Monique. Is everything all right?"

"I thought you were coming to see Quran?"

"I know. I'm trying to rearrange some things so I can get away," KoKo stated.

"I know there is a lot of important shit going on in your life, but nothing is more important than your son," Monique said.

After giving a little thought to Monique's request, she said, "You're right. I'll board a plane tonight."

"See you when you get here. Travel safe."

"Will do." KoKo hung up the phone. "Is there anything else I can help you with?" KoKo turned her attention back to Boa.

"Nah, handle ya business. I'll get at you later." He got up and walked out the room with an attitude.

As he walked out the office, KoKo gave him a hard stare. She tightened up her office and moved out to execute the next level of her plan.

Dead Niggas Can't Send Messages ...

KoKo stormed into the room around 10:15 p.m., pissed that she had to leave Quran and rush back to New York for a surprise meeting. "So what's on the table?" she asked as she took a seat next to Night.

Night looked over at her with disappointment, and then looked back over at Feliciano.

"There is nothing on the table," Feliciano responded.

"So what the fuck have we been doing for the last forty-five minutes?" She looked around the room in search of answers.

"My father said we no longer have the same deal. And he no longer wants to work with a woman. But he will work with any other member of your team," he revealed, careful not to upset the situation more than it was.

KoKo sat for a minute. "Tell your boss I said suck my dick." She stood up. "Get the fuck outta my office." The rest of the crew stood up next to her, and Chucky opened the door so Feliciano and his crew could exit.

When Feliciano reached the door, he turned and said, "When I leave here everything changes."

"Muthafucka, if you don't walk out that door while you still have the chance, I'ma change your wife's status from married to widowed."

Feliciano stared at her for a minute and then was escorted down the stairs. When he got to the car he tried once again to make an offer. "Man, look. I know y'all want to do shit on y'all own. Branch out. Come from up under this woman's tit." He looked at Chucky for confirmation.

They stood in the parking lot of KoKo's office, air thick with tension and a crisp chill from the winter breeze. Chucky looked at him with eyes black and cold like the night. "The only thing I want separate from my sister is my body count and you just made the list." Chucky pulled his gun and shot Feliciano right between the eyes. His crew began scrambling for their guns, but they were too slow. There were more guns on them than they could count. "We don't leave no witnesses!" Chucky spat.

One of the guys looked like he'd just shit in his pants. He raised his hands up in surrender and was talking fast. "I'm just an escort. This is my first time. I don't want to die."

"You shoulda called in sick," Chucky said, putting one between his eyes, and repeated the process on the other three guys with them. They pulled the van up and threw the four bodies inside and drove off. Chucky gave the orders and headed upstairs to deliver the verdict.

When he got upstairs, KoKo was in a heavy conversation with Night. KoKo and Night looked up as he entered.

"They ain't going to be able to pass that message on, but when they don't show up he'll get the point."

KoKo nodded.

Chucky took a seat and lit up as KoKo and Night wrapped up their conversation.

Then she gave the next instructions. "Have the bodies dumped on the Russian's territory. Tighten up all our spots. Put everyone on point. Close this spot down. We done here. I have to secure some shit for a couple days. Until then, Night is in charge. You're second in command, Chucky. Don't let shit miss his ear."

"You already know," Chucky responded.

"Don't take this as an open opportunity to fuck my secretary while I'm gone either," KoKo joked.

Chucky laughed. "I got you. You know we about to go to war, right?"

"We ain't never stopped being at war. We just changing the battlefield." She got up and walked to the door.

Night and Chucky followed suit. They needed to strap up tight for the fall out.

*****

Over the next couple of weeks shit was tight. The Russians and the Italians went to war. KoKo made the proper arrangements for her crew to be out of sight. With all the side deals she had cut, she was able to still earn while everyone else was feeling the fall out. When the smoke cleared, the Russians and the Italians had crippled each others' camps, forcing them into hiding, and leaving KoKo the only one standing for the Columbians to do business with.

Revelations . . .

KoKo felt worn out from flying back and forth, handling her business and spending all her free time with Quran. She lay comfortably in her bed when Boa barged into her room.

"I need you to take a ride with me real quick," Boa stated firmly as he entered the room.

KoKo lifted her head from the pillow, "Boa, I'm tired. I don't feel like taking a ride."

"I know, but this is important. Just come on." He gave her a serious look that let her know that whatever it was had to be important.

I should put his ass out, she thought. But something in his eyes told her she needed to go with him. "Let me make a few calls, then I'll be ready."

"I'll be downstairs," he responded and left the apartment.

*****

When they pulled up into the estate, KoKo's brows lowered as she glanced around. "Hello, Sir. Who are you here to see?" the guard asked Boa.

"Latreece Simmons," he responded as he handed the man his driver's license.

The guard took his identification and walked into the booth. He checked Boa's credentials and then returned with two visitor's passes. "Have a good day," the man said and raised the arm to the security barrier.

As they approached the parking area, KoKo's curiosity rose off the meter. "What is this about?" she asked as he put the car in park.

"Don't worry. It will all be clear in a minute." He got out the car. Walking over to KoKo's side, he opened the door. "Come on," he said, reaching for her hand. KoKo now had an apparent attitude.

"I know you didn't drive me three hours to see your bitch."

"Chill out and come on."

When they got inside, Boa checked in at the front desk and asked to see Latreece.

The nurse looked at him with hungry eyes. She had been trying to get Boa to pay her some attention, but he had been so distracted his last couple of visits. "Is that your sister?" she asked in a sneaky tone.

"Do I look like his fuckin' sister?" KoKo turned to the woman and met her face to face, wiping the smile completely off her mouth.

"I was ju—"

"You was just what?" KoKo growled. She could see the chill bumps rise up on the bitch's skin. "I *hate* a punk bitch."

"KoKo!" Boa called her in an attempt to calm her down.

"Don't call my fucking name. You and this bitch is about to get it."

"Nona, just chill. I got this," he said to the nurse who then turned away.

"Can you chill the fuck out for a minute?"

KoKo leered at him with her nostrils fully flared as her frown line deepened. "I'ma give you a fucking minute and not a minute more." KoKo walked over to the empty chair.

Boa was taking a hell of a chance bringing KoKo up there,

but he was ready to show his hand and fuck the consequences. Boa turned and walked into Latreece's room.

KoKo sat fuming, conflicted about everything surrounding the trip. A question arose in her mind, *What the fuck is this nigga up to?*

Fifteen minutes had passed, and KoKo was ready to kill something. Then her phone started vibrating. She grabbed it from her jacket pocket. "Hello," she answered with frustration in her voice.

"Where you at?" Night asked.

"Why?" She got up and walked into the big room with all the couches and stood by the window looking at the grounds.

"We have that meeting at 9:30."

"I'll be back by then."

"You a'ight?"

"Yeah, I'm good. Everything cool on that end?"

"For now."

"See you at 9:30," she said, ready to hang up.

"KoK?"

"What's up?" She brought the phone back to her ear.

"You seen that nigga Boa?"

"Nah. But when you see him tell him to hit me up." She quickly threw shade on the situation, knowing Night was searching for information. He was no closer to getting it than a Muslim getting some nun pussy. She swiftly disconnected the call before he could ask anything else. KoKo tucked the phone back down in her pocket, folded her arms, and continued to enjoy the view. She took a deep breath and decided she was about to bring this little visit to an end. When she turned, a woman was standing right behind her. She looked into the woman's eyes and they were an exact match to hers.

The woman glanced at KoKo and then down at the medallion on her chain. She smiled as she reached out and touched it. KoKo's breathing picked up as she looked over all the woman's features. She wanted to speak, but she couldn't.

"Shhh . . . come here," the woman whispered as she took KoKo by the hand and pulled her out of the sight of the nurse at the front desk. KoKo moved behind the woman like a puppy on a leash. When they got to a side hallway, the woman kept looking around KoKo with fear in her eyes. "I have one too," she whispered.

"One what?" KoKo found herself whispering right along with her.

"Shhhh . . . Don't let them hear you." She continued to look around. Then she reached in her shirt and pulled out an identical medallion from her bosom. The woman rubbed it as if it was her lifeline. "See. I have one." A tear fell from her eye. "He loved me," she said, nodding her head. "He loved me."

KoKo stared at this woman as thoughts began to rush her mind. She wanted to move, but her feet were planted to the floor.

"I've been waiting for you." She touched KoKo's face.

KoKo's heartbeat threatened to explode from her chest. She swallowed hard and then whispered, "What is your name?"

The woman paused and looked around again. "Keisha," she responded.

Tears began to run down her face. "Mommy?" KoKo said.

The woman smiled. "You gotta get me outta here. He loved us," she said as two orderlies approached.

"Mrs. Davis. What are you doing out here?" They gave KoKo a curious look. KoKo glanced up, wiping her eyes. "Is she bothering you, ma'am?" the orderly asked.

"No. She just thought I was somebody she knew," KoKo replied. Keisha quickly tucked the chain into her shirt."

"It's time to get back to your room, Mrs. Davis."

Keisha threw her arms around KoKo and hugged her tight. "Don't leave me here," Keisha whispered in KoKo's ear.

"I'll be back." KoKo tried to comfort her.

"Promise?"

"On my life," KoKo said as the men pulled the woman away.

Keisha looked into KoKo's eyes as she was led away by the two men.

KoKo covered her face with her hands and wiped away her tears. She took a few deep breaths in an attempt to compose herself. As she started back toward the sitting area, she looked up and saw Boa.

"You all right?" he asked.

"Yeah, I'm good," KoKo said with a little crack in her voice.

"That's why I brought you here."

KoKo looked up at him. She didn't know what to say or think. She rattled off her usual line of questions, but there were other questions a little more important. Like who put her mother there and why?

KoKo walked over to the desk and asked Nona, "Who was

that nicely dressed female?" The woman looked at KoKo and then at Boa. He nodded, prompting her to reveal her hand.

"She is like royalty around here. From what I know she has been here almost twenty years."

"Does anyone come visit her?"

"No."

"Who pays for her care?"

"I can't tell you that."

"Don't fuckin' play with me. I'm that bitch you most definitely don't want to play with." KoKo leaned in, giving her that 'bitch, try me' look.

"Let me handle this," Boa said, placing his hand on KoKo's arm and pulling her back.

KoKo looked down at his hand, and then back up at him. "You wanna draw back a nub?"

"Let me handle this," Boa asserted himself.

KoKo reluctantly turned and walked toward the door and stood with her arms folded. She tried to talk herself into a happy place. She wanted to pull out and put bullets in everything. But she knew if she acted up she would have mass murder on her hands and put her mother's safety at risk. Boa went in his pocket, pulled out a gwap of money and slid it to Nona.

"Look, I need you to do this for me," he told Nona.

"I could get into a lot of trouble," she said.

"Please. For me." He put his hands together.

"This shit can't come back to me," she pleaded.

"I got you. Just do this favor for me." Boa flashed that sexy smile.

Within seconds, she was smiling back at him. Nona turned to the file cabinet and pulled Keisha's file. She flipped through the pages and found the information and headed to the copy machine. After Nona copied a few pages, she placed them into an envelope and walked back to the cabinet and replaced the file. When she returned, she slipped Boa the envelope.

"Thanks, ma."

Nona tucked the money in her uniform pocket and replied, "Anything for you." Boa grabbed KoKo firmly by the hand and pulled her out the door and down the walkway.

Once outside, KoKo asked, "So you knew all along?"

Boa looked over at her as he began to filter what it was that he would reveal. "No. Not all along. A few weeks ago, Treece tried to kill herself and I brought her out here. I saw that the woman looked like you, so I stopped to talk to her and spotted her medallion. I wanted to tell you, but I didn't know how, with all that shit jumping off."

"So you been all in my face hiding something like this from me?" She looked at him with disgust.

"Now you know. Here." He passed her the envelope.

KoKo snatched the envelope and looked over the papers. It appeared to be just as she was told. Keisha had been there for almost twenty years, and they had her on a cocktail of medicine. KoKo searched the papers to see who was paying the bill. When she got to the last page she saw that a company by the name of Wells Inc. was paying in checks and had been doing so for over fifteen years. KoKo's head was spinning. She needed to get to the bottom of who put all this shit together and then put together a plan to get her mother out of there.

Missing Pieces . . .

It took a few days but KoKo had tracked down the company in Ohio that was paying Keisha's bill. She decided to pay the CEO a visit, determined to resolve all of the issues. When she got to the building, fury drove her every step. Boa's confession, Monique's revelations, and all the other shit plaguing her soul made KoKo ready to tear somebody a new asshole. She walked in the building, signed in, and got on the elevator. KoKo slid the receptionist a couple hundred dollars and in seconds was seated comfortably in his office and waiting.

"Have those files been sent to corporate?" Mr. Wells asked as he exited the elevator.

"Yes sir, Mr. Wells."

The tall, handsome older gentleman closed the door and headed toward his desk while looking down into a black leather folder. He reached the other side of the desk and pulled out his chair and instantly bucked his eyes. KoKo was sitting in the corner of his office.

"Who let you in here?"

"I'm the one asking questions today," KoKo said. As she sat staring at him, she realized he was the man in the picture shaking hands with the man with the scar.

Who is this beautiful young woman? Tyquan wondered. *And why is she in my office?* "I don't know who you are, but I will tell you this—I'm the wrong man to fuck with." He unbuttoned his jacket, still maintaining eye contact.

"What the fuck is that? A threat?" KoKo shot back.

Tyquan smiled, pulled out his chair, and sat down. "I'm not a man that needs to make threats."

"Good. I'm not a bitch that takes threats lightly."

"Look, I'm a very busy man. If you have something to say, say it."

"Let me explain something to you. There are a lot of lives in the balance, and yours is one of them. I have a very important question to ask you, and if you don't answer them to my satisfaction your wife is about to be a very rich widow."

Tyquan smiled. "Is that right?"

"I don't know how right it is, but it's damn sure critical."

The two sat in an intense stare down. "What does the name Kayson mean to you?" KoKo threw the question on the table.

The smile dropped from his face as well as a little color. "Why?"

"Answer the fucking question?" KoKo demanded.

"You think you know what's going on? You don't know shit."

KoKo grabbed her nine and cocked it. "You don't know who the fuck you dealing with," she emphasized with intense venom. "I'ma bitch that ain't got shit to lose. I strongly advise you start bumping your gums or bleeding out your ass. Either way I will get what I came for." She sat forward with her gun pointing in his direction. Her hardened gaze told him that dismissing her was not an option. He reached forward and hit the intercom.

"Hold my calls," he said this to alert security.

"Yes sir, Mr. Wells," the voice came blaring back through the speaker.

Tyquan stroked his chin, contemplating what this determined woman wanted to hear and what part of his hand he should reveal.

KoKo sat patiently waiting, knowing what he knew and what he didn't know. She waited to see what would slip from his tongue.

"I will say this. You're a bold young lady," he said in a calm voice. He reached for a mahogany cigar box and grabbed a cigar. He clipped its end and lit it up. KoKo kept silent. She had placed the ball in his court and wasn't saying anything else until he did.

Tyquan blew on the lit end of the cigar to increase the fire as he decided to lay his first card on the table. "Kayson was my son. What does his name mean to you?"

"Who I am only becomes important to you after my next question."

"Ask," he firmly stated.

"What does the name Malik mean to you?" KoKo watched Tyquan's brow fold as he took in a little air through his nose.

"Why?"

"Answer another question with a question and I'ma put something hot in that ass."

"Are you KoKo or Star?"

"Who do you think I am?"

"Who you are is incumbent on your inheritance of this information."

"I'm Mrs. Wells."

Tyquan smiled. That information had changed everything. He stood up, and his quick movement brought KoKo to her feet. "It's okay. There is no danger intended. I have been waiting for you." Please sit back down.

"May I?" he asked as he reached toward his desk and hit a button that slid the wall open next to him.

"Walk lightly," she warned. KoKo's finger caressed the trigger, itching to release. She watched Tyquan carefully walk toward his safe. He manipulated the numbers and the safe popped open. He pulled a large white envelope from inside and then closed the safe and spun the dial. He walked back to the desk and hit the button and the wall closed. Tyquan took a deep breath and sat down.

"I'm not going to bullshit you."

"Like you did my father?"

"Your father crossed me. Was it deserving of death? Hell yeah. He ran up in my woman. But business and money is much more important to me than pussy. So I didn't kill him. I wish my son would have shared my same ideas and maybe he would be alive."

KoKo squinted and shifted her jaw. "Maybe if you were slinging better dick he wouldn't have been in your pussy."

Tyquan cracked a sly smile. "My son had the right idea dealing with you. In a couple more years you just might be brilliant."

"You don't know shit about me."

"I know you're naive. I know you have surrounded yourself with your enemies and can't even sort them out." His riddles had KoKo's mind all over the place. "I'ma hand you this envelope, then I don't want to see you again."

"If I blow your fucking head off you won't see me again."

"Maybe. But I'm sure the DA would love to know about that robbery down in GA."

"So you're a sorry muthafucka and a snitch."

"Nah, just a little insurance." He rose from his seat. "Take this and do what you gotta do. Protect my grandson and my son's investments. From what I understand, he was in love with you." He buttoned and straightened out his suit jacket. "Remember, our business is done. I've given you all you need in this envelope. The only advice I can give you is, open your eyes." He extended his arm, handing her the envelope.

KoKo internalized his advice as she moved toward his desk. Reaching out for the envelope, they both held an end and locked eyes.

"Also, never threaten the life of a man who isn't afraid to die," Tyquan said.

"And never threaten a bitch who ain't afraid to kill. Today you get a pass." She snatched the envelope and moved to the door.

"Open your eyes, KoKo," he said again as she left out the door. Tyquan picked up the phone and pressed the intercom button. "Julie, have my car brought around front and cancel all my appointments for the rest of the day. I have to leave town."

"Yes sir, Mr. Wells."

Tyquan stood there for a few minutes and then moved out.

— 43 —
Trappin'

Boa was tired as hell from running the streets for the last couple days. He wanted to just hop in the shower and then get some much needed sleep. He opened the door to his new apartment, amazed by what he saw. Huge red candles were lit all around the room, and approximately twenty bouquets of black roses filled up tall vases wrapped with big red ribbons. A remnant of red carpet with black rose petals scattered on it led to his bedroom. He followed the trail. When he got to the door, he saw KoKo wearing a black negligee, holding a Moet flute in one hand and a bottle of champagne in the other. Vases of black roses aligned his bedroom and a dark red satin comforter and many huge pillows decorated his bed. Music playing in the background set the mood.

"I figured you might need something hot," she said in her sexy voice.

Boa kept a serious face as he looked around. Her flawless body glowed. Her hair was pulled back off her face.

"What's all this about?" Boa said, trying to maintain a serious demeanor even though his dick was talking to him.

"I don't want to fight with you, Boa," KoKo stated as she seductively set down the glass and bottle and strutted over to him. Standing right up on him, she searched his eyes for some warmth. Boa grimaced, still mad about Rock coming to the city.

"I know you're not going to stay mad at all this." She placed her hands on his chest and kissed his lips. Closing her eyes, she parted his lips with her tongue and he received her well. Turning her head to the side, she grabbed him by the back of his neck. Now she could feel him heating up. She reached down and rubbed gently on that steel. *That's what I'm talking about*, she thought.

"So you think you can just show up, get a nigga dick hard, and all that shit you was popping just magically disappears?" He moved her hand.

KoKo looked at him and smiled. "You still trippin' over that? Fuck you on? Your period?"

Boa stepped back. "I don't have time for this shit. Watch out." He moved past her and headed to the bathroom.

KoKo immediately went to plan B. She had anticipated Boa not easily just rolling over. Not only had she cussed him out, she had been turning down his offer to be his woman. She was too scared of feeling for someone. At that moment, she realized she needed to calm down and surrender some of her power. Too much shit was at stake. As KoKo stood there thinking, she heard the shower come on. She swallowed her pride and walked to the nightstand where she poured herself another glass of champagne. After drinking it down, she grabbed the remote, turned up the CD player, and then headed to the bathroom.

Luther Vandross' "If only for One Night" played in the background as KoKo watched the water run over Boa's body. Turned on by the splendor of his muscular frame, she slowly removed the straps of her nightie off her shoulders, stepped out of it, and then entered the shower behind him. He looked over his shoulder and then turned back around. KoKo placed her hands on his back and placed tender kisses up his spine.

Boa took a deep breath as he prepared his mind to talk to KoKo.

"I meant what I said. I don't want to fight with you," KoKo said a little above a whisper. She reached around his waist and firmly caressed his steel in her hand. The water ran over their bodies as her hand slid effortlessly up and down the length of his dick.

Boa came to attention as he closed his eyes and enjoyed her wrist play.

KoKo kissed along his back and soothed his mind. "Baby, I know I can be a bitch sometimes, but you gotta be patient and ride with me. I promise it'll get better." She turned him toward her, took him by the back of his neck, and placed soft kisses on his lips. "Be nice, baby." KoKo moaned as she rubbed the head of his long, thick, massive dick on her clit.

He broke their kiss and looked down at her rubbing him in her wetness. "He look delicious, don't he?" he said, his voice dripping with confidence.

"Yep, and I want to feel him."

"Nah. You on knock off."

"I got something for you to knock off."

"You don't get it, do you?"

"Lay it out for me, Boa."

"You always want what you want when you want it. And you can't have no more of Boa." He moved her back and stepped out the shower.

"Hold the fuck up. You serious?"

"Hell yeah, I'm serious. I told you I need to have all of you. And I know you fucking with that nigga down in the 'A'."

"What nigga? What the fuck are you talking about?"

"What am I? Stupid?" he asked, getting charged up. "I know what the fuck goes on between you and that nigga Rock when you down in the 'A'."

KoKo kept quiet.

"Yeah, I thought so." He turned to walk away.

"Boa, don't." She grabbed his arm.

"Don't what? I can't share you, KoKo. I want all of you." He gave her that intense stare.

"Boa, I'm sorry," she responded.

The room fell silent as Boa looked into her eyes. The Whispers "Chocolate Girl" filled the empty space when words could not.

Boa moved closer to KoKo and then took her into his arms, picking her up off her feet. Boa kissed her lips as she wrapped her arms around his neck. Boa hadn't had any of that sweet chocolate in weeks, and he was ready to devour her. As he laid her on his bed, the coolness of the sheets comforted their sexually ignited bodies.

"Let me love you, KoKo," Boa said as he kissed her neck and eased inside her inch-by-inch.

"I'm afraid," KoKo responded, showing all of her innocence as her very words caused a tear to fall from her eye.

Boa looked down into her eyes. "You ain't got to be afraid of me."

"You can't hurt me. I can't do it again."

"I won't hurt you. I promise," he whispered as he stroked her nice and slow.

KoKo closed her eyes and squeezed him tight.

"From this day forward, all this belongs to Boa. Am I clear?"

"Yeeesss. Make me feel like it's yours, Boa," she moaned, sending him into overdrive. He stroked and moaned as KoKo put that wet on him until he came long and hard.

Boa placed sensual kisses all over her face and neck as he whispered, "I love you."

KoKo just lay there with her eyes closed, enjoying the feel of his lips as they moved around her body. It was official . . . Boa was trapped.

This is My House . . .

With shit getting thick, KoKo sent Monique and Quran back to Dubai. She took a little time out of her already busy schedule to check in on them.

"Mommy!" Quran yelled as he ran to KoKo. She scooped him up and placed him in her arms.

"Hey, my little prince. What you doin'?"

"Playing," he said as he placed kisses on her face.

"You love your mommy?"

"Yeeeees . . . " he said. Quran put his lips on her cheek and blew, making a loud sound, which always caused him to crack up with giggles.

"Ewwww . . ." KoKo said and tried to wipe her face.

"Noooooo . . . Mommy, don't. It's my power."

"Your power?"

"Yes," he said, shaking his head up and down.

"You're a silly little boy," she said, putting him down and walking toward the kitchen.

Quran ran to the couch, picked up his remote control, and continued playing his game.

"Hello, Miss KoKo. We didn't expect to see you today," Monique said as she kissed KoKo on the cheek. KoKo faked a smile.

As Monique pulled back, the sight of the large hickey on KoKo's neck immediately angered her. She quickly turned to the sink and began washing the dishes. "I know you have moved on from my son. I'm a woman and I understand. But I didn't think you would come to my son's home with another man's mark."

"I'm a grown woman. And if you haven't realized it, this is my house."

"You're right." she said. Monique chuckled for some reason. Then, with her back facing KoKo she mumbled, "I guess when you know a person's weakness you can get whatever you want." Those words shot through KoKo like hot lava. Her hands trembled forcibly.

"Excuse me?" KoKo said, burning a crater in Monique's back with an intense gaze.

Monique smiled and took a deep breath before turning to face her. "Maybe I misspoke. You and Quran are all I have. I just want the best for you. Kayson would want me to do that for him. You understand?"

KoKo fought to speak through the lump that had now formed in her throat. "Yeah, I understand," she said, mustering a smirk. Monique began drying the dishes.

"Quran, get your stuff. I want you to go with mommy for a little while," she shouted. She summoned all the willpower she could in order to not grab a knife and cut Monique's throat.

"Go with you?" he asked, looking up at her and pulling on her hand.

"Yes, baby. Out with me," she said, looking at his little face. She used the last bit of kindness inside her to keep her composure.

Quran took off, grabbing his little backpack and stuffing things inside. "What time will you be back? Quran and I have an appointment in the morning," Monique asked.

"I'll call you."

"I'm ready." He ran up to KoKo all excited. He had been really missing his mom. "Come on, Mommy." He pulled her hand in his direction.

Monique turned and bent down, placing her hands on her knees. "Come give your grandmother a kiss." Quran ran to her and threw his arms around her neck. Monique hugged him tight as if it was her last time. "Grandma loves you."

He pulled back and kissed her cheek. "I know. I'll be back." He ran back to KoKo.

She made eye contact with Monique and mentally fought off her killer instinct. She knew that if she didn't leave now her son would witness his first murder.

Puzzled ...

315

Spring had set in and the leaves were beginning to form on the trees as the budding flowers began to decorate the city. KoKo had been spending everyday with little Quran. It felt good to have him with her. She took him to all the local museums and aquariums, and of course, his favorite, Dave & Buster's. They had just finished lunch and were driving back to the house when she got a call.

"Hello?"

"Mrs. Wells, your chain is ready," the jeweler said into the phone. She had dropped it off weeks ago after the attempt on her life.

"I'll be right there." She hung up and headed to the shop.

Thirty minutes later, she walked into the Cartier jewelry store on 5th Avenue in Manhattan. "You want something, Quran?"

"Yes. I want that, that, and that." He began pointing at several pieces of jewelry.

"You trying to break my pockets." She looked down at his smiling little face.

"Good afternoon, Mrs. Wells," the jeweler said in his French accent.

"Good afternoon."

"My wife is cleaning it. She will be right here."

"Okay, can I see that little watch for him?" She pointed at the small black men's Fendi with the diamond face. The jeweler removed it from the case and she tried it on Quran. "I like it. Fit it for him and put it on my bill." She handed him her American Express card and sat down.

"Here you go." He handed her a bag with the chain and watch inside.

"I want it," Quran said, holding out his arm as his little face beamed with joy. She reached in the bag and began placing the watch on his arm.

"You satisfied?" she asked. Quran eagerly shook his head yes.

"Okay, have a nice day," she said to the jeweler.

"Oh wait!" the jeweler's wife came from the back.

KoKo turned around.

"The little key." She came over to the counter holding a little gold key.

"What is this?"

"It was in the medallion," she replied.

KoKo's brows folded with curiosity as she reached out for the key. "Thank you," she said as she held it in her hand. *What does this go to?* Whatever it went to she was about to find out. She jumped in the car and headed home.

*****

Once KoKo got Quran bathed and fed, she put him to bed. She went to her office and pulled out all the information she collected in her search for her parents' killer and spread it out on her desk. She went through everything carefully to see if there were any links. Exhausted after a couple hours of poring over the files, KoKo rose from her seat and rolled a blunt. She lit it and sat back down, puffing and staring at the papers. The various conversations she'd had with Nine, Pat, and Tyquan played in her head. The thing that stuck out the most was Tyquan saying, "Open your eyes." She took another look and realized the signatures on the insurance policies and the one on the checks to the facility where Keisha resided, matched. Then she thought about that key. Shit just wasn't adding up. She gathered the paperwork, placed it back in the envelope, and headed up stairs.

"Open your eyes," she repeated as she walked into her bedroom. Then it hit her. Her heart started to race when she thought about Monique coming to the mansion with Quran. She ran to the closet, turned on the light, and began looking through everything. First, she checked the secret drawer that was under the jewelry case. Then she began going through every drawer. She stood in the middle of the closet and looked around. "Think KoKo," she said aloud.

Just as she turned, her eyes settled on Kayson's chair. She remembered Monique standing over there when she came in the closet. She moved to the chair and pressed her foot on the rug. KoKo got on her hands and knees and pulled at the corner of the carpet. It began to lift. She pulled back each layer until she saw a gold safe. Reaching in her pocket, she pulled out the key and stuck it in the lock. It cracked. KoKo grabbed the handle and pulled it all the way open. It was filled with stacks of hundred dollar bills. In between two stacks was a brown folder. She grabbed it and opened it up. There it was. The missing piece to the puzzle.

∽ 44 ∽
The Boss is Back

KoKo carefully went through each one of the envelopes she received from all parties involved and possessed all the information she needed to serve justice. She figured she would handle the inner circle first, and then go after the big dog when the drama settled. The last couple of months she had lost a lot of good men. But with what she had learned from Kayson, she was able to build a whole new crew. Everyone was tense, not knowing their fate. But KoKo was calm, handling shit like a well-groomed puppet master. She called a meeting to make a much-needed announcement.

"Is everyone here?" She looked around the room to take count. She had the new crew on one side and everyone else on the other side. Those who were left after the fallout. In a small section in the opposite corner were Goldie, Chico, and Zori. Seated across from her spot at the table were Night and Aldeen. Aldeen sat there full of pride as he thought that maybe this would be his chance to get back near the top of the throne.

"Okay, we have a lot of business to handle. We're making huge moves. Goldie and Zori will continue to run the clubs, answering only to me. The men you see on my right will now head each borough. Y'all on my left fall in under them and make them aware of all goings on. Night is still second in charge. All reports go to him. Chico is still in charge of

Atlanta. You are to also report to Night. Chucky, you have been bumped up. You are now in charge of the DMV area."

Aldeen began to move around in his seat. The whole situation appeared to be excluding him, and he could no longer remain silent. "So where do I fit in this picture?"

"Oh, you. We have something very special for you, but I will not be the one giving it to you."

Aldeen looked over at Night. "What? I gotta take my orders from him again?"

"No, you have to take them from me," Boa barked as he moved from the shadow by the door.

All the color immediately drained from Aldeen's face. Boa moved over to KoKo's side of the table, sat down and stared Aldeen right in the eyes. "What, you ain't happy to see me?"

"What the fuck? You got this nigga sitting at the head of my brother's table?" he complained.

"I sit at the head of this muthafucka. And as for your brother, you decided to kill him?" KoKo calmly replied, as her team looked on in shock, ready to make their move.

"You don't know what the fuck you talking about," he said, looking over his shoulder.

"I know everything I need to know." She crossed her legs and sat back.

Night was on edge. He had made a promise that if he found out Aldeen had anything to do with Kayson's death he would kill him.

"You think you know everything? You don't know shit!" said Aldeen.

"School me," she shot back.

"All you and Kay ever concerned yourself with was y'all and your come up. Neither one of y'all gave a fuck about who you had to step on to get to the top."

"So you figured you would take out the top?"

"I ain't got time for this shit. You know exactly what the fuck I'm talking about, and if not, figure that shit out after I'm gone," he said like that would get him out of the shit he was in. Aldeen got ready to rise from his seat.

"Oh, leaving already? Well, hold up. Somebody wants to talk to you," KoKo said, holding eye contact with him.

Aldeen's heart beat fast in his chest. He heard the door creak open. He wanted to turn around, but fear kept him bound in his seat. Just as panic started to set in, he jumped up. "Fuck this! I'm ghost." He started to walk away, but heard a deep voice come up from behind.

"Nah nigga. Remain seated. You been sitting on your ass all this time. Don't get up now." Baseem placed his hand on Aldeen's shoulder and forced him back to his seat.

"What's the matter?" KoKo asked, watching sweat form on Aldeen's forehead.

"Shit, what you think. I thought Bas was locked up."

"When you get out?" he asked Baseem with a nervous chuckle.

"Why? You missed me?" Baseem stood next to him.

"Missed you? What the fuck you talking about?" Aldeen became uneasy.

"Missed me. You know. When a nigga attempts to do something but isn't successful."

Aldeen got quiet as Baseem moved behind him and stood

there peering down at him. "You put my life at risk. You put this family's life at risk. Then your coward ass tried to move into a spot made for boss type niggas."

"Bas," Aldeen turned to face him and tried to plead his case.

"We would have given you anything you wanted. But you crossed us. And the only thing that can settle treason is blood."

Aldeen sat petrified, searching for the right words. "Bas, Night, KoKo, we can fix this." He made eye contact with each of them.

"Tell your boy Terrance, we said suck our dick," Baseem said, grabbing him by the head and stabbing him repeatedly in the throat. Aldeen grabbed Baseem's hand as pain shot through his body. Blood and flesh sprayed out onto the table as Baseem stabbed him until there was no more movement. He released his head, pushing it onto the table.

Baseem stepped back, blood dripping from his knife. "Let this shit be a lesson to all you muthafuckas." He pointed his bloody knife around the room. "I am not to be fucking played with. And crossing this organization will get you killed." After making sure he connected eyes with each man, he put his arm down and gave his last warning. "You see the people on the other side of this table?" He pointed at KoKo, Night, and Boa. "We in charge of this muthafucka. We see all and we know all. Don't fuck with us. I looked death in the face and told that bitch to kiss my ass. Y'all nigga's ain't got shit for me. Me and that dead nigga right there ate off the same plate. I'll never show that kind of loyalty again. Cross me and I'll make closed caskets a fashion statement." He pulled his arm down, looked at KoKo and said, "Let's go, you know a nigga been on lock. I gotta spend some time with my baby." He turned and smiled at Zori.

KoKo got up, pushed in her seat, and moved toward him. "Don't get carried away. My gun bust just like yours."

"Whatever! You just like to be the only one being mean." Baseem pushed KoKo when she got close to him.

"You remember what happened to the last nigga that pushed me."

"Yeah, he can't wear hats." Baseem looked down and they both burst out laughing.

"Night, make sure these niggas do they job, and send somebody over to Adleen's hotel to give Vanessa a surprise visit. It's time for her to take a few sleeping pills," she announced on her way by. "I'll see you later," she said to Boa.

He winked and then walked over to the crew to pass out new assignments.

When Baseem and KoKo reached the elevator, he asked, "You really trust that nigga like that?"

"If the puppet master is working the strings, somebody gotta be the puppet," she said and walked on the elevator.

Revenge . . .

"Bring me a drink, gal," the thick Jamaican accent carried throughout the room. The waitress hustled to fill his request. Scarie was seated in a booth at his restaurant on the south side of Chicago surrounded by family and friends. It was a beautiful fall night. The women were dancing and laughing while the men slammed dominos and talked shit at several tables. Scarie was smoking a fat spliff as he engaged in conversation with the waitress. KoKo pulled up a chair and sat down.

"Me a know you?" he asked.

"You about to." KoKo grabbed her gun and rested it on the table.

Two of his men rushed to KoKo's side. "Hold on." Scarie put up his hand. "You dare come sit 'pon these snakes, gal." He pulled on his spliff and blew a heavy cloud of smoke in her face.

"I came to bring you a message."

"Message? What that be, gal?"

"You forgot one." She tossed the picture of the man with the scar on his face that she got from Nine on the table in front of him.

"You must be de bitch dem call KoKo." He chuckled. "You tink me forgot? Me a know ya every move, gal. Ya mistake mercy for dementia?" He grabbed his glass and took a sip. Placing it on the table, he picked up the picture and threw it in the ashtray.

He said, "What dis gal want? Revenge? Payback?" He laughed as he looked around the room. The smile dropped from his face as his eyes met hers. "Me a give ya de same deal me gave ya father. Maybe ya smarter than he."

"Let me have your soul and I'll let your family live," KoKo stated with a serious expression.

"This gal foolish!" he yelled, causing his men to come to attention. "Even with death upon ya, ya tongue still wicked."

He sat staring at her, eyes wide and nostrils flaring.

"My offer expires at midnight." She rose from her chair.

As KoKo turned to leave, he said, "Ya mother's pussy was sweet. But me hear yours is sweeta."

Without turning around, KoKo said, "Make that, two souls. I'll surprise you with the other one."

"Little gal. Big dreams. She'll die like the rest," Scarie announced.

As she approached the door, she heard a roar of laugher. She jumped in her car, ready for revenge.

Scarie dropped the smile from his face as KoKo's words played in his mind.

"Don't let her upset you, baby. I need you focused tonight." His wife came over and sat on his lap and placed a kiss on his cheek.

Scarie squeezed his wife tight. "That gal already dead. Me just have to bury her."

*****

Later that evening, Scarie lay back caressing his wife's ass while she worked that pussy reverse cowgirl.

"Just like dat," he whispered, watching her glide up and down his dick making it nice and creamy.

She leaned forward and continued to ride. Scarie licked his finger and massaged her asshole while pulling her down on him. "Ahhhh . . .   baby," she moaned in pleasure.

After a few deep strokes, he felt her muscles tighten. He squeezed her waist and thrust fast. Her moans filled the room accompanied by his deep grunts. Just as he was about to release, a figure moved toward him. "What da fuck?" he said, adjusting his eyes.

"It's 11:49 p.m." KoKo appeared, holding a cell phone in one hand and a gun in the other. His wife jumped off his dick and crawled beside him.

"Me not afraid to die," he said, looking KoKo in the eyes.

She dialed a number and then put the phone on speaker. "Night?"

"Yeah," he answered.

"You already know." She tossed the phone on the bed.

"Daddy please! Help me," a piercing voice came through the phone.

"Your daughter is though," KoKo said, twisting a silencer on the end of her gun.

"You can have my life. Spare my wife and daughter," he pleaded.

"Oh, your wife? No problem. She works for me." KoKo looked over at Shameezah as she rose to her feet. "But your daughter . . ." KoKo looked at her watch that read 12 a.m. "Her time's up," she said as screams came through the phone, causing chill bumps to rise on KoKo's skin. "Hell is where she'll meet you," she said as she began to fill Scarie's body with holes. When she stopped shooting, Scarie's blood leaked all over the gold satin sheets.

KoKo walked over to his lifeless body. Then she reached in her pocket for her knife and cut off his dick and stuck it in his mouth. "See, your mouth got you fucked." She looked over at Shameezah.

"Let's go. We have a plane to catch." She gathered her things and trailed right behind KoKo.

*****

When KoKo got back to New York, she set up a meeting with the Colombians. She had managed to shake the city upside down. And with the deception she manipulated between the families, she put herself in a position to dictate how the dope would move in the city and receive the biggest profit.

KoKo had invited the Columbians for a meeting that would be conducted in a penthouse suite of Trump Soho hotel. She rolled with her usual crew, Night, Savage, and Mugsy along with several men of Night's security team. Alejandro arrived with a team the same size. They arrived and were searched then led into the meeting area. Once every one was seated in the luxurious room, the meeting began.

"Miss KoKo. You are a brilliant woman," Alejandro said, sitting across from KoKo as he puffed his cigar.

"I'm a business woman. And when I see something I want, I go after it," she replied.

"This is true. And I will say I never want to become your enemy." He smiled. "And please don't ever become mine." The smile dropped from his face.

"The best advice should always be taken first, by the one giving it." She smiled.

Alejandro nodded his head in agreement and went into business mode. "First, thank you for taking care of the Russians and the Italians." He turned to his bodyguard who was standing next to two black duffle bags.

"Juan." He waved him over.

Juan set the two bags on the table in front of her. KoKo didn't move. She waved over Night and Baseem. They looked in the bags then removed them from the table.

Alejandro smiled. "You trust me enough not to count it?"

"To a man of your caliber that would be an insult. Plus I know where you live," she stated.

Alejandro chuckled. "Beauty and brains is a deadly combination for a woman. Glad you're on my side." He sat up and grabbed his glass. "To longevity." He raised his glass.

KoKo grabbed her glass and raised it.

"Salute." They clinked glasses and took the fist sip sealing the deal. However, in KoKo's mind she was already devising a plan to get rid of him as well. KoKo knew all too well that if a man could have you kill another, then the next person he came for might be her.

*****

As KoKo and Night drove from the meeting with the Columbians, his head was full of questions. "You authorized Boa to do that hit on the the Russian's son?" he said, looking over at her.

KoKo smiled. Not only had she allowed Boa to hit the Russian's son, Vladimir, which jumpstarted the war between the Russians and the Italians. But she was also behind all of Boa's reckless behavior that caused the organization to question his loyalty and her leadership. A mere smoke screen illusion so KoKo could move undetected. Weeding out the weak from the strong. A few casualties came with the price of power, but fuck it—what war doesn't?

328

"Why didn't you tell me about your plans?" Night questioned.

KoKo looked over at him. "If everybody knew it wouldn't have seemed real." Then she turned forward and reclined her seat.

Night had to chuckle with disbelief. Because he thought he was on top of everything, and all behind his back she was able to destroy the competition and solidify herself as the boss.

"I know you always say you're a bad bitch. But today. You wear the crown." He turned up the music and continued to drive, holding a whole new respect for KoKo and the power she held.

~ 45 ~
The Pick Up

KoKo was fifteen minutes away from the Connecticut assisted living facility. As she drove, she thought about the information inside the envelope that she got from Kayson's dad. Here it was, all these niggas were hiding money, committing murder, and using deceit to manipulate the lives of many. Monique, the woman she had took in and loved in Kayson's absence was secretly behind everything.

KoKo thought her mother-in-law was weak and fragile, when in fact she was only using KoKo as an insurance policy and had not only been fucking her dad, but Scarie too, causing a riff in the organization. Not only had Monique helped with the assassination of Malik and his crew, but she was the link between the heads of the families. She was actually the one calling the shots.

Because of the life that Malik lived, he put insurance policies on Sabrina, Keisha, and himself that would roll over to the children at age twenty-five for twenty million a piece. Monique carefully devised a plan to remove KoKo and not only collect on the policies, but also get everything that Kayson and KoKo worked for. Knowing Kayson would never stop searching for KoKo's murderer, she had him killed first. Even though Malik crossed Tyquan, once Tyquan pinpointed all the players in the game, he had Nine tell Pat about Keisha and manipulate the information that was given to KoKo. He knew that one day the smoke would clear and she would seek revenge.

The lies and manipulation left KoKo, a wild child of the streets, walking in darkness and feeling alone and abandoned, only to find Keisha tucked away like a dirty secret. That bitch Monique had a bounty to pay, and KoKo was getting ready to hand her the verdict.

KoKo walked into the lobby and went up to Nona. Unlike the last time, Nona was actually grateful to see her. KoKo was paying her a king's ransom to keep her eyes on Keisha and take good care of her.

"Is everything ready?" KoKo asked as she stood next to the nurse's station.

"Hi, Mrs. Wells." Nona came to attention and handed KoKo a small gift bag, which contained Keisha's chart and information.

"Hold that until I come back," KoKo ordered.

Nona put the bag under her desk.

KoKo walked out the door and toward Keisha's small bungalow. When she got within listening distance, she heard a female voice talking to Keisha.

"It's okay. You can come with me."

"No! I have to go with my daughter," Keisha yelled back.

"No Keisha, this is your daughter," the woman responded.

KoKo moved to position herself for a look inside. All she could see was Pat. KoKo moved again and caught a glimpse of another woman but couldn't see who she was.

"Please, KeKe. I really want you to come home with me."

"No, if I leave she won't be able to find me."

Pat put her head down in exasperation. She had been trying to convince Keisha for over thirty minutes to leave with her.

KoKo couldn't take it any more. She pushed the door open and there they all stood. Keisha's face lit up when she saw her. KoKo squinted her eyes for a minute, and then she realized who the other woman was. Right around the time Kayson got killed there were a few occasions when that woman had been following her.

Pat jumped when she realized KoKo was standing there and the other woman also became alert.

"You came for me," Keisha said, moving to KoKo's side.

Pat reached out to grab her arm.

"Stop it! My baby came for me. I can leave now." Keisha stood behind KoKo, who gave Pat a look that said 'bitch, if you make one move it will be your last.'

"So, we meet again," KoKo said.

"I came to get my niece. You don't have shit to do with this."

"I don't have shit to do with my mother? Bitch, you must have bumped your head on the way over here."

"This is Keisha's daughter." She grabbed the woman next to her and pulled her forward. The woman had a shy look in her eyes that were now tearing up.

"That is not my daughter. This is my Ce'Asia. She wears the medallion," Keisha cried. "You can't take our baby." She put her face in her hands and bawled.

"Calm down, ma. It's okay," KoKo said without taking her eyes off Pat.

The tone of KoKo's voice brought Keisha to a tranquil state.

"Your niece?" KoKo stated. "With family like you, a bitch wouldn't have need for enemies." She paused and chuckled. "Yeah, it took me a while to figure all this shit out, but being the boss bitch that I am here I stand."

"I don't know what you're talking about."

"You never respected the fact that my mom had Malik. So you snuck and slept with him one night when he was drunk and became pregnant. When Monique found out, she offered you a piece of the pie if you could pass your daughter off as me in order to collect the money."

"How dare you!" Pat said.

"How dare you fuck my father, have his baby, and try to convince my mom that she's her daughter. You're a dirty bitch. How much was Monique paying you?"

"You don't know shit."

"Yeah, and you ain't worth shit. The only thing keeping me from killing you right now is traumatizing my mother. So today you get a pass, however, the next time I see you we gonna dance."

"KoKo, please let me talk to you." Pat folded her hands and brought them to her mouth.

"Now you wanna talk to me? I came to you. I gave you the opportunity to tell me your side. So fuck you! Come on, ma." She grabbed Keisha by the hand and turned to the young girl who appeared oblivious. "I feel sorry for you, but if you really are my blood I'll contact you. That's your mother, no doubt, but as long as you're close to your mother, I ain't got shit for you." KoKo turned to walk away and Pat came toward her.

"Please. You don't understand." She began to cry and plead her case.

"I don't understand what!" KoKo yelled, changing the mood in the room.

"I had no choice. You don't know what you're up against. These people . . ." She grabbed KoKo's arm and looked at her for some pitty.

"Death is better than deception." KoKo snatched away and kept walking.

"It was Nine and that damn Tyquan," she blurted out. "They're behind all this shit," Pat continued to ramble.

"Well, I hope those muthafuckas have pity on you. 'Cause I don't give a fuck about you."

"What am I supposed to do?" Pat cried out. "KoKo, we're blood," she yelled.

"And that's the only reason you're still alive." KoKo took a now trembling Keisha by the arm and left, slamming the door behind her.

Pat fell to her knees and cried.

All Scores Settled . . .

Monique sat across from KoKo on the couch waiting for Quran to come back from a basketball game with Night. KoKo peered at the woman who had stolen her whole life, wanting the satisfaction of torturing her to death, but patience was the key to winning this game.

"I'm so glad I came. That spa treatment was amazing."

Monique set her tea on the saucer and then placed the cup on the table.

"Yeah, I think we needed to have some time alone together." KoKo struggled to keep the conversation going.

"So what have you been up to, KoKo? From the looks of it you been eating," she commented on the few pounds KoKo had put on.

"Just been chilling and celebrating."

"Celebrating? What we celebrating?"

"You will see soon enough," KoKo said and then rose to her feet. "Go get dressed. I'm taking you to dinner."

*****

Later at dinner, KoKo sat across from Monique as she asked KoKo a million questions. KoKo answered what she could and the rest she left alone. Even though Monique seemed happy to see her, the whole night she felt uneasy.

"I know you are still a little upset that I brought Quran to New York without your permission. I put him in harm's way and I'm sorry. How do we move forward?" she asked.

"Well, I still have a lot of things to straighten out," KoKo responded.

Monique picked up her glass of water and took a few sips. "Would you like any dessert?" the waitress asked, smiling down at them.

"No thank you. I'm good. You can bring the check," KoKo responded.

"Wait, KoKo. Let me see what they have." Monique picked up the menu.

"You know you don't need it, Mo."

"I am still grown, or have you forgotten?" She looked over at KoKo and smiled and then glanced at the menu.

"You're right. Bring her whatever she wants."

"Thank you. I'll have a slice of cheesecake, and wrap me up a piece of chocolate cake to go. I want to bring Quran something back." She closed her menu and passed it back to the waitress.

Within minutes the waitress returned with the two desserts and the check. KoKo handed her two one hundred dollar bills and told her to keep the change. "Thank you, drive safely."

Monique began eating her cheesecake. KoKo sat watching and wanting to blurt out all her findings, but endurance would prove to be rewarding.

"That was so good." She wiped her mouth with the napkin, and then took another sip of water. "You ready?" she asked as she went for her purse.

"Why'd you do it?" KoKo asked as her whole mood changed.

"Do what, baby?"

"Even though the reality of me sitting here confirms you fucked up, you sit across from me acting as if nothing has happened."

"If you got something to say, say it." Monique was now on the defensive.

"I ain't got shit to say. Your mood change says it all."

"You think you're so smart. Just like your father. He thought he was smart too."

"Yeah, and so did you by fucking his friends." KoKo sat

quietly looking at Monique with a smug grin.

"Been doing your homework, huh?" she asked.

"I loved you. I sacrificed a huge part of my life to make you happy and keep you safe."

"Well, if I ever taught you anything I taught you war has no friends."

"Yeah, and if I learned anything from you, I learned trust no man or bitch." KoKo glared at her, eyes blood shot and nostrils flaring."

"Look—" Monique got ready to say, but a pain struck her stomach causing her to lean forward. "Ahhh . . ." She grabbed at her waist.

"What's the matter?" KoKo asked, wearing a wicked smile.

"What did you—Ahhh . . ." Monique sqawked as blood trickled from her nose. KoKo sat there watching her suffer. Monique could no longer take the pain. She fell from her seat on her hands and knees gasping for air and coughing up blood. The patrons in the restaurant became alarmed. The manager ran over.

"Oh my God! I'll call 9-1-1." He ran back to the front of the hostess station and frantically dialed.

KoKo got up from her seat and kneeled down beside her. She watched Monique struggle to hold onto life with poison surging through her system.

"How does death taste?" she whispered in her ear. "You took my mother and father away from me. That in itself is unforgivable. But to take the life of your own son makes you the most heartless bitch on the planet."

"What did you give me?" Monique mumbled, still holding

her stomach and coughing up blood. "My son would never forgive you," she whispered.

"I'm not looking for forgiveness. And I'm not worried about him. What we had was real, and your death is my gift to him."

"Fuck you!" Monique managed to say, with blood now coming from her mouth and nose. "You're weak. And you know what happens to weak people?" She wanted to continue but the pain in her gut took her breath.

KoKo whispered in her ear, "Yes, I do. You can kill them when you know their weakness."

Monique feebly lifted her head and looked at her. Tears fell from her face as her head hit the floor.

KoKo stood up as the EMT rushed in the door in their direction as they kneeled at her side and immediately began working on her. KoKo knew that was a mission that would prove to be futile.

∽ 46 ∽
Back on Track

As summer set in, so had peace and calm in KoKo's crew. She had Night running the out of town affairs, and Boa running the city while she took over only dealing with the exchange of money between her and the Japaneese. With all the deception, she relocated from Dubai to St. Croix and tucked Keisha and Quran safely away so she could move back and forth. Even though she kept rejecting Boa's quest to be his, it didn't stop her from getting that dick from time to time. However, her heart would not allow her to love anyone but Kayson.

"Mooove . . . Boa!" KoKo giggled as they rushed into her Park Avenue apartment-soaking wet.

"Oh shit!" Boa yelled as he slipped on the hardwood floor from the water dripping from the bottom of his pants.

"That's what you get," KoKo said, pulling her shirt over her head.

"You know you had fun. Stop frontin'." Boa had talked KoKo into sneaking into a pool and taking a late night swim.

"Here we are running all over the country into all kinds of bullshit, and you got me about to go to jail over breaking and entering into a fucking swimming pool," KoKo said as she stepped out of her pants.

Boa laughed and then stepped out of his jeans. "You

talking shit, but you know your ass had fun," he said as he walked toward her. Seeing her in her bra and thong instantly aroused him. Taking her in his arms, he began kissing her deeply and running his hands up and down her baby soft skin.

KoKo pulled back a little. "Down boy, I have to take a shower."

"Let me get you dirty and then we can shower together," he stated while trying not to release her from his grip.

"Don't worry, I'ma let you get whatever you want." He took the opportunity to continue to touch and kiss every part of her that he could get his hands and mouth on.

"Stop, Boa. I have to wash this chlorine outta my hair." She pulled back again, this time breaking his grip. She smiled at her victory as she walked off.

"Yeah, a'ight. You got that off," he said, grabbing his steel. Boa watched her grab the wet clothes, head to the laundry closet, and then toward the shower. He left the room to lay out his wet money. "Hurry up and wash your hair so I can come make that pussy moan," Boa yelled as he heard the shower come on.

When he entered the room, he turned on the light and got the kind of shock that was paralyzing.

"What the fuck you doin' in here?" Boa went right into killer mode.

"Sitting here listening to you make plans for pussy that ain't yours."

"Who you talking to?" KoKo asked as she entered the room wrapped in a towel. When she reached the door her heart stopped.

"Who the fuck is this nigga?" Boa turned toward KoKo, who stood comatose.

"Usually an introduction isn't necessary, because in most circles they call me the Boss," Kayson said smoothly as he sat there looking at KoKo. As far as he was concerned, she was the only one in the room.

"KoKo, come here," he said. She wanted to move but couldn't.

"She ain't going no fucking where!" Boa got in front of her.

"Muthafucka, you must be crazy." Kayson got up and walked toward him.

"Do what the fuck you gotta do," Boa said.

"I plan on it." He pulled his nine, cocked it, and stood nose-to-nose with Boa. "This right here is boss pussy and I came to collect." He grabbed KoKo to his side. Reaching in his pocket, he pulled out a wad of money and threw it at Boa's feet. "You can go buy you a woman. This one right here belongs to me." He stood with KoKo on one side, and his nine on the other.

KoKo felt her legs weaken. Her heart pounded vigorously. As she looked up into Kayson's face, her eyes glossed over with tears. She wanted to speak but couldn't. Her eyes slowly blinked as the tears that threatened to leave them were now rolling down her face. She stood thinking, *Was this another nightmare, or had her dreams just come true?*

The Burning Bed

By: NeNe Capri

My desire has my sexual emotions off the Richter scale and
that desire is you.
Hot memories between pillow and sheet,
Your presence has embodied my soul.
The heat of breath ignites the very heart of me.
Intensity of your gaze is a brazing elliptical of passion from
the top of my head to the tip of my toes.
While lying in my bed, thoughts of you clouds my head, your
essence embraces my spirit as I become impassioned in a gulf
of flames called you.
I want to tongue kiss the depths of your mind.
So gently, the tip of your tongue traces my silhouette.
The arch in my back,
A deep inhale.
Lift the veil of my innocence with hot liquid kisses
that paint the crease of my inner thigh.
As we become intertwined in rhythmic flow,

NE NE CAPRI

Scented moans caress my inner drum.

Shhhh. . . be quiet so you can hear the drip of my passion

carried on a slow knowing thrust.

Fingerprints left behind from your incline to push deeper.

Perfect friction,

Long deep strokes from behind . . . mmm . . . can you feel my

slippery wet pleas?

I want to feel you up against my spine.

Let it go baby . . .

So you can write your name on depth of my walls.

Is this fantasy? No my body says it's real.

Beautiful and Complete, Oh baby, pour me a whole cup

full.

And on my way to mental ecstasy,

My feelings for you get the best of me,

Sizzling thoughts of your touch and how I miss you so

much,

All while lying here alone, in my burning bed.

Book Club Discussion Questions:

1. Was KoKo justified for killing Monique?
2. Why do you think KoKo is keeping Boa around?
3. Was KoKo wrong for sleeping with Rock?
4. What is Rock hiding?
5. What else do you think is hiding in KoKo's past?
6. Will KoKo ever change or will she always be a roofless killer?
7. Should KoKo take her little sister under her wing?
8. What will come of KoKo's relationship with her mother?
9. Will all of the traps KoKo set, trap her? or will she be victorious?
10. The Enforcer is back. What will happen between KoKo and Kayson?

WAHIDA CLARK PRESENTS

FLIPPIN'
The Hustle

A Novel by
TRAE MACKLIN

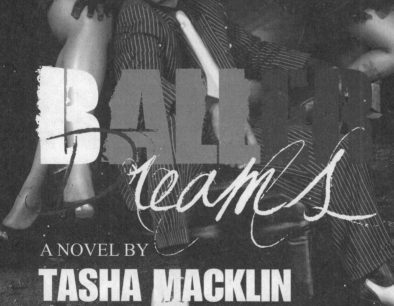